On the bridge all eyes, including Nero's, were focused on the forward viewscreen.

As time passed and nothing happened, a hesitant Ayel stepped forward to venture a comment. He did not do so lightly. As much as he respected his captain, as much as he held him in awe, he knew that Nero would not hesitate to kill him in an instant if he thought his trusted second-in-command had for a single moment faltered in their common purpose.

"Perhaps, Captain, our calculations were incomplete. Considering that it was necessary to plot the energy distortions involved against the projected time frame under such conditions and involving physics that are as much theoretical as proven, it would not be surprising if the delivered result is imperfect."

"No." Nero spoke with the confidence of one for whom science and mathematics were intimate servants of self. "It is now. Now and here. We wait."

As it turned out, both Romulans were right. The calculations *were* slightly off, and the now was only slightly postponed. The great ship trembled perceptibly as space warped before it. The distance between them was substantial, but not in interstellar terms. Opening, a vortex spat energy and stripped particles. Scrambled subatomic matter fountained forth in every direction. In the midst of the particulate chaos something notably larger and intact emerged. Remarkably, it was a ship—in one piece and moving fast. The uniqueness of its shape rendered it instantly identifiable. Nero needed no technical confirmation.

"Our wait is over." He stared at the screen with a terrible longing. "Welcome back—*Spock.*"

STAR TREK®

A NOVEL BY
ALAN DEAN FOSTER

WRITTEN BY
ROBERTO ORCI & ALEX KURTZMAN

BASED UPON "STAR TREK"
CREATED BY GENE RODDENBERRY

POCKET BOOKS

NEW YORK   LONDON   TORONTO   SYDNEY

Pocket Books
A Division of Simon & Schuster, Inc.
1230 Avenue of the Americas
New York, NY 10020

This book is a work of fiction. Names, characters, places, and incidents either are products of the author's imagination or are used fictitiously. Any resemblance to actual events or locales or persons, living or dead, is entirely coincidental.

This book is published by Pocket Books, a division of Simon & Schuster, Inc., under exclusive license from CBS Studios Inc.

All rights reserved, including the right to reproduce this book or portions thereof in any form whatsoever. For information, address Pocket Books Subsidiary Rights Department, 1230 Avenue of the Americas, New York, NY 10020.

This Pocket Books paperback edition September 2010

POCKET and colophon are registered trademarks of Simon & Schuster, Inc.

For information about special discounts for bulk purchases, please contact Simon & Schuster Special Sales at 1-866-506-1949 or business@simonandschuster.com.

The Simon & Schuster Speakers Bureau can bring authors to your live event. For more information or to book an event, contact the Simon & Schuster Speakers Bureau at 1-866-248-3049 or visit our website at www.simonspeakers.com.

Manufactured in the United States of America

10 9 8 7 6 5 4 3 2 1

ISBN 978-1-4391-9487-4
ISBN 978-1-4391-6339-9 (ebook)

For Bjo and John Trimble
Because hospitality is forever and so are memories . . .

1

The star was a supergiant and very old. Over billions of years the forces that had powered it throughout its long life had finally exhausted themselves. Now it was falling in upon itself. The cataclysmic gravitational collapse triggered the spectacular explosion known as a supernova. What was left at the core of the supergiant was a neutron star, cold and dense and dead. Everything else was blown outward, creating a brilliantly glowing shock wave traveling at nearly a tenth the speed of light that swept up everything in its path. For a day or two this supernova remnant would shine more brightly than any other corner of the galaxy. A star had died.

Elsewhere in the cosmos, in an unremarkable corner of one galactic arm, a child was born. Such is the balance of existence.

Though his arrival was considerably less dramatic than the passing of the supergiant, it was in its own way no less remarkable. As some stars have unusual origins, so too did the squalling infant. At the moment this was not a concern of the pair of medical specialists who were attending the delivery. Reflecting as well as honoring their own ancient culture, the actual birthing was a combination of the traditional and the ultramodern. The former ensured that the occasion would be memorable for the mother while the latter precluded any possibility of miscarriage. Though they had overseen hundreds of birthings, the medical team in attendance was especially focused on the one that was taking place this morning. This was not because the father happened to be of high status and held various important positions within the government.

It was because the mother—was different.

As she cleaned the newborn, the older of the two specialists noted the infant's steady breathing as well as the force with which he kicked. His occasional squalling rose above the soft traditional music that filled the room.

"He is strong, this one."

Carefully she passed it to the mother. As she took her offspring in her arms, tears appeared at the corners of her eyes and began to trickle down her smooth cheeks.

"Hello," she whispered to her child.

Taking her superior aside, the younger specialist murmured softly as she studied the tender bonding—and the peculiar weeping.

"The baby is healthy. Why does she cry?"

The older woman replied, as if it explained everything, "She is human."

It did explain everything.

A distant buzz caused both of them to turn. "Sarek arrives," the senior of the two specialists observed.

His breathing was labored from the haste with which

he had traveled, but Sarek remained completely under control. In other words, for a new Vulcan father, he was normal. Though he regarded the exhausted mother of their child without smiling, the pride and affection he felt shone clearly in his face.

Though they betrayed no emotion, all the attendants in the room strained for a better look. Details of the pregnancy and subsequent delivery were hardly conventional and the attendants' curiosity was understandable.

As her respiration returned to normal, Amanda Grayson regarded her newborn proudly. Though she was the only human in the delivery chamber, she did not feel isolated or alone. It was a state of affairs to which she had grown accustomed and one that she had willingly embraced. Besides, she was hardly alone. Sarek was there. Her husband was there.

And about time, too.

Pushing back his hood, Sarek approached the bed and knelt beside it. Having completed her duties, the medical specialist stepped back to allow the parents their first moment together as a complete family. Like her companions, the specialist said nothing. It was not her job to comment on the singular circumstances of the birth and certainly not the time to do so. Her task and those of her associates was to bring newborns safely into the world. This they had done, with skill and precision and caring. Any personal opinions they might hold they kept entirely private. To do otherwise would have been . . . impolitic.

Sarek knelt beside the bed. Beside his wife and child.

"Well done."

Through the joy and pain she still managed a sardonic reply.

"Thanks."

The awkwardness of the moment caused him to momentarily look away.

"Your tone suggests disappointment. I fully understand. To be absent at the critical moment was not my wish. The Science Council required my presence for a session regarding . . ."

She interrupted him. "Don't do that. You knew I wanted you here."

Catching the two birthing specialists exchanging a look, Sarek threw them one of his own that caused both of them to hurriedly excuse themselves. Reaching across to a small touchpad, he slid one finger across the pressure-sensitive surface. The music that had filled the birthing chamber ceased.

"As you are aware, the Vulcan male is traditionally not present at the moment of delivery."

She was not mollified. "Well, *traditionally* I'm the one giving birth. I moved here, to another *planet,* to be with you. I need you to be with *me* today. Holding my hand and telling me I'm doing great, even when I'm just—*breathing* the best I can."

For a long moment it was silent in the chamber save for the baby's burbling and soft crying. Then Sarek moved as close to the bed as possible, as close to his wife as possible, and lowered his voice.

"You are correct. Our love has already proven itself stronger than tradition. I should have been here. I am sorry."

The smile that broke out on her face was radiant. Using her free hand she pulled him to her, and they kissed. Together, they contemplated the wonder they had brought into the world.

"Look—look at our boy. He's so beautiful. . . ."

"I had a thought," Sarek began.

"You often do." Her smile widened.

Even for a human, she was incorrigible, he thought fondly. "I thought we might name the child after one of our respected early society-builders. His name was Spock."

Regarding her striking newborn, Amanda pondered the suggestion until Sarek began to stir uneasily.

"Your silence does not suggest overwhelming enthusiasm."

"No . . ." She hesitated a moment longer and then her smile returned. Reaching out, she lightly touched the baby's nose. "*Spock.* It's fine. It's a *good* name. 'Spock.' "

"The child has your eyes," her husband murmured lovingly.

Reaching over, she carefully pulled aside the upper swaddling. One forefinger pushed gently at a still-curled ear until it unfurled like a tiny flower—a flower that was pink and pointed.

"And your ears," she added affectionately.

The *U.S.S. Kelvin* was not alone. That bothered Captain Pierre Robau almost as much as the fact that it was presently sharing this part of Federation space with an as-yet-unidentified intruder. Judging by his expression, Lieutenant Pitts was even more troubled; the other officer was clearly unsettled. Whether by something that was thus far inexplicable or something else, Robau could not tell.

Well, they should have some answers soon enough.

Even though Pitts had little of substance to say, he couldn't stop talking. Robau chose not to upbraid his subordinate. When excitement slammed up against concern, it was best whenever possible to allow those submerged in the resultant mix the opportunity to vent. That way when an actual crisis did manifest itself, reason would have a better chance of supplanting emotion.

". . . We don't know why our sensors didn't detect the anomaly earlier. It doesn't make any sense, since its gravitational reading's off the charts. We should have picked it up at much greater range than we did. Our people are going crazy trying to classify it, an . . ."

Pitts's exposition continued as the lift doors parted to admit both men to the *Kelvin*'s bridge. No one there was taking their ease. Some were moving quickly from one station to another to check readouts or confer with their colleagues. Everywhere, hands and eyes were in constant motion. Old reports were being processed and new queries initiated.

One day, Robau told himself, *we'll be able to do away completely with the primitive inputting of information via repeated digital impression and just talk to a ship's central data processing system about everything.* But not yet. Voice recognition technology was fine for handling basic ship operations, but not for handling the immense complexities involved in directing the more intricate activities of a starship. A command wrongly interpreted by a toaster might result in burnt toast. A command wrongly interpreted by a starship as powerful as the *Kelvin* might result in consequences rather more serious. Starfleet was working on the problem, he knew, and such technology was improving by the day. For example, there was a new ship under construction that . . .

It wasn't his ship, he reminded himself as he approached the *Kelvin*'s first officer. Whatever they were facing, they would have to make do with existing technology.

"Report."

"Readings show gravitational distortions on an astronomic scale, Captain, but we can't localize the source. I know that's contradictory, but the anomaly is irregular and—I don't know how else to say it—all over the place. We're still trying to identify a nexus and—" He broke off as his instruments demanded his attention. "Sir, new contact, bearing zero-three-four."

An alarm began to sound throughout the bridge and the rest of the ship. *Proximity warning*, Robau knew. But proximate to what? How could the *Kelvin*'s sensors be overwhelmed by a gravitational distortion they couldn't pinpoint?

Glancing in Robau's direction, the helmsman imparted information that was also an opinion. "Captain, we're a full light-year outside the Klingon Neutral Zone. Unless this is another of their probes or provocations, it doesn't seem reasonable the distortion would have anything to do with the Empire."

Approaching the helm, Robau directed his attention to the screen that showed the view from the forward sensors. There was nothing to be seen there but star field. Yet unless the *Kelvin*'s instrumentation had been impossibly compromised or had otherwise suffered a massive failure of indeterminate cause, something *was* out there. Something imposing. And according to the sensors, not nearly as far distant as the readings suggested it ought to be.

"Could the anomaly be reflecting the presence of a new type of ship drive?"

"If it is originating from a vessel, then it's not Klingon, sir." The first officer was very certain. "The distortion that's being generated doesn't match any recorded profile."

"As I said—something new, then." Robau continued to study the forward view.

"Something different, anyway," the science officer murmured under his breath as he scrutinized his own instruments.

"There!" It was the communications chief who spoke first.

Ahead of the *Kelvin* a gigantic ring of energy flared explosively to life. To many it looked like a lightning storm in space. That in itself would have been enough to draw the attention of everyone on the bridge. But the dazzling disruption of otherwise empty space was not what fixed the gaze of all who were present. Their attention was focused on the shape that was materializing from the center of the anomaly.

"Is that," the science officer whispered in awe, "a *ship*?"

Someone—or some*thing's*—idea of a ship continued to emerge from the precise center of the circular gravitational distortion. And continued to emerge. An immense construct of paralyzed geometry rendered solid in metal and composite and materials the *Kelvin*'s sensors could not fully explicate, it completely dwarfed the Federation vessel. Staring at it, the science officer was put in mind of a gigantic mutated squid that had been unable to stop itself from growing more and more tentacles than it needed. In vast sweeping curves of dark material lit only intermittently by internal illumination, these "arms" curved toward the tiny *Kelvin* as if reaching out to grab the much smaller ship.

"It looks," the science officer declared, "as if whoever designed it couldn't stop building. I've been in a couple of historical structures like that, where the owners just kept adding room after room without any thought as to whether or not they were needed or would ever be utilized." He nodded in the direction of the forward viewscreen. "I don't know what it is or where it came from, but if it's Klingon I'll swallow a *d'k tahg* points first."

While impressed by the intruder's immensity, Robau was more concerned with its purpose. "Are they transmitting anything? On any frequency?"

Gazing at his console, the communications chief shook his head. "Negative, Captain. All hails meet with silence. As near as I can tell, they're not even talking to themselves."

Too quiet, Robau thought uneasily. Whoever was behind anything that big ought to have something to say. And the vessel, if that was indeed what it was, was showing too much internal illumination to suggest it might be a ghost ship. Was its crew even now studying the *Kelvin* and thinking similar thoughts? It was hard to formulate any reasonable assumptions, given the paucity of information. Just as it was difficult to decide how to respond to the intruder's continuing silence.

"Keep hailing them. You're sure there's nothing on the registry at all, not even speculation about an experimental craft of this size?"

"No, sir," replied the first officer.

Robau understood that putting up shields could be interpreted as a hostile gesture. But doing nothing could be a fatal one.

"Go to Yellow Alert, shields up."

"Shields up, yes, sir!" As the tactical officer inputted the command, the relevant telltales on the bridge responded accordingly. Throughout the *Kelvin* meals were abandoned, conversations terminated, and entertainment venues both general and private automatically shut down as the crew scrambled to battle stations.

The communications officer's frustration was clear in his voice. "Captain, they're still not responding to our hails. Even if there's a language problem, they ought to acknowledge our abstracts."

Once again Robau considered the possibility that they were confronting a ghost ship. But if that was the case, then why had it emerged so near to them from the depths of the gravitational anomaly? Coincidence? Had the craft possessed a functioning crew on the other side of the anomaly that had only just this moment gone silent?

"Maybe they can't," he hypothesized. "I know it's a radical configuration we're looking at, but I'd still think our sensors could discern any identifiable damage. Atmosphere bleed, excessive radiation discharge, visible hull violation— something to indicate that they're disabled."

The first officer was quick to shoot down the possibility. "Negative. It may be distinctively peculiar, sir, but it appears to be intact."

Robau looked toward Pitts. "Lieutenant, signal all departments and add a special alert to science detail. First contact protocols to be initiated. We might have someone new on the block."

Pitts nodded his comprehension. "Should we initiate a scan?"

Despite his desperate desire to know more about who or what they were confronting, Robau did not have to ponder the officer's question. He replied immediately.

"No. Could be seen as an act of further provocation. That they haven't responded in a hostile fashion to us raising our shields is a positive sign. Let's build on that." He nodded toward the helmsman. "Take us in for a closer look—nice and slow. Passive scans only. No maneuvers that could be interpreted as aggressive."

Slowly and on impulse power the *Kelvin* began to approach the gargantuan creation. Given the continuing lack of information, no one could even be certain as yet that the visitor was a ship. For all they knew at this point, it might be a comatose inorganic life-form. Despite himself the science officer again had visions of reaching tentacles.

"The size of the thing," the first officer was murmuring. "Even its construction materials are unrecognizable. If it is a ship, its internal power supply must be off the charts. The amount of dilithium alone required to—"

Speculation was cut off by warning signals. Pitts's eyes grew wide as he stared at his instruments. "Sir, I have a reading—they've locked weapons on us!"

Robau's expression tightened. "Are you *absolutely certain,* Mister Pitts?"

"Yes, sir! The pertinent signatures are new but not unrecognizable." He whirled to face the captain. "There's no doubt!"

That answered the question as to whether or not they were dealing with a ship, Robau decided. "Red Alert! Arm weapons systems!"

Anyone on board who had neglected to fully comply with the previous alert needed no further urging to drop whatever they had been doing and respond to stations. Lights and warnings flared and blared throughout the length and breadth of the *Kelvin.*

"Incoming!" Pitts yelled the warning as an almost familiar energy schematic appeared on his main monitor. An instant later the first officer confirmed his fellow officer's reading of the newly detected signal.

"Torpedo locked on us at three-twenty degrees, mark two, incoming fast! Type unknown, propulsion system unknown, capability unknown!"

Those not seated scrambled to brace themselves for impact as Robau roared orders.

"Evasive pattern delta five. Return fire, full spread! Prepare to—!"

There was no time to prepare.

Unexpectedly, the incoming weapon seemed to shatter. Instead of a single missile it devolved into a spray of smaller yet still immensely powerful projectiles. Slamming into the *Kelvin,* the unknown weapons ripped open several decks before finally concluding their path of destruction near the main engine room. Men and women were sent flying by the massive explosion that ensued. Others died almost instantly as the hull in their vicinity was breached and they were sucked out into the vacuum of space. Supports were twisted, sensitive instruments shattered, lines of communication severed. Precious atmosphere was consumed by fire that the ship's automatic suppressors struggled to keep from spreading.

From the command chair on the bridge a tense Robau hailed engineering. "Damage report! What's our main power?"

The technician who replied was not the chief of section. That venerable and respected senior officer lay somewhere farther toward the stern, having perished instantly when the torpedo had struck.

"Our shields did nothing. All weapons systems off-line. Decks nine through fourteen report hull integrity compromised and numerous casualties." He paused to glance at a handheld monitor. *"Main power at thirty-eight percent, and I don't know how long we can maintain that!"*

Dragging himself back to his station, the first officer slammed a hand down on the open communicator. "Deck nine, bridge here—report."

"Plasma seals activated and holding. Can't say for how long, but for the moment we're tight."

The first officer fought to gather himself—both his wind and his wits. "Winona—is she okay? My wife?"

The reply steadied him. *"Yes, sir. That's the good news. Bad news is, she's gone into labor."*

Eyes wide, the officer turned sharply in the direction of the captain's chair. Robau had also heard the reply. He was preparing to respond when a cry from Pitts filled the bridge.

"They're firing another, Captain!"

Engineering's report had been devastatingly accurate: for all the protection they were offering against the current attack the *Kelvin*'s shields might as well have been made of aerogel. Barely deflected, the blast from the second torpedo tore a gash along the Federation vessel's primary hull. Flames flared and vanished as the oxygen that fueled them was consumed or dissipated into space. Every deck was rocked and, if not directly impacted by the explosion, suffered subsidiary damage that was life-threatening and ongoing.

"Life support failing on decks seven through thirteen!" the helmsman shouted.

"Get Starfleet Command on subspace!" Robau fought to make himself understood over the growing chaos and confusion. "Emergency power to communications!"

"Shields at eleven percent." Somehow the first officer had managed to stay at his station and monitor what remained of his instrumentation. "Eight percent! *Six!*"

"That was like nothing I've ever seen." The tactical officer was staring at his own readouts and shaking his head. "Velocity and condensed explosive capacity—we can't take another hit!"

Robau forced himself to stay calm. He had been through situations like this many times previously—in simulations. To the best of his knowledge no one had ever been through it in actuality. Gigantic unknown ship, unknown weapons, dead silence: nothing to do but wait for . . . what?

The answer arrived more quickly than he expected.

"Captain," declared the first officer with obvious surprise, "we're being hailed."

Shoot first, talk later. An inauspicious way to commence embryonic negotiations. Especially when your side couldn't shoot back. Still, he mused, no matter what happened next, talking was better than dying.

"Open communications." Settling back into the command chair, Robau tried to compose himself. No matter what ensued, he wasn't going to let their unknown enemy see that he was rattled. "And keep our transmission tight on me. No need to let them see the damage they've inflicted."

There was a moment of distortion before the forward screen cleared. The face that appeared on the monitor was humanoid. It featured heavily tattooed skin, pointed ears, and, in parallel primate terms at least, an unpleasant expression. In excellent Federation lingua franca it addressed its audience in a tone that was unapologetically severe.

"Starship captain. I am Ayel. My captain requests the presence of your captain in order to negotiate a cease-fire. He will speak to you only in person. Face to face. Come alone. You come aboard our vessel via shuttlecraft. It is unnecessary to provide docking coordinates. Once you are within pickup range, your craft will be acquired and directed to the appropriate location."

Well, Robau thought, *at least now they finally had some information. Even if none of it was good.*

"And if I refuse?" he responded appropriately.

The visitor was remorseless. *"Your main engines have been severely damaged. You can no longer achieve warp speed. Your weapons are disabled. Your refusal would be unwise."* The screen went blank.

For a moment dead silence reigned on the *Kelvin's* bridge.

"Not a very talkative bunch," the communications officer finally murmured.

Pitts looked sharply at the command chair. "Sir, who are they?"

A dissenting voice sounded from the vicinity of another console as the first officer continued to study his flickering instrumentation. "I think he's Romulan."

Robau blinked. He was processing information, details, statistics that had not been reviewed in a long time, because there had been no reason for him or anyone else to do so.

"We haven't had contact with any Romulans in over fifty-three years, how can you identify—?"

Apologetically, his first officer cut him off. "They're the closest known genetic cousins of Vulcans." He nodded in the direction of the forward monitor. "The body markings that were visible on this Ayel's face and neck, epidermal coloration, attire, all point to him being Romulan and not Vulcan. And one more thing, sir."

"What's that?"

"Even though he was brusque and only relaying orders, this Ayel was very, very emotional."

All eyes remained on the captain as everyone waited for Robau to come to a conclusion. It did not take long. When you're down to a single option, decision-making becomes simple.

"As long as they want to talk, there's a way out of this. Has to be. Only logical. If their intent from the beginning was to destroy us, we wouldn't be sitting here discussing their motivation now." Rising from the command chair, he gestured at his first officer. "Commander—walk with me."

As the two most senior officers on the ship strode its damaged corridors their passing drew only occasional glances from the rest of the crew. Much as they might wish to inquire of their captain and first officer as to the nature of the situation in which they presently found themselves, and desperate as they were for news, not one crew member stepped in their path, shouted a query, or otherwise tried to engage the two men. It was in situations such as the one they were currently facing that Starfleet training proved its worth.

Robau addressed his second-in-command evenly. "If this goes bad, I mean really bad, I'm granting you authority to execute General Order Thirteen."

The younger man at his side momentarily lost his stride. "Sir, we could issue a mayday call to . . ."

Robau was too human not to show that he was at least a little afraid. That did not in any way affect his resolve. "There's no help for us out here. Even if someone responded they'd never get here in time. If we're going down we're taking them with us. Do as you're told. Save as many as you can." Stepping into the waiting turbolift, he turned to face the other man. The first officer's expression was stricken. Both men knew what was at stake. Both men looked at each other for what each suspected might well be the last time.

"Aye, Captain." Stepping back, the younger man saluted sharply.

Punching the lift control, Captain Robau left his first officer with one last directive.

"You're captain now—Mister Kirk."

II

*G*eorge Kirk continued to stare at the lift long after the door had closed. There being no time to spend on lingering remembrances, much less paralysis, he turned smartly and headed across the corridor toward the nearest communications panel. It was in moments of crisis that a captain's mettle had to assert itself. Which meant that he had to assert himself—since he was now the captain.

A finger slid over a control as he spoke toward the pickup. "Kirk to medical."

Deep in the thus far undamaged portion of the *Kelvin,* a very pregnant Winona Kirk was wheezing slightly as she underwent yet another in a series of progressive checkups with one of the ship's physicians. The call that had been put through now came over the examination room's speaker.

"George? What's going on? No one will tell me anything. The ship . . ."

He cut her off. *"Are you okay? Is the baby okay?"*

She looked helplessly toward the doctor, who, despite

the desperate situation that had engulfed the *Kelvin*, responded to the incoming query with the kind of reserve and calm aspired to by every physician who had ever uttered a healing mantra, picked up a willow branch, and twirled it widdershins over a queasy patient.

"Everything's fine. She's had a few contractions, but the inhibitors should suppress labor long enough to get back to Earth—as long as you don't give us any more bumps."

Bumps. The doctor was being discreet for the sake of his patient. *"No promises,"* Kirk replied. *"I'll be there as soon as I can."* Cutting the link, he forced himself to focus. He *had* to force himself.

It is not easy for a man to tell himself that his wife and unborn child would have to wait.

On board the chosen shuttle the door sealed tight behind Captain Robau as he settled himself into the pilot's seat and commenced programming the departure sequence. He did not check the compact craft's power reserves or whether its life-support system was fully charged. He would worry about both when it was time for him to return to the *Kelvin*.

All eyes were on Kirk as he entered the bridge and settled himself into the command chair. On another occasion it might have been comfortable. Today it was not.

"Lieutenant Pitts, transfer the captain's vital signs to the main viewscreen. Assuming that we are receiving the standard relay from his shuttle."

"Aye, sir."

As the shuttle departed through the stern bay doors, Robau's heart rate and respiration showed steady and normal. They only began to increase as his craft left the *Kelvin* and headed toward the enormous intruding vessel. Kirk told himself the rise was to be expected. Robau was as experienced an officer as could be found in Starfleet, but he was also human. Captain or no, he was not immune to the state of affairs in which they all presently found themselves.

"Heart rate's elevated," Pitts reported in a monotone. "One ten per minute."

"High, but within parameters, given the situation," Kirk murmured to no one in particular.

If anything, Robau thought as his shuttle was drawn deep into the heart of the alien craft, *its size is even more implausible and unreasonable when seen close up.* What could be the purpose behind so much construction? What Romulan or Vulcan group would have need of a vessel of such magnitude? It struck him as wasteful, excessive, even megalomaniacal. Where had the behemoth come from, and why had it attacked his ship without the slightest provocation? What were they up against?

Or who.

Two of them were waiting for him as he stepped off the shuttle. Without being ordered to do so, he had come unarmed. The necessity had been implicit in the tone of the individual who had issued the original demand. In any event, they would surely have scanned him for weapons before greeting him in person.

Though bulkier than the spokesperson who had communicated the order that he appear in person, his guards were plainly of the same species. Up close, there was no denying Kirk's analysis: if these were Vulcans, they were unlike any Robau had ever encountered.

The interior of the gigantic vessel was as chaotic as its exterior. Possibly it did not seem so to its crew or builders. Every species, he reflected, viewed matters of starship interior space and design from their own unique perspective and built according to their own needs and desires.

For example, though replete with instrumentation, the enemy ship's bridge had the look of barely organized bedlam. Alien eyes followed him as he was urged roughly forward before finally being brought to a halt before a seated individual whose visage was already known to him: the one who had called himself Ayel. Another sat behind him—a bodyguard, perhaps? Or someone of greater importance?

An image appeared between Robau and his interrogator. Hovering between them was a ship soaring through space. If it was nothing like a Federation vessel, it was also nothing like the gargantuan monstrosity on which he presently found himself. Larger than a shuttle yet far smaller than the average starship, its most prominent feature was a large rotating torus in the vicinity of the stern. He could only speculate on its function. The movement and design intrigued him so much that for a moment he forgot the dire circumstances in which he found himself.

Ayel brought him back to reality. "Are you familiar with this craft? What do you know of this ship and its—crew? Its origins, its designs, its intentions?"

Eyeing his interrogators, Robau ignored the question. Two could play the game of protocol. "Who is your commander?" He indicated the unblinking figure sitting behind Ayel. "Is it him? I will speak only with your captain."

"You will speak only to me," his questioner replied sharply.

Robau replied as steadfastly as he could. "Then ask him what right he has to attack a Federation vessel operating in open, free, unclaimed space."

The valiant verbal maneuver was brushed aside. "What has just occurred can hardly be called an attack. My captain will easily destroy your ship if you do not respond to the question."

Robau regarded the schematic anew. At that moment, at least, he hoped there was a truth monitor trained on him. "I've never seen it before. Don't recognize the type. Is it one of yours?"

His interrogator barely held his frustration in check. "Are you familiar with—or better—know the location of the individual, Ambassador Spock?"

The image of the ship was replaced by one of an elderly Vulcan. Robau found himself gazing at a face that had plainly seen many years and experienced much. Wise, knowing, yet typically enigmatic in the way of Vulcan-kind. Robau decided it was the face of someone he would *like* to know. Once again he shook his head.

"No. I am unfamiliar with the individual you identify as 'Ambassador Spock.' I've never seen him before."

Ayel hissed in exasperation. "What is your current stardate?"

Yet another in a series of bizarre questions that seemed to be proceeding from the curious to the merely inexplicable. "Stardate? Twenty-two thirty-three oh-four." Turning his gaze away from the questioner he scanned the alien faces that were focused on him. All were intent, unblinking, and driven by a purpose he could not divine. *"Who are you people? Where are you from?"*

Something in the captain's tone, perhaps. Or maybe it was his innocent ignorance. Whatever the cause, it triggered an explosion of movement in the individual who had been sitting behind Ayel. Eyes wide, he sprang forward straight at Robau. At the same time his fingers clutched tightly around the staff he was carrying. Four ceremonial blades sprang forth from the top of the instrument. Charging alien and quadruple blades converged . . .

On board the *Kelvin* the portion of the monitor that was tracking the vitals of Captain Pierre Robau flatlined suddenly and in unison. George Kirk's fingers tightened on the arms of the command chair.

"Oh *God.*"

He did not have time to think, to reflect, to mourn. The voice of Lieutenant Pitts rang out as alarms blared throughout the bridge.

"They're launching again!"

"Evasive!" Kirk snapped. "Delta-five maneuver! Fire full spread!"

Only because the desperate helmsman managed to execute a maneuver that was rarely if ever carried out with success did the ship avoid a direct and fatal strike. Even so, the glancing detonation caused additional damage. Intact, the *Kelvin* might have shrugged it off. Wounded as she was, it was a struggle for those on board the starship simply to maintain power and life support.

"Sir, multiple decks report damage," Pitts called out. From the other side of the bridge the science officer provided unwelcome confirmation.

"They won't have to hit us with another weapon, sir. As badly damaged as we are, a stiff breeze could shake us apart."

The acting captain leaned toward the command chair's pickup. "Kirk to medical. Get my wife to medevac shuttle thirty-four. I'll meet you there."

Internal explosions shook the medical bay as the *Kelvin* shuddered. Techs scrambled to maintain stability as artificial gravity flickered. On the examination table Winona Kirk screamed, and not just from the pandemonium that had broken out around her. A wireless monitor had begun beeping loudly. Breathing hard, trying to keep her respiration steady, she gazed at the ceiling as tears streamed down her face.

"What's *happening*? Please—is the baby okay?"

"Heartbeat's dropping." The medtech who was reporting did not address himself to her. "Late variable decelerations, could be umbilical cord compression. . . ."

Reverberating from the bay's speakers, Kirk's voice rose above the general bedlam. *"All decks, this is the first officer. Evacuate the ship. This is a general evacuation order. Get to your designated shuttlecraft. I repeat, this is a general evacuation order."*

The doctor in charge was already moving, gathering up instruments and what equipment he could shove into a single bag. "Pack it up, we'll deliver in the shuttle!"

Firm, caring hands eased the patient onto a mobile

gurney. Moaning, and with techs in attendance, a confused and struggling Winona was hustled out of the disintegrating medical bay.

So many future prospects, Kirk was thinking. So many plans unrealized, so many hopes and dreams unfulfilled. The rest of a life unlived passed before him in seconds. He was frightened. No—he was terrified. But he was also in command, and little of what he was feeling slipped out.

"If we're going down, maybe we can take these bastards with us." He leaned slightly forward. "Mister Pitts, set autopilot. Plot a two-minute intercept course. We know where they've been firing from. Target those weapons systems and let's see if we can buy the shuttles some time."

The lieutenant's voice was tight. "Aye, sir."

"Targeting." As the tactical officer spoke, another tremor ran through the *Kelvin's* superstructure. She was threatening to break up, Kirk realized. Hopefully she would hold together just long enough.

"Sir," the helmsman reported despondently, "autopilot's off-line. Can't tell if it's internal damage or disruption being beamed from the hostile vessel. We have manual control only."

Manual control only. Kirk thought back to his time at the Academy, to all the simulations he and his fellow cadets had been forced to run through, over and over and over again. Dull, boring, repetitious, useless simulations—until you needed those skills. He knew what the lieutenant's declaration meant. Everyone still on the bridge knew.

"Transfer manual control to the command chair. All functions: helm, tactical, science—everything." His gaze swept the bridge. "All of you, get to your assigned shuttles. *That's an order.*"

Different faces, same expression. Just as none of them wanted this moment to come, none of them wanted to forget it. Assuming they lived to remember it, which none of them would do unless they got moving. As the ship's officers rushed to evacuate the bridge, Kirk slumped back into the captain's chair and tapped the verbal communications link. He spoke slowly and clearly, so that there would be no misunderstanding between man and machine.

"Computer, initiate directive element addendum document, General Order Thirteen. Set auto self-destruct sequence for maximum matter-antimatter yield on two-minute count." He took a deep breath. *"Mark."*

Something pinged. So simple, yet so fraught with significance. He settled himself into the chair. Better to go out with a bang than a ping, he told himself. Every monitor on the bridge now replaced prior information and readouts with a single, simple countdown sequence.

"Kirk to Shuttle Thirty-four pilot." He was more relieved than he could say when a slightly shaken but still confident voice replied.

"Standing by, sir."

"As soon as my wife's on board I'm *ordering* you to leave. Don't wait for me, *no matter what she says.* Understood?"

"Aye—sir." The pilot's tone as well as his words indicated that he definitely did.

As the last of the bridge staff staggered out and the lift doors shut behind them, Kirk found himself alone. A strange calm settled over him now that he had done what was necessary. It was the kind of calm that comes from knowing one's fate—and that he would not have to make any more decisions.

Well, maybe one more.

He had ordered the now absent helmsman to set a course for the hostile ship's weapons center. The kamikaze maneuver might hit there—or it might run into an incoming torpedo. But lower down on the strange vessel, in the direction of its drive components, there would be considerably less chance of that happening. And perhaps an even better chance of saving what remained of the *Kelvin's* crew. Swiftly he began manually entering the commands necessary to change course.

The doctor was not happy when he and his team arrived at the entrance to the shuttle. Why did Nature always have to be so contrary? He bawled instructions at his technicians.

"Her water broke—this baby's coming *now.*"

Eyes wild, head lolling, a dazed and disoriented Winona Kirk tried to focus on surroundings that were changing rapidly around her. "George—*where's George?*"

She screamed, pushed instinctively, pushed again. Between her spraddled legs the delivery physician and his assistants scrambled to adjust.

"He's stuck," the doctor muttered grimly. "I need to free his shoulder. Push on her abdomen."

Glancing back at a monitor that showed the continuing countdown, an agitated tech spoke through clenched teeth. "Doctor, we have to *leave.*"

The physician ignored the warning. He was busy. "Winona, I'm going to use my hand to free his shoulder. *Bear down and push.*"

"Everyone get ready," the pilot told them from his position forward. "We can't wait any longer. I'm initiating departure sequence."

Struggling through the pain and confusion, Winona managed to raise her head slightly. "George, the shuttle's leaving! Where are you? No! I'm not leaving without my husband!"

Swallowing hard, the pilot concentrated on his instrumentation and the task at hand. "I have my orders, ma'am. I'm sorry."

"Winona!" The doctor strove to command her attention. "I need you to *push.*"

Her convulsing body overriding her thoughts, she screamed again as she pressed her head back into the gurney's cushion and contracted the muscles in her abdomen.

It was almost as if she were pushing the shuttle clear of the *Kelvin.* Clamps snapped back and the medevac craft found itself expelled from the starship. Impulse engines sprang to life as the small vessel dropped away from the flickering, mortally damaged mother ship. The pilot concentrated on adjusting course so that the shuttle moved to join up with the other escape shuttles. Clustering in loose formation, they accelerated away from the *Kelvin* and the gargantuan vessel looming before it. Everyone on the fleeing craft knew that phasers mounted on the multilimbed malignity could sweep them from the star field in an instant.

Unless . . .

Winona screamed yet again—only this time there was

an echo. Softer, filled with life instead of pain. Rising above both voices were the triumphant words of the relieved doctor.

"That's it, he's out! Winona, you did it! You did it!"

The pain was already starting to fade, to be replaced by joy and thankfulness as she reached for the newborn that was being cleaned and treated by the tech team. Weakly but with increasing determination, she stretched out her arms toward her child—her son.

As the wounded *Kelvin* picked up speed and the countdown on the monitors shrank toward zero, a voice sounded over the speakers on the bridge. Thin and distorted by static though it was, he still recognized it instantly.

"George? George!"

He could not cry. He could not spare the time. "Right here, sweetheart. So what is it?"

"It's a boy."

"It's a boy? Yeah! Tell me—tell me about him. Please."

His wife was sobbing, but this time not in pain. *"He's beautiful, he's so beautiful. He looks like you. George—you should be here."*

Don't cry, dammit, he told himself. *Hold together.* He had only seconds left, and it was vital that anything he said be understood.

"I know . . ."

"You have to get out of there! George, listen to me—get off that ship right now!"

"Winona—I can't. This is—there's no other way. I'm sorry—I'm so sorry. Tell me—tell me what he looks like." Directly ahead and shutting out the star field now, shutting out everything else, was the mass of the alien monster that had brought him to this moment. An engineer might have thought the view beautiful. George Kirk did not.

"Brown eyes." She struggled to remain coherent, realizing now that nothing could change what had been set in motion. Nothing could roll back time or circumstance. *"God, they're your eyes."*

He swallowed. "So what should we call him, huh?"

She blinked. *"Name—we have to name him. What about—after your father, Tiberius?"*

He would have laughed except that he might have choked. "Tiberius? Are you kidding me? That's no name for a kid. We'll name him after your father—Jim."

On board the shuttle, and in spite of everything, the new mother smiled. *"Jim. Jim it is."*

"Sweetheart? Sweetheart, can you hear me?"

"Yes. Yes, I hear you."

"I love you. I love you. I lov—"

For one moment an isolated corner of space flared with a light more brilliant than that of the surrounding stars. Matter and antimatter came together in a fiery outburst that would have delighted physicists, had any of those in the immediate vicinity been in a state of mind to carry out standard scientific observations. At the moment, however, they were more concerned with surviving the expanding shock wave that blasted outward from the point of disruption as the *Kelvin* smashed into the underside of the enormous alien craft and detonated its drive.

Every one of the fleeing shuttles was kicked forward and shaken by the concussion as a tsunami of ravaged particulates slammed into them from behind. The disruption did not last long. One by one, the small craft soon steadied. Rearward-facing monitors showed an intense glow fading rapidly behind them. Of the gigantic, hostile alien vessel and the Federation starship that had crashed into it, there was no sign.

On board one shuttle a new mother cradled her son. He was as quiet and peaceful as she was devastated. *No matter,* she thought.

She would cry for both of them.

|||

*T*he learning center was full. The room itself was dark, the better to allow the participants to concentrate on the work at hand. Each student stood alone in one of multiple concave depressions in the floor, the sides of each individual bowl forming a single continuous screen upon which was projected an uninterrupted stream of information. While questions were asked, multiple images relevant to the respective queries were projected on the sloping interior of the hollow. It was therefore possible for a budding scholar to be answering one question while the data that underlined several others was already appearing. A learner's objective was to absorb an avalanche of information as rapidly as possible. A wrong answer would cause the encircling information stream to run backward, freeze, or, worst of all, draw the attention of a supervising teacher. To prevent this from happening too frequently, the flow of information could be slowed or accelerated according to the abilities of each individual student.

One junior scholar in a particular learning concavity

drew more than usual attention from the instructors. Sometimes they would even gather in pairs to look in on him. Not to criticize or correct but to admire. The occupant of the bowl was progressing so rapidly that some discussion had begun among his tutors as to whether or not it might be judicious to advance him to another level of instruction entirely. There were also instances when their attention was required elsewhere.

It was on such occasions that the eleven-year-old Spock's tormentors gathered.

"What is the square root of two million, three hundred and ninety-six thousand, three hundred and four?" the learning bowl asked.

Facing the continuously changing encircling screen, Spock replied with his usual lack of hesitation. "One thousand five hundred forty-eight."

"Correct. What is the central assumption of quantum cosmology?"

"Everything that can happen does happen, in equal and parallel universes."

A few notes of music momentarily filled the aural boundaries of the concavity.

"Correct. Identify the twentieth-century Earth composers of the following musical progression."

"John Lennon and Paul McCartney."

"Correct. What is the . . . ?"

Question, answer, question, answer—on and on in steady unending procession until the learning period was over.

"Your score is one hundred percent. Congratulations, Spock."

Gathering up his personal effects, the young student quietly emerged from the instructional concavity. As he started to leave, a trio of classmates came up behind him. All three were older and bigger. Unable to avoid them, he confronted them with the sullen air of every child who has ever been picked on by bullies and knows what is forthcoming: living proof that at least a small portion of the future can, indeed, be predicted.

"I presume," he declared resignedly, "that you've prepared new insults for today?"

The first adolescent spoke up without hesitation. "Your mother is a human whore."

The subject of this unimaginative but nonetheless stinging imprecation simply nodded. "I have no such information."

The second lump of insensitive bipedal protein tried another tack. "You are neither human nor Vulcan, and therefore have no place in the universe. You should be expunged."

The younger boy patiently filed the second insult alongside the first. "This is your thirty-fifth attempt to elicit an emotional response from me. Logic dictates you would realize the futility of your efforts and would cease by now."

It was hard to tell which was more infuriating to his tormentors: their prey's calm indifference to their efforts or the realization that he was right. At least one of them was not willing to give up.

"Look," one of the older boys sneered, "he has human eyes. They look sad, don't they?"

"Perhaps an emotional response requires physical stimuli," commented another of the boys. "Consider this attempt thirty-six."

Before the eleven-year-old could dodge, the bigger youth gave him a hard shove that nearly sent him toppling backward into the instruction bowl.

"It still doesn't react," observed the third bully. "Perhaps stimulus of a different kind is required." He loomed over the smaller boy. "He's a traitor, you know. Your father. For marrying her. That human whore."

His eyes widened as the younger boy suddenly slammed into him. Caught off balance, the bigger boy tumbled down into the education bowl with Spock on top of him. As they both struggled to their feet the older youth tried to execute a nerve pinch. Avoiding the clumsy attempt, Spock flipped his tormentor over his shoulder and slammed him to the ground. On top once more, he began flailing away with both fists.

Green blood appeared, and it was not his.

Chastened, his lower lip swollen, Spock sat on a bench in the exterior corridor of the learning center and tried not to look up as his parents stood at a distance away from him. They were arguing. Or at least his mother was arguing. His father was discussing. Another difference between them, Spock knew. One that he had difficulty reconciling. One that, when it occurred, he always tried to avoid.

Except this time he could not avoid it because he was at the center of it.

"Where I'm from, when someone hits you," his mother was insisting, "you hit back. How is that *logical*? As far as I know, masochism does not exist in Vulcan society. They pick on him, they *tease* him, every day."

Sarek was unrelenting. To his wife, he was simply being stubborn. "Spock had no *reasonable* expectation of being physically injured. The instructors arrived to separate them before any real harm could be inflicted."

"He's a *child,* Sarek! We can't expect him to be *reasonable.* Especially given the uniqueness of his situation. Doesn't logic allow for any exceptions, even for personal defense? It's not a *reasonable* state of affairs."

"Which is precisely," her husband replied with infuriating composure, "when reason must guide his actions above all. The more serious the situation, the more vital it is to be able to control one's emotions in order to render the best possible decision and ensure the most efficacious outcome."

Turning away, she shook her head in frustration. "I want him to embrace Vulcan, you know that. But he has to be himself. Which means occasionally being human. When Vulcans get disgusted with each other, they never just walk away, do they?"

"No!"

She glared at him. "Well, humans do!" she said back over her shoulder. "Here—in case you've forgotten, I'll show you how it works!"

Turning, she marched off in the opposite direction, to disappear through an open portal that closed tightly behind her. Sarek followed her departure, then exhaled softly. He stood there for a long moment, until his wandering gaze eventually encountered that of his son looking back at him. Spock hastily dropped his eyes, but not quite fast enough.

When next he looked up, it was to find his father peering down at him.

"I did not mean to create conflict between you and Mother," the boy murmured in his customary soft tone.

Sarek gazed down a moment longer. Then he blinked, seemed to slump slightly, and sat down behind his son. There was no anger in his expression. Of course. No clue to what he was feeling. Or rather, thinking. He tried to explain.

"Do not take that which you have just witnessed to heart. It is a common and natural thing not to be feared. In marriage conflict is . . ."

"Constant?" the youngster ventured hesitantly.

"Natural. You will learn that emotions run deep within our species, though it is far less in evidence than it is in humans. Long ago, such emotions nearly destroyed us. That is why we decided to follow the teachings of Surak. The result is the calm, controlled, and contented civilization you see around you. Had we not changed, perhaps we could have accomplished more. But general content would not have been among those accomplishments. Now, *you* must choose."

Insofar as he was able—or allowed—Spock looked alarmed. "Between you and Mother?"

Sarek almost smiled. "Never, my son. Though the universe suddenly collapse in upon itself and all living things be faced with extinction, I promise you that is one choice you will never be required to make. But you may choose for yourself the ethic of logic. This offers a serenity humans seldom experience. It is not the absence of feelings, but control of them. So that they do not control *you*."

The boy started to protest. "They called you a traitor. You suggest I should be completely Vulcan—and yet you married a human. Why?"

It was not a question Sarek had anticipated, and it took him a moment to properly formulate a reply.

"As Ambassador to Earth my duty is to observe and understand human behavior. This led to a deeper involvement on my part than either I or anyone else on the council expected. Given the depth of that involvement and the personal attraction I developed to . . ." He hesitated, gathered himself. "Marrying your mother was only logical. It was a decision that, to my own surprise, I was capable of making for myself.

"What you *are* fully capable of is choosing your own destiny. Despite what you may think, you are old enough to do so. The question you are faced with is which path you will take. That is something only you can decide." Reaching out, Sarek put an arm around his son's small shoulders. It was an entirely physical gesture. Logical, in fact.

"No one can make that decision for you, Spock. Not your mother, not I, not your peers. Not all of Vulcan or all of Earth. Only you."

As he sat silent and contemplative by the side of his father, Spock did not reply, the two of them gazing together down the corridor. Thoughts, however, he could not suppress.

But . . . I'm eleven . . .

The Corvette was old, red, and well preserved. It was not cherry. Time and loss had required the replacement of missing or nonfunctional parts with more modern components.

But thanks to loving modifications, it looked right, felt right, drove right.

The hands that picked the dripping wet sponge out of a nearby bucket and slopped soap and water against the gleaming fiberglass did not belong to the owner of the classic car. For one thing, they were too small. For another, their actions and the motivation behind them were indifferent to the work at hand.

The Iowa sun was hot, and he was glad of the cool water as he worked. He would far rather have been out playing. But in Frank's household, his word was law. Unfair law, unreasonable law, but at Jim Kirk's age there was little he could do except suffer under it. His stepfather, Frank, was not a particularly benign dictator.

More evidence of this arrived in the form of the loud disputation that was currently emanating from the nearby farmhouse. The irritated voice of his stepfather soared to a peak of exasperation.

"Big man, huh? Go, then! Have a nice life out there! Run away! You know I could give a damn!"

As Jim looked on, the front door slammed open and his brother emerged. Not walking. Stomping. As the younger boy looked on, George shouldered his backpack and headed right past him, down the driveway and out onto the empty country road. Dumping the sponge back in the bucket, Jim followed.

"George, where are you going?"

"Going away. Anywhere but here. Far as I can get." His brother spoke without looking down. "I can't take it anymore. Frank, I mean."

Jim had to struggle to keep pace with his brother's longer stride. "But . . . leaving for where?"

His sibling seemed not to hear. "Gives me orders like he knows who the hell I am! That's not even his car you're washing. That was *Dad's* car. And you know why you're washing it?" He finally looked around to meet his anxious brother's gaze. "Because he's gonna sell it! Without even telling Mom!"

"You can't leave." Jim was growing increasingly frantic. The thought of him being left behind was bad enough. The thought of being left with his mother and stepfather . . . "We can talk to Mom about it."

His brother whirled on him. "You can't talk to Mom about Frank! I can't take another five minutes!" It was then that he saw the apprehension in his younger brother's eyes. "Look," he continued reassuringly, "you'll be okay. You always are. Frank—he pretty much ignores you. You're not like me, Jim. Always doing everything right, good grades, teachers' pet, doing everything you're told."

From the house a distant and angry voice reached them. "When you're done with the wash I want a nice coat of wax. You hear me, Jimbo?"

The younger boy looked pleadingly at his brother. "George, don't go, please!" He held out a floating disk. "You can have my flo-yo!"

A hand slapped it away. "Sorry, Jim." Looking back, George squinted against the sunlight. "This isn't about toys. It's Frank. Mom has no idea what he's like when she's not here. D'you hear him talking like he's our *dad*?" He shook his head. "You can't be a *Kirk* in this house."

Spinning back around, he lengthened his stride. Behind him his younger brother slowed, stopped—lost. Then George whirled and hurried back. A quick, hard, guilty hug. Jim clung to him, until at last George pulled away and resumed his march toward the utterly flat horizon. Nowhere to go, lacking any options, Jim watched until the older boy was almost out of sight. Then he turned and ran back toward the only home he had ever known.

He took it out on the Corvette, shoving the sodden sponge against the paint as if he could scrub away the recent memory of his brother's departure along with the dust and grime. Front hood, front doors, windshield—he was leaning across to wipe away the suds from the latter when a glint of metal caught his attention.

The keys were in the ignition.

It was possible that Frank heard the metallic whirr of the Corvette's specially customized replacement engine as it started up. It was possible that the sound caused him to rise from where he had been sitting engrossed in the real-time transmission of the big game from Cairo. But he did not emerge in time to see the costly vehicle blast out onto the road and fishtail as it roared away from the isolated residence. Even if he had stumbled out of the house early enough to watch the big red road machine vanish into the distance, he still might not have seen the driver.

After all, that individual was awfully short.

As determined as he was panicky, Jim Kirk clutched the wheel in a death grip as he steered the Corvette down the empty, ruler-straight road. The longer he drove, the faster he went, and the faster he went, the easier it became, until it felt almost . . . natural. Reaching down, he activated the radio and let the channels spin until the add-on insert

settled on a stream of heavy music the likes of which Uncle
Frank rarely allowed to fill the house. A verbal command
cranked the volume up, way up. As exhilaration replaced
fear, he nearly lost control of the machine. A moment away
from Not Being, he floored the ancient accelerator. A huge
grin spread across his face as the car's updated engine responded. *What do you know?* he thought delightedly to
himself.

Going fast was . . . *fun*.

Fun, but confining. He knew that the roof slid back—
somehow. There were mechanical fasteners of some kind.
With one small hand still manipulating the steering wheel,
he reached up and undid first one roof latch, then the other.
The roof retracted, all right. The wind ripped it right off its
rear mounts and sent the aerodynamic sheet of fiberglass
flying like an out-of-control kite. Wide-eyed, the car's
young driver managed to look back in time to see it smash
into the road far behind him. For a moment he was despon-
dent.

But there was wind in his hair now, the bright sun il-
luminating the car's interior, and speed—the overwhelming
sensation of speed.

It was the same speed that drew the attention of the
highway patrol officer standing by the side of the road as
the Corvette thundered past. He did not need to check the
readout on his hoverbike to know that everything about the
antique vehicle's passing was wrong. Climbing aboard his
bike, he shot off in pursuit, the wheel-less bike accelerating
over the old road a couple of meters above the pavement.

Even at the velocity the Corvette was traveling, it didn't
take long for the modern police bike to overtake it. Face

shield in place, the officer peered down into the car's interior. What he espied in the driver's seat caused him to put aside the angry reaction he had prepared. Amplified by his mask speaker, his command rang out clear and firm.

"Son, you pull over that car—*now.*"

Jim turned the car's speakers all the way up as he replied innocently, "What? I CAN'T HEAR YOU!"

Backpack slung over one shoulder, an irate George Kirk was moping down the same road, hoping to hitch a ride. His outstretched thumb dropped in concert with his jaw as first the Corvette and then the police bike roared past. His composure returned rapidly, augmented by a considerable dollop of disbelief.

"*No—way . . .*"

Half in terror, half in control, and with no notion of which way to go or what to do next except that he knew it was not going to be back home, the Corvette's diminutive driver wrenched the wheel around and shot straight back in the direction of his pursuer. Gaining altitude to avoid the oncoming car, the highway patrol rider managed the sharp turn and resumed the chase. As the officer was doing so, Jim sent the Corvette careening down a side road. Perpendicular to the country highway and all dirt, it was churned into clouds of grit and grime beneath the wheels of the fleeing 'Vette.

Kirk saw the gate but couldn't avoid it. The car shattered the old wooden barrier into splinters. No warning electronics sounded, further indicating the age of the fence line he had just crossed. Where was he? Too preoccupied with trying to keep control of the car on the dirt track, he had no time for supplementary contemplation. He did not even see the fading sign that loomed in front of him and quickly disappeared in his wake.

DANGER—QUARRY AHEAD
IOWA MINING CO.

Anxious now, the pursuing officer had his bike's siren and lights on. Neither had any effect on the wildly careening Corvette.

Having been mined for construction stone for hundreds of years, the quarry was over a hundred meters deep. Its sheer sides dropped straight down into the pool of turgid rainwater that had accumulated at the bottom. No vehicle and no driver could survive such a plunge. An easy way and a convenient place for a distraught child to put an end to anger, confusion, uncertainty, and despair. All Kirk had to do was keep going and gravity would do the rest. Keep going and . . .

At the last possible instant he jammed his right foot down on the brake. But the 'Vette didn't stop. At the speed it was traveling it only skidded and slewed—not slowing enough. Unbelted and unfamiliar with the internal handles, the driver reflexively pushed himself up, out, and over the side of the open-topped vehicle. As he landed hard in the dirt, the car continued to slow, slow—and slip sideways over the edge.

The pursuing patrol officer was stepping off his bike even before the classic vehicle exploded against the floor of the quarry.

One hand hovering in the vicinity of his sidearm, mask

still in place, he approached cautiously as the car's elated, adrenaline-pumped driver spat out dirt and struggled to his knees.

"What's your name, son?" the cop asked curtly.

The boy straightened until he was standing. He was bruised, aching, scratched, dirty, swaying slightly, and alive. Very much alive. More alive than he had ever been in his young, heretofore limited life. He did not speak but rather spat his response.

"My name's *Kirk. James Tiberius Kirk!* What's yours?"

With its soaring ceiling and stark, sere walls unadorned by paintings or color, even the antechamber of the Vulcan Science Academy was impressive. It was also daunting to those who dared seek formal admittance, as the retching noises coming from a nearby hygiene chamber indicated. Waiting outside the doorway, Amanda Grayson listened with concern as she waited for her son to emerge from the restroom.

"Spock, come here—let me see you."

"No."

"Spock . . ."

She put on her most sympathetic maternal smile.

"Honey, it's perfectly understandable that you're nervous. I would be, too. There's no need to be so anxious. You'll do fine."

Mouth set, posture perfect, dark hair recently trimmed, her son gave no indication that he had just spent several minutes violently upchucking his most recent meal. He appeared completely in control of both his mind and his body, even in the face of recent audible evidence to the contrary.

"I am hardly 'anxious,' Mother. And 'fine' is unacceptable."

Her smile widened. "Of course. Please pardon my presumption. The Science Academy is only the most prestigious institute of higher learning on Vulcan. Why on Earth—or on Vulcan, for that matter—would you be anxious?"

No responding smile, as expected. No understanding chuckle, as expected. The lack of both did not trouble her. She was more than used to their absence: she was comfortable with them.

"Your provocations," he declared equably, "are quite juvenile."

She pursed her lips in a faultless imitation of a Vulcan mother. "Yet my maternal instinct quite accurate." She continued to fidget with his attire. "Your collar is crooked—here . . ."

Reaching up, he grabbed her wrists and firmly moved them away, much as small boys are wont to do when embarrassed by a mother's attention. But unlike the child he no longer was, he did not let go of them. His eyes locked onto hers.

"May I ask you a personal query?"

She smiled. "Anything."

"Should I choose to complete the Vulcan discipline of *Kolinahr,* and purge myself of all emotion—I trust you will not feel it reflects judgment upon you."

Gently disengaging her wrists from his hands, she gazed back at him. One palm reached up to lightly touch his face and slowly caress the smooth skin.

"As always, Spock, whoever you choose to be, whatever

course you decide to take through life, your journey will always be accompanied by a proud mother."

They eyed each other for a long while. Not for the last time as mother and son, but for the last time as mother and child. Then a commanding musical tone echoed through the antechamber and he stepped back. It was time to go. Forward, always forward. But knowing now for a certainty that there would never be any difficulty in looking back.

"You have surpassed the expectations of your instructors, Spock."

From his position atop the impressive dais, the chairman of the Vulcan High Council gazed down at the applicant standing patiently before them. The soaring atrium was reflective of all that was admirable and noble about Vulcan and its people, a chamber where reasoned aesthetics melded seamlessly with logical design. Several members of the Council were present, Sarek among them. Outwardly the applicant's father exhibited no special interest in the singular young man standing before the dais, nor did he betray any emotion.

That did not mean he felt nothing.

The chairman continued. "You have excelled in every field you have studied, including physical achievement. I believe that it will be some time before a number of the standards you have set in the course of your matriculation will be equaled. I can do no more than say that your final record is flawless." The speaker paused. "With one exception: I see you have applied to Starfleet as well as to the Academy."

Several of the other councillors leaned forward slightly. Spock did not miss the movement, nor was it intended that

he should. Another time, an earlier time, it might have dis-
concerted him. Not anymore. He had always had confidence in his individual talents. That was now equaled by
the confidence he had in himself. He responded without
hesitation.

"It was logical to cultivate multiple options."

"Logical but unnecessary," the science minister countered a little too quickly. "You are hereby accepted into the
Vulcan Science Academy with full academic and associated
privileges. A distinction all the more significant given that
you will be its first half-human member." The minister was
watching the applicant closely. "Does this surprise you?"

Spock did not hesitate. "Your question presumes an
emotional investment in the outcome I do not have."

Satisfied, the minister sat back and nodded approvingly to Sarek. The formality signified by the brief interview
was all but over. Almost.

"It is truly remarkable, Spock," ventured another of the
councillors, "that you have achieved so much despite your
disadvantage. Welcome to the Academy."

Almost, Spock thought. *There it is. Almost.*

"If you would clarify, Minister, the nature of the 'disadvantage' to which you are referring?"

Not a hint of emotion was present in the minister's
voice as he replied. "Your human mother, of course."

The conflict that boiled forth within the applicant did
not manifest itself visibly. Only the glance he threw in his
father's direction hinted that anything other than rote accep-
tance was present within the young man's mind. Ever the
consummate diplomat, Sarek said nothing. His eyes widened
slightly: suggestion or command, it did not matter. As the

councillors were preparing to rise and disperse, Spock made the first spontaneous decision of his life. He did not feel entirely comfortable with it, but it felt . . . right.

Even if it was not entirely logical.

"Council, Ministers—I must decline."

Preparations to return to other daily duties were instantly forgotten. Confused looks gave way to cold stares. His colleagues on the Council left it to the science minister to respond. Where previously his tone had been complimentary and welcoming, now it was flat with disbelief. But, of course, not with anger.

"Are we to understand that you are refusing the honor that has been granted to you? No Vulcan has ever declined admission to this academy."

Completely at peace now with himself and his decision, the applicant replied coolly. "Then, as I am half-human, your record remains untarnished."

Sarek had held his peace as long as he was able but, confronted with his son's astonishing demurral, could no longer remain silent.

"Spock. You have made a commitment to honor the Vulcan way, even in the face of unreasoning prejudice." At this the councillor who had made the pivotal comment shot a look in the diplomat's direction. Sarek ignored him.

"At the moment, Father, I can think of no greater way to honor our species than to attend Starfleet as its first Vulcan. Given a choice between 'firsts,' I have decided to opt for that one."

The councillor who had spoken last raised his voice without altering his tone. He did not have to. His choice of words was sufficiently accusatory.

"Why did you come before this council today? Why did you waste our time? Are you playing at some sort of irrational game? Or was it to satisfy your *emotional* need to rebel?"

Spock betrayed not a hint of what he was being accused of displaying. He was as calm and collected as if addressing a group of close friends. "I came with the intention of enrolling, as my father wished. However, your . . ." he hesitated long enough that no one could fail to get the point, ". . .'insight' has convinced me that my destiny lies elsewhere. You have persuaded me that for the foreseeable future at least, my life does not lie in the pursuit of pure academics. Therefore, the only emotion I wish to convey is . . . gratitude." He nodded ever so slightly. "Thank you, ministers and councillors, for your consideration. Live long and prosper."

No emotion in those words, not even in the last few. But just a hint, perhaps, of a nonverbal suggestion best exemplified by a distinctively human digital gesture with which those on the Vulcan High Council were not familiar.

As he turned, Spock's eyes met those of his father. Sarek's disappointment was evident in his expression. Yet in addition to the disappointment there was a trace of something else, of something more. As he departed, head high, Spock could not be at all sure he had interpreted it correctly. His uncertainty was understandable.

It was not customary for Vulcans to take pride in any kind of repudiation, whether propounded by themselves or by those whom they love.

IV

There were bigger dives in Storm Lake, with better music and cheaper booze. Some attracted construction workers, others engineers, still others visiting suits from Washington and Moscow and Beijing. The Shipyard bar was the favorite of the majority of cadets.

The young East African woman entering now had a back as straight as an arrow, black hair done up in a contemporary coif, legs that would not quit beneath a short skirt, and calves tucked into high black boots. The combination drew appreciative stares from every man present who saw her, from a few women, and even from a couple of visiting non-humanoids—there being a certain universality of physical aesthetics that in exceptional instances transcends species. Nodding and smiling to those she recognized, she ambled up to the old-fashioned bar and leaned gloriously toward the bartender.

"*Habari* and hi. Any recommendations tonight?"

The bartender smiled a greeting. "How about a Slusho Mix? A little powerful, though."

She nodded agreeably. "Sounds intriguing. I'll give it a try." As the bartender nodded, admiring both her smile and her capacity, a nearby voice more admiring than accusatory commented cheerfully.

"That's a helluva drink for a woman wearing those kinds of boots. Or is that where it all ends up?"

The face of a young man leaned toward her. Not a cadet, she saw immediately. A welder, maybe, or a driver. Possibly even younger than her. He had nerve, if not brains. Typical ladies' man, she decided: muscular, handsome, stupid. His grin confirmed it. She straightaway banished him from her reality.

"And a shot of Jack," she finished instructing the bartender, "straight up."

Kirk turned toward the barkeep. "Make it two—her shot's on me."

"Her shot's on *her*. Thanks but no thanks."

He made a face at her. "I don't hear 'no' very often."

She replied politely and without smiling. "Then it's evident the universe is out of whack and I have to take it upon myself to redress the imbalance. When I say 'no,' I mean it."

A woman who could respond with more than a nervous giggle or an outraged slap. One who could construct a coherent sentence without having to engage in a conference call with friends. He liked her already. "My name's Jim. Jim Kirk." A great echoing lack of response ensued. It threatened to continue until the sun winked out. "If you don't tell me your name," he finally prompted, "I'm gonna have to make one up. I can be pretty inventive, but I doubt it'll be as appealing as the real one."

She stared at him, wishing her order would arrive. He remained where he was, the same silly grin on his face, and she wished she had opted for a less complex drink. Had she done so she would by now be on her way and free of him.

"So—what's your name?"

She replied without looking at him. "Uhura."

"Uhura?" His lower jaw dropped precipitously. "No *way*. That's exactly the name I was gonna make up for you." His smile returned. Practiced, charming, usually irresistible—until now. " 'Uhura' what?"

"Just Uhura."

He looked dubious. "They don't have last names in your world?"

She sighed. "Uhura *is* my last name."

Kirk didn't miss a beat. "They don't have *first* names in your world? Wait, let me guess. Is it 'Jim'?"

Where is my drink? she wondered. The guy was good-looking and playful rather than overbearing, but the conversation was growing as tiresome as it was predictable. She had heard variations of it a hundred times before, in bars and shops from Dar-es-Salaam to Des Moines.

"I could tell you my first name, but you'd forget it by the time you're halfway through your next shot and then I'd be insulted."

Lowering his voice, he did his best to edge closer. "Baby, I will *never* forget anything you tell me. In fact, I remember the first time you rejected me. Remember that? When we first met?"

She smiled in spite of herself. He was still intrusive, still goofy, but . . . charming. As long as he didn't get physical . . .

Where *was* her damn order?

"Okay, so you're a cadet," he was saying. "Studying, preparing to go . . . ," he waved an indifferent hand skyward, "out there. Thataway. What's your focus?"

"Xenolinguistics." If she expected that to draw a mask down over his eyes, she was mistaken. Surprisingly, he didn't blink. "Lemme guess: you don't know what that means."

"Let *me* guess. Study of alien languages: phonology, morphology, syntax, variability in different mediums of aural conveyance, symbology . . ." He broke off, smiled afresh. "It means you've got a talented tongue."

She pursed her lips, regarding him in at least half a new light. "And for a moment I thought you were just a dumb hick who only has sex with farm animals."

He looked away demurely. "Well, not just."

A shape materialized on the bar floor. Massive enough to generate his own eclipse, the bearded cadet was nearly bigger than both of them put together. While his words were addressed to Uhura, his eyes were locked on the man standing next to her.

"This guy bothering you?" he rumbled.

"Beyond belief," Uhura admitted. "But nothing I can't handle."

Smiling benignly, Kirk leaned toward her. "I'm sure you *could* handle me. And that's an invitation."

At least her drink had finally arrived. Picking up the Jack, she downed the shot in a single swallow. Gathering up the rest of her order, she turned and started to walk away. Kirk followed her departure with a wink. One that was more hopeful than knowing. The big cadet caught the gesture, and didn't much care for it.

"*Hey.* You mind your manners."

Turning, a smiling Kirk reached out and clapped a friendly hand on the cadet's shoulder. He had to reach up to do so. "At ease, cupcake. I didn't touch her and I didn't say anything weal bad. It was a *wink.*" He batted his eyes. "Or are you just jealous I didn't wink at *you*?"

Seeing that conversation was starting to diminish around her, Uhura looked back. Several other cadets were assembling around their big compatriot. It did not take a specialist in motivation to sense what was happening. Wondering why she should bother—hell, she didn't even *like* the guy—but feeling somehow sort of responsible, she retraced a step.

"Hey—*Jim*. Enough."

The oversized cadet was still steaming over the local's last comment. He took a step closer. "*What* was that?"

Kirk didn't retreat. Not that he could have gone far anyway, with the bar pressing into his back. "You heard me, moonbeam."

Jerking his head in the direction of his assembled cohorts, the cadet continued to restrain the impulses that were rising to a boil within him. "You know how to *count,* farm boy? There's five of us—and one of you."

The smaller man straightened, a posture that put him virtually in the big cadet's face. "Well then, get another five and it'll be almost even." When the other man failed to respond, an uncaring Kirk pushed it one step further. "Y'know what I always wondered? Do they beam those uniforms right onto you guys? 'Cause they're so *form*-fitting and . . ."

The bigger youth swung. He was faster than Kirk expected, but not quite fast enough. Ducking the hook, Kirk charged forward. Once locked tight to his antagonist, the cadet's friends couldn't get in a clean swing at the local pro-vocateur. As they wrestled, a now fully engaged Kirk kept up a steady stream of biting commentary.

"Please tell me you haven't taken combat training yet, 'cause that would be so embarrassing to Starfleet. That last punch was *adorable."* As he finished delivering this assess-ment, two of the other cadets wrenched him away from their friend. Drawing back his fist, this time the big cadet connected. Rocked by the blow, Kirk's head snapped back, then forward. Sucking on his lower lip, he spat blood, eyed the dribble speculatively.

"Okay—definitely better."

Scowling, the larger man took another swing. At the last instant, Kirk ducked, almost as if he had managed to shrink his torso into his hips. The punch sailed over his head to connect with one of the cadets pinioning his arms. This allowed the younger man to break free, spin, and slam the edge of his right hand into the other cadet who was holding on to him. Poleaxed, the cadet's eyes rolled back into his head and he went down like a sack of local onions. An instant later the other two cadets were on top of Kirk. What had begun as a straightforward bar fight now threat-ened to get truly ugly as more blood was spilled.

A razor-sharp, penetrating command stopped it cold.

"ATTENTION ON DECK!"

Regardless of their position and irrespective of their condition, every cadet in the bar immediately snapped to attention. Not being one of them, Kirk was not obliged to do so. This was fortunate, as he was currently flat on his back on a table, out of breath, badly battered, and bleeding from at least two different orifices.

Starched and straight, with close-cropped hair and rugged features, a single figure entered the room. Someone had thoughtfully turned off the music. It was so quiet you could have heard a barfly drop. In addition to being considerably older than the majority of those present, the newcomer also evinced considerably less patience. As he scanned the collection of faces present, those clad in the uniforms of cadets did their best to avoid his gaze. He let the uncomfortable silence linger for a moment longer, then snapped a single directive.

"Outside, all of you. *Now.*"

The younger crowd cleared the room with impressive speed, leaving behind only those who were not part of the military. Espying the body on the table, the new arrival walked over and peered down.

"You all right, son?"

"Ye—yeah." Wincing in pain, Kirk rolled over on the table. This also provided him with a better look at the new arrival. "Why'd you have to barge in? I had 'em right where I wanted 'em."

Repressing a smile, the newcomer looked away. "Yes, I could see that."

Kirk grimaced anew as he slid off the table. His face was bloodied and there were bruises in places he did not want to visit. "Who the hell are you?"

"Captain Christopher Pike." Tilting his head slightly to one side, the Starfleet officer studied the bruised face of the much younger man. "I swear, I'm looking at you—and I'm staring right at him."

Kirk eyed the older man sharply. *What the hell . . . ?*

In the course of the ensuing conversation Kirk realized

he had absorbed more alcohol on his injuries than found its way to his stomach. Wary but riveted, he listened in silence to the visitor's delineation of a history he barely knew.

"Your father didn't believe in no-win scenarios," Pike finally concluded.

Kirk nodded slowly. All the telling of old stories, all the relating of past incidents, had done nothing to temper his attitude. "He sure learned *his* lesson."

The youthful sarcasm had no effect on Pike. "Depends on how you define winning. *You're* here, aren't you?"

Kirk looked away. "Not sure I'd call that a win."

The captain replied coolly. "Time will tell. That instinct to leap without looking, to take a chance when logic and reason insist that all is lost—that was his nature. It's something Starfleet's lost. Yeah, we're admirable. Respectable. But in my opinion we've become overly disciplined. The service is fossilizing." He leaned forward across the table.

"Lemme tell you something. Those cadets you took on? Ivy Leaguers or the overseas equivalent, all of 'em. Oxford omelettes. Sorbonne sisters. They'll make competent officers. Run their departments with efficiency and class. But command material? People I'd trust with my life when confronted by a couple of Klingon warbirds?" He shook his head dolefully.

Kirk considered before replying. But only briefly. "What the hell are you telling me all this for?"

Pike sat back. There was a gulf between them considerably greater than the tabletop. "I've got a bear-trap memory for promising individuals, and I know your history. Your aptitude tests were off the charts. Every one of 'em."

Kirk grunted and felt for a possibly loose tooth. "What d'you do—memorize test results in your spare time?"

"I make it my business to know who I might have to work with." Pike's stare was unblinking—and unsettling. "Who I might have to trust with my life. I don't remember everybody's results. Only," he added meaningfully, "those that strike me as exceptional. Tell me, Kirk—d'you *like* being the only genius-level repeat offender in the Midwest?"

The younger man's response was defiant. "Maybe I do. Maybe I love it." He sneered. "Everybody needs a hobby."

Pike shook his head sadly. He offered up neither simple platitudes nor fake smiles.

"Let me ask you something, son. Do you feel like you belong here? In *Iowa*? Do you feel that just because your daddy died you can settle for an ordinary life? What do you want to do with the rest of it? With all of it, really. Spend it making the acquaintance of every jail between Chicago and St. Louis? Or perhaps you're planning on reforming and settling down, maybe getting into macrotic farming?" Fixing his eyes on the younger man, he lowered his voice.

"Or do you feel like you might be meant for something better. That maybe you're supposed to do something *special*?"

The older man had hit a nerve, but Kirk did his best not to show it. Whenever he was uncomfortable he covered it with bravado, and this time was no exception.

"Come to think of it," he shot back shamelessly, "I do want to feel special. But she walked out on me. Thank you for your insights, Captain Pike. You know what? I'm going to take your advice. I'm gonna start a book club."

Once more Pike ignored the younger man's clumsy attempt to perturb him.

"Enlist in Starfleet."

Kirk just gaped at the figure seated on the other side of the table. "Enlist in— You must be *way* down on your recruiting quota for the month."

Pike refused to give up. He was less than encouraged, but Kirk was still there, still sitting across from him. There had to be a reason—besides his superficial injuries—why the younger man had not yet fled the room. He might not be eager, but it was just possible that he was curious. The captain continued to play on that possibility.

"If you're half the man your father was . . ." He stopped himself mid-sentence. Nostalgia wasn't working. Perhaps promise would be more tempting. "Jim, Starfleet could use a guy like you. You're headstrong but you're smart. One without the other is useful. Both employed in tandem point toward a potentially dynamic career. You could be an officer in four years. Have your own ship in eight. Unusual, but not unheard of. I know people as well as ships. I believe you could do it."

He was getting to him, Pike could see it. Just when he thought he might be having a real impact, the younger man stood and clutched at his jacket. The faint flicker of interest Pike had aroused was once more replaced by attitude.

"We're even, right? I can go? Or do I have to sit through more of the sermon?"

Pike nodded reluctantly. "We're even. You're welcome for the bailout. Enjoy your next bar fight." Pushing his chair away from the table, he also rose.

"Yeah, that should be some time later tonight. Varies according to the fullness of the moon."

They were done here, Pike saw. But he couldn't let it go without adding one last bit of information, more hopeful than expectant.

"We're at the Riverside shipyard inspecting construction of a new vessel. Shuttle for new recruits leaves tomorrow oh-six hundred." He hesitated, then locked eyes one last time with the younger man standing across from him. "Your father was the captain of a starship for twelve minutes. He saved eight hundred lives, including your mother's and yours. I *dare* you to do better." Pivoting sharply, he headed for the door.

"Ooo," Kirk muttered mockingly, "you *dare* me. What's that—the playground version of Starfleet? Gonna take your uniforms and your bonus and go home if I don't play?" But Pike was already through the door and out of earshot.

Which left a conflicted Kirk stewing in his own thoughts, and in more confusion than he would have thought possible.

Flat, featureless, and largely empty save for the isolated Starfleet installation, there was no denying that central Iowa was boring during the day. Exceeding all posted speed limits did not alleviate the boredom: excessive velocity only made the interminable vistas whip past faster. Iowa scenery cubed was still Iowa scenery dominated by endless fields of cornstalks and the occasional sleek grain tower. He had grown up with it, Kirk mused as he leaned forward on the spokeless electric cycle. That did not make it any less repetitious.

Like the fight last night. Different antagonists, different venue, similar outcome. As he sped southward, an uncomfortable vision presented itself: him, lying on the floor of another unnamed bar, in an unknown town, at some unspecified date in the future. Dazed, beat-up, and doing boozy complex calculations in his head for the amusement of laughing patrons in order to cadge a few credits to buy a bottle. It was not a pretty picture. With no one else present to bear the brunt of his trademark sarcasm, it did not seem quite so amusing as it had in the past.

Then there was the other past—the one that damned Captain Pike had dredged up. Anecdotes about the father he had never known. Tales of heroism. Stories of accomplishment. Parables of achievement. As the bike cruised along the otherwise empty road he glanced skyward. Blue was beautiful but empty, whereas the night sky was full of stars. Go outside after the moon had set and you could not escape them. His jaw clenched. What else couldn't he escape? Until Pike had dredged it back up, Kirk had managed to escape his past.

Did he also want to escape his future?

The fence was not particularly high, but it was strongly charged. The invisible energy beams that hummed through the traditional metal latticework and rose higher than his head could not be interdicted without setting off multiple alarms. Vertically aimed beams meant that a would-be intruder could not simply soar over it. Kirk made no attempt to do so. Instead, he pulled up just outside the perimeter. Within, wrapped in a web of metal and composite scaffolding, a starship was under construction.

Its presence was no secret. Starfleet had chosen central Iowa as the site of this particular construction yard not only because of its proximity to Mississippi shipping and the industrial-commercial hubs of the Midwest but because if something blew, few people outside the yard itself would be at risk. There was ample room to work, plenty of territory for subsidiary firms and support industries to set up shop, and the ground was flat and tectonically stable.

His bike idling almost silently, Kirk gazed at the great ship. While the superstructure was largely finished, it was still a long way from being complete, and internal fitting out had barely begun. The service yard was filled with crates, containers, and boxes, some of them enormous, each stenciled or otherwise branded with the name of the new vessel for which their contents were destined.

U.S.S. ENTERPRISE

As he observed the flurry of activity, he sought the right words to describe the ship. She was the newest model and represented the latest Starfleet designs. Not that he paid regular attention to such things, oh no. He had been far more interested in which female performers happened to be dancing or singing at the regional bars. Physical beauty had always been important to him. That and natural charm, stance, and grace.

With a start he realized that he was unconsciously applying the same parameters to the ship under construction.

What the hell do you think you're doing? he asked himself. *You sleep* on *a starship, not with it. Why are you wasting your time here? What makes you think they'd accept an overage delinquent like yourself? Because one slumming Starfleet captain said so? You haven't even contemplated filling out the necessary forms, let alone making formal application. Get away, get going, get gone.*

Spinning the bike, he accelerated away from the fence and the inaccessible metal temptress within. But which way to go? Which way to flee? He was nauseous with indecision.

Just go, his inner self screamed. *No particular direction. Thataway.*

In the heart of the construction and assembly complex, Captain Christopher Pike found his gaze sliding repeatedly toward the main gate. No reason why it should be so, he knew. No reason to expect anything out of the ordinary. Still . . .

The shuttle pilot wandered over. "We waiting for something, Cap'?"

Pike shook his head. "No. I guess not." The pilot nodded and headed off in the direction of his waiting craft.

There was final data to check. Always more paperwork, even in the absence of paper. Reports to sign off on, statistics to confirm, requests to answer, procedures to follow . . .

He couldn't wait to get out of the atmosphere.

Something was wending its way through the bustle toward him. A bike, a slick and elegant model, whirring powerfully. He did not recognize the machine, but its rider was familiar. Pike allowed himself a grin, and waited.

Dismounting, Kirk came toward him. The younger man carried no baggage save for unfulfilled expectations. He looked as cocky as he had that night in the bar, albeit somewhat less weather-beaten. As he strode purposefully toward Pike, a passing worker paused to glance in the direction of the parked bike.

"Nice ride."

Without looking in the man's direction Kirk tossed him the ignition and identification card. "Live it up."

Reflexively catching the toss, the man gaped at him. "Hey, you kidding me . . . ?" Kirk did not even look at him. Did not look back. In the course of some very serious introspection, he had made a significant discovery.

He was tired of objects.

Halting directly in front of Pike, he regarded the captain evenly. For a moment neither man said anything. For a moment neither needed to do so. A good deal passed between them without having to be put into words. Pike eventually broke the silence.

"How did you get in here? Past security?"

The attitude was still present. "Told 'em I was your nephew. Came to say good-bye, not enough time to fill out the necessary requests, and they could check me with a retina scan. The guard-in-charge had her buddies go over my bike while she checked me out personally." Kirk grinned broadly. "Guard-in-charge was a gal. I can be very persuasive."

"Yes," Pike replied dryly, "I believe I saw ample evidence of that the other night." Turning slightly, he indicated the waiting shuttle. "You're here: that's what matters. No time to fit you with a uniform, I'm afraid."

"That's all right," Kirk assured him. "I'm not real big on uniforms. They tend to get in my face."

"Nevertheless you'll be required to wear one. And not,

if you please, over your face. Any last questions before you board?"

"You mean like, any last wishes? Just one. What's the Academy's policy on fraternization between cadets?"

Pike didn't crack a smile. "You'll find out. Just like you'll find out the Academy's policy on everything else."

Kirk started past him. "Won't some poor psion-pusher get upset when I show up on board without appropriate paperwork?"

"If there's any problem, use me as a reference," Pike told him. "Just try not to reference me too often, okay?"

Smiling, Kirk snapped off a farewell salute. Or to be more precise, flicked one finger at the captain from the general vicinity of his forehead. Then he was gone, lost among the crowd that was preparing the shuttle for departure. Left to his thoughts, Pike smiled to himself. He had not exactly countermanded proper procedure in recruiting young Kirk. More like danced around it.

He hoped fervently that it was not a decision he would come to regret.

Pushing his way past technicians and engineers, Kirk boarded the small spacecraft. It was crowded inside, the majority of seats already occupied by uniformed cadets. Some of them were non-human.

Pike probably thinks that includes me, he ruminated philosophically.

Uhura was there. Her reaction when she saw him among the other recruits was almost worth enlisting, he decided gleefully. One of the cadets seated nearby sported a bandaged nose, and Kirk remembered him from the earlier night's altercation. He grinned cockily as he strode past.

The rest of the smackdown bunch were present as well. As he walked by he repeated the casual finger salute with which he had farewelled Captain Pike.

"At ease, gentlemen." He lingered near Uhura. "Never did get that first name."

She fought to repress a grin and was only partly successful. "And you never will."

A whine began to rise from the vessel's stern. *Time to find a seat slot or get off,* he told himself. Locating an empty chair, he sat down and began to strap himself in. Behind and beneath him the seat's integrated ergonomics responded to his presence by molding themselves to the back of his body. As he worked to prepare himself for liftoff, he was distracted by a commotion from the rear of the craft.

Florid-faced and clearly upset, a slightly older gentleman was being forced out of the bathroom by one of the shuttle's crew. He looked to be about thirty, and his steady litany of complaint was tinged with an accent that identified his origins as southeastern North America. The expression he wore as he continued to protest was familiar to Kirk. Having himself been hauled before a judge on several occasions, he recognized it as the look common to all prisoners who had just been sentenced to an unexpectedly long spell in the regional lockup.

"Are you people *deaf*?" the objector was loudly declaiming. "I told you I don't need a doctor, dammit! I *am* a doctor!"

Gently but firmly, the member of the shuttle's crew was wrestling the man forward. "You need to find a seat. Sir, for your own safety, sit down, or I will *make* you sit down. Right *now.*"

"I *had* one," the man insisted vociferously. "In the *bath-*

room, with no *ports.* I suffer from aviaphobia, which, in case you don't understand big words, means 'fear of flying.'"

Wrenching the complainer around forcefully, the tight-lipped crew member pushed him in the direction of one of the few remaining empty seats. As this happened to be right next to Kirk, the frustrated protestor found himself dropping down beside the casually clad younger man. Muttering to himself, the dyspeptic newcomer adjusted his straps. When he was finished, he gripped both armrests so tightly his knuckles went white. Despite the shuttle's excellent climate control, he was perspiring noticeably. He also, finally, took note of the unashamedly inquisitive passenger seated beside him. The greeting he offered was unconventional.

"I might throw up on you."

Kirk replied pleasantly. "Nice to meet you, too. Wouldn't be the first time someone's thrown up on me." He tapped his own armrest. "I think these things are pretty safe. Starfleet's been using this model for a long time."

"Don't pander to me, kid," his new neighbor growled. "One tiny crack in the hull and our blood boils in thirteen seconds. Unpredicted solar flare might strike when we leave the magnetosphere and cook us in our seats. Hell, some of the damn passengers are *blue.* Wait'll you're sitting pretty with a case of Andorian shingles, see if you're still so relaxed when you're bleeding from your eye sockets, tell me if you're still feeling good when ship gravity fails and your intestines start wrapping themselves around your stomach, ask yourself—"

Sensing that the ghoulish recitation of potential physiological disasters was liable to continue until they reached their destination, Kirk tried to put a stop to it.

"I hate to break this to you, but Starfleet operates in

space. Are you sure you didn't apply for a position with the Chicago Transit Authority?"

His traveling companion subsided a little. "Yeah, well—my ex-wife took *everything* in the divorce. You'd think that a species that's succeeded in reaching the stars could have managed by now to devise a more equitable method for dividing communal assets. Sometimes I think the Klingons have the right idea. Anyway, I got nowhere to go but up."

Smiling, the younger man extended a hand. "Jim Kirk."

The exasperated physician eyed him warily, then nodded and took the proffered hand. "Leonard McCoy."

"Took everything?"

McCoy nodded again. "Yeah—everything of mine, including the planet. All I got left is the skeleton, and I wouldn't be surprised if she put a lien out on that."

The whine at the stern rose to a fevered pitch. The shuttle rocked slightly, rose to a predetermined height, and then swerved. As it cleared the construction and administration complex it accelerated rapidly, shoving its passengers back into their protective padding. From where he was seated Kirk had only a partial view out one of the ports. Beneath the ascending craft the surface of the Earth was falling away rapidly. Iowa was falling away rapidly. He settled himself back in his seat. He was leaving behind everything he had ever known, every vestige and reminder of his life to this point in time.

Good riddance.

V

*T*hough the multiple kisses Kirk was deploying along the length of the body beneath him were going off like very tiny photon torpedoes, neither they nor the effect they were having were simulated. The exquisite feminine shape bucked and twisted beneath his hands and his lips. Moaning, she forced herself to push his head away as she raised her head to look down at him. Her eyes were bright, her lips red, and her skin as green as the fabled city of Oz.

"I can't stand it anymore, Jim."

His head hovering in the vicinity of her stomach, he grinned up at her. "That's the general idea."

Dropping down, he resumed his previous activity on her left leg and was soon advancing steadily northward. Lying back, she writhed in delight. A normal enough state of affairs for an Orion female, but one of which they never grew tired.

"How did you know?"

"Voodoo, baby, voodoo."

She gasped, head thrown back and eyes half closed. "What—what is this 'voodoo'?"

"Ancient secret Terran technology. Very complicated. I'll elaborate on some other occasion." His mouth moved against her. "One course of instruction at a time."

Her lips parted in ecstasy. "You—you are amazing."

He smiled to himself. "You just wait till we initiate warp drive."

At which point the door to the dormitory room dinged softly and slid aside.

Sitting straight up on the bed, her green-swirled black underwear pulled taut against her, the Orion cadet looked wildly toward the front of the room. "Hide! Under the bed! Quick!"

Naked save for his underwear, he rolled to a hard landing on the floor. "Under the bed? Isn't this kinda clichéd? I mean, I could . . ."

"Under the bed, now!"

Approaching from the front of the room, footsteps grew louder as he hurried to conceal himself. Peering out from his prone position, he saw feet enter. They were clad in black boots. That style, simple yet elegant—where did he know it from? And the legs that fit so precisely and perfectly and, yes, beautifully into them—didn't he know them as well? At least they were neither male nor Orion.

"I thought you were taking finals," his erstwhile paramour inquired. *A bit too loudly,* Kirk thought.

"I finished early. I was working in the language lab. We're picking up a lot of chatter, something about a prison escape and a stolen vessel that destroyed an entire Klingon fleet. Why? What's wrong?"

That was all it took for him to match the owner with the boots. The voice was as unforgettable as the legs. A skirt fell to the floor, followed by a shirt. Squirming against the floor in hopes of getting a better look, he tried to move forward without making any noise.

"We've been running simulations all week," the green girl atop the mattress explained. "I'm just catching up on some rest. Tired. Very tired." She yawned prodigiously.

It was not quite dramatic or loud enough to muffle the sound of something moving beneath her. Uhura's expression contorted.

"We have a proverb where I come from. 'A sweet taste does not remain forever in the mouth.' Were you running simulations with the mouth-breather hiding under your bed? Or did you mean 'stimulations'?"

Not in the least embarrassed despite being caught in *flagrante delicto*—or at least in *dishabille*—Kirk emerged from beneath the bed and stood up on the far side. Uhura's underwear, he noted with a touch of regret, was disappointingly conventional.

"Hey, I got one, I got one," he volunteered. " 'A man on the ground cannot fall.' "

She didn't know whether to laugh or applaud. "That's a South African proverb. I'm not from Southern Africa."

He raised a hand, his voice solemn. "And thus by such stealthy means we draw ever nearer to your actual first name. Your hearing's pretty good. You *sure* both your parents are human?"

She shook her head and sighed. "Get gone, Jim. It's my ass too if Administration catches you in this room." She nodded in his direction. "Never mind in that condition."

"In what condi—oh." Having the grace to finally look somewhat abashed, he began climbing into the pile of clothes that had been discarded on the far side of the bed. While he put on his clothes, Uhura addressed her roommate in Orion Prime. Already she had sufficient command of numerous alien humanoid tongues to render her tone disapproving. She was utterly indifferent to her current state of undress.

"You know he's been through half the cadet corps since he got here? There are rumors not all of them were even humanoid."

Such a comment might have drawn an emotional response from another human female. To an Orion the veiled accusation amounted to little more than a straightforward, utterly uncontroversial statement of fact. Cadet Gaila's response was tart and matter-of-fact.

"Which half are *you* in?"

Uhura shrugged. "He's not my type. Too abrasive, too self-centered, too much in love with himself. I prefer someone capable of a little more self-effacement and a lot less impetuosity." Shifting back to standard Federation English, she looked at Kirk. "Stop staring. Put your pants on."

Kirk pulled his shirt down over his head.

Nude from the waist down save for his underwear and boots, he smiled at her—and spoke in Orion Prime. "I would, but you're standing on them." Switching back to English he added, "And hardly *half*. You're rounding up that number. Not that I'm not flattered, mind."

Taking a step back, she picked up his pants and threw them at him. He caught them easily, hoping she would notice the grin he flashed in return. He took his time pulling on one leg, then the other. When he was done he strode confidently past the two women: a disapproving Uhura with her arms folded over her chest, a winsome Gaila with arms behind her back.

"And," he added as he made his exit, "they were *all* humanoid—I think."

The communications officer's tone was more than bored: Uhura sounded almost resentful. "We are receiving a distress signal from the *U.S.S. Kobayashi Maru*. The ship has lost power and is stranded. Starfleet Command has ordered us to rescue them."

Whipping around in the command chair, James T. Kirk hastened to correct her.

"Starfleet Command has ordered us to rescue them— *Captain.*"

She glared at him sharply, then turned back to her console. From another station, McCoy recited in a resigned monotone.

"Klingon vessels have entered the Neutral Zone and they are firing upon us."

At this point in the simulation cadet responses varied from panicked, to confused, to nonexistent. On this occasion Kirk succeeded in providing one that, insofar as any present could recall, was entirely original. Not necessarily sensible, not even wholly coherent, but original.

"That's okay."

His fellow cadets gawked at him. Even Uhura turned from the communications station. It was left to McCoy to comment.

"It's *okay?*"

From the command chair, Kirk waved diffidently. "Yeah—don't worry about it."

Above and to one side of the simulation bridge, puzzled test administrators and technicians exchanged a number of profoundly bemused looks.

"Did he just say 'Don't worry about it'?" one administrator asked his colleague.

Turning back to the simulation chamber, his cohort's eyes narrowed as they focused tightly on the cadet presently occupying the command chair.

"What's he doing . . . ?"

"Three more Klingon warbirds decloaking and targeting our ship," McCoy reported from his position. He glanced toward the command chair, occupied by a friend who possibly had lost his mind. "I don't suppose that's a problem either?"

Kirk let himself slide a little lower in the chair. "Nah."

The cadet manning tactical reported in. "They're firing, Captain. *All* of them."

Kirk nodded in understanding. "Alert medical bay to prepare to receive all crew members from the damaged ship."

"And how do you expect *us* to rescue *them,*" Uhura pointed out sharply, "when *we're* surrounded and under attack by the Klingons?"

Briefly, he sounded like someone in command. *"Alert medical."*

Visibly annoyed, she complied.

"We're being hit," McCoy reported. "Shields at sixty percent."

"I understand," Kirk replied blithely.

How have I let myself be roped into this farce? McCoy found himself wondering. "Should we at least, oh, I dunno—fire back?"

Kirk's brow furrowed as if he were deep in thought. "Mmm—no," he finally replied.

"Of course not," McCoy muttered under his breath. "What an absurd notion. Forgive me for bringing it up."

Above and outside the perfectly replicated command deck, a number of technicians busied themselves at their consoles fine-tuning simulation variables according to the responses propagated by the crew training in the room below them. Computer programs could be learned, predicted, and defeated. Computer programs undergoing continuous modification by live participants possessed critical aspects of ongoing variability that could not be memorized. In other words, the simulation technicians supplied the real-life responses no program could provide.

As they followed the progress of the simulation, the test administrators and technicians were careful not to get too close to the tech seated slightly off to the left at the main console. With her bright green skin she was immediately identifiable as an Orion humanoid. Since it was both visually and chemically unavoidable, admiration of such beings was permitted, so long as the admirer did not linger in the vicinity. It was recognized that extended proximity to an Orion female was distracting to other humanoids. In fact, it could be downright dangerous.

Anyone who happened to be looking in her direction suddenly found themselves wrenched back to reality.

Instrument consoles suddenly went berserk and died. Information that should have been transmitted was not. Commands to the simulation consoles below died aborning. Perplexed monitors and baffled instructors struggled to redirect, reassign, and reboot important instrumentation, all to no avail.

Then, as abruptly and inexplicably as every monitor had gone blank and every console had died, lights came back on, monitors winked back to life, and telltales resumed spitting out information.

Below, Kirk continued to relax in the command chair, waiting. The report he anticipated was not long in coming.

"The *Kobayashi Maru* is still in distress," Uhura reported, "but—the Klingons have stopped firing. They are dropping shields and powering down their weapons!" The astonishment in her voice verged on the childlike.

"Imagine that." Kirk finally straightened in the chair. "Then I guess we might as well respond. Arm photons. Prepare to fire on the Klingon warbirds."

"Jim," McCoy reported, "their shields are up."

Kirk turned innocent eyes on his friend. "Are they?"

McCoy looked back at his console. Blinking, he leaned as close to it as he could without losing focus. "Uh—no," he finally admitted.

Kirk nodded with satisfaction. "Fire on all enemy ships. One photon each should do. No reason to waste munitions."

"Yes—yes *sir.*" The tactical officer complied. Unable to resist turning from their own instruments, every one of the cadets on deck momentarily put aside their individual assignments as they looked toward the forward screen. Unimpeded by shields, five photon torpedoes struck five Klingon warships head on. Each warbird exploded with satisfying brilliance. As the resulting fragments filled the monitor,

McCoy once more looked toward the command chair. Only this time he was smiling.

The simulation was not quite over. Kirk turned toward the communications station. "Signal the *Kobayashi Maru*. Tell them they are now safe and their rescue is assured. Begin rescue of the stranded crew." He glanced toward the helmsman. "Bring us in close and arrange for shuttle transfer at leisure, beginning with the most seriously wounded." As he let his eyes rove around the simulation room, his gaze was met by a succession of flabbergasted stares.

"So. We've eliminated all enemy ships, no one on board was injured, and the successful rescue of the *Kobayashi Maru* crew is under way." For the first time he let his attention wander upward to the windows of the administration room. "Anything else?"

The stunned silence among the administrators was no less profound than that which had settled over the simulation chamber below. Finally one turned to the figure standing ramrod straight alongside him.

"How'd that kid beat your test?" the administrator inquired in disbelief.

Spock's gaze did not swerve from the simulation bridge. In particular, it was locked on one participant: the grinning cadet who occupied the command chair. The test designer's tone was in no way properly reflective of what was going through his mind.

"I do not know . . ."

The immense ship was alone. Continually expanding, never to be finished, the *Narada*'s automated constructors labored in the cold and silence of deep space to add still more capacity to the vessel's interior while rendering its appearance ever more intimidating. In this it reflected its captain's ambition as well as his aims.

They had been waiting for this moment for a long time. Not so long in galactic terms; a quarter century in terrestrial years. On the bridge all eyes including Nero's were focused on the forward viewscreen. At the moment it showed nothing but star field. It had been thus for two days now. As time passed and nothing happened, a hesitant Ayel stepped forward to venture a comment. He did not do so lightly. As much as he respected his captain, as much as he held him in awe, he knew that Nero would not hesitate to kill him in an instant if he thought that his trusted second-in-command had for a single moment faltered in their common purpose.

"Perhaps, Captain, our calculations were incomplete. Considering that it was necessary to plot the energy distortions involved against the projected time frame under such conditions and involving physics that are as much theoretical as proven, it would not be surprising if the delivered result is imperfect."

"No." Nero spoke with the confidence of one for whom science and mathematics were intimate servants of self. "It is now. Now and here. We wait."

As it turned out, both Romulans were right. The calculations *were* slightly off, and the now was only slightly postponed. The great ship trembled perceptibly as space warped before it. The distance between them was substantial, but not in interstellar terms. Opening, a vortex spat energy and stripped particles. Scrambled subatomic matter fountained forth in every direction. In the midst of the particulate chaos something notably larger and intact emerged. Remarkably, it was a ship—in one piece and moving fast. The uniqueness of its shape rendered it instantly identifiable. Nero needed no technical confirmation.

"Our wait is over." He stared at the screen with a terrible longing. "Welcome back—*Spock.*"

VI

No one knew why the assembly had been called. It was unusual but not unprecedented. Called from their classes, hundreds of cadets streamed across the manicured lawns and free-poured walkways of the Academy campus. It was a beautiful day, the towers of downtown San Francisco gleaming in a blue sky that had been cleared of fog by a light offshore breeze.

A perfect day for a coronation, Kirk thought as he paced McCoy toward the assembly hall. Not that they would give him a crown. He would settle for an official commendation in his record. And maybe a plaque. A plaque would be nice, preferably one with an integrated holo projector so that visitors could admire the ceremony in three dimensions, complete with accompanying sound. He would settle for that, yes.

"I made valedictorian," he surmised boastfully. "I bet that's what this is. Or they're going to give me special notice for being the first cadet to solve the *Kobayashi* scenario. Or they're going to announce a commendation on top of the valedictorian award."

His friend regarded him with his usual jaundiced eye. "You know you might be constipated, on account of you being so full of yourself. If you elevate yourself any more you risk breaking gravity and drifting off the planet. I don't think even you can accomplish much in space without a ship."

"You're wrong there, Bones. I don't need a ship." Kirk radiated confidence as they started up the steps leading to the assembly hall. "A simple spacesuit'll do me."

A doubtful McCoy shook his head. "Where will they ever find one big enough to fit your head?"

"C'mon, Bones. Don't be jealous."

The older man gaped at him. "Jealous? I'm not jealous of you. I'm expectant. I look forward to being able to write the first scientific paper on a cadet who died from brain hemorrhaging due to a surplus of ego."

"Fine with me." Kirk winked at the doctor as they entered the building. "Just make sure I'm co-credited as the author."

McCoy sighed deeply. "Jim, you're incorrigible."

"No I'm not. I'm in the assembly hall. Let's find some room down front."

"Don't you want to sit in back so you can walk the entire length of the hall and bask for as long as possible in the glory you expect to receive?"

Kirk demurred as they entered the rapidly filling amphitheater. "Not a good idea. I might trip. Bad for thy image."

"Trip over what? Your own teeth? You might even try keeping your mouth closed for a change."

"Why?" Kirk asked innocently. "False modesty never did me any good before." When this time his friend failed to reply, Kirk added, "Bones, you always have permission to speak your mind, even in the face of my growing power."

"Thanks," McCoy replied wryly. "Just don't forget that the one person on a starship who can relieve an officer of duty is the ship's doctor. And that's not you, Mister Omnipotent Farm Boy. That's *me.*"

Kirk conceded the point as they searched the lower tier of seats for a couple of empty places. "And don't you forget the one person who can relieve the ship's *doctor* of duty." McCoy frowned in puzzlement. Kirk let him stew a moment before reminding him. "The ship's doctor's ex-wife."

His friend moaned.

Muted discussion filled the amphitheater as cadets continued to arrive from distant corners of the campus. Every available opening at the Academy was filled, Starfleet constantly being in need of competent trainees. Only when the exalted members of the Academy council began to arrive did conversation start to fade. When the senior officers and school advisers took their seats, so did every one of the cadets. At the same time and without the need for a command, all conversation ceased. Kirk was delighted to see that his mentor, Captain Pike, was among those seated at the long table facing the risers. One more good sign, he felt. The Academy commandant, Admiral Richard Barnett, spoke crisply into the silence.

"James T. Kirk. Step forward."

Kirk threw his friend McCoy a look that said "See?" as plainly as if he had voiced it. Confident, beaming, he marched down onto the floor and halted at attention. The commandant was gazing evenly at him. The big man was not smiling, but that meant nothing. Joyous as it promised to be, the assembly was still a formal occasion. The expressions on the faces of the other members of the council were unreadable, Pike's included.

The commandant began speaking. And the longer he spoke, the more Kirk felt his illusions as well as his conclusions collapsing in a confused heap around him.

"An incident has occurred," Admiral Barnett began, "that concerns the entire student body. Academic immorality by one is an assault on us *all*. It will not be allowed to stand. Cadet Kirk, evidence has been submitted to this council suggesting you violated Regulation Seventeen four-three pursuant to the Starfleet Code of Ethical Conduct. Is there anything you care to say before we begin?"

Rapid decisions. A good part of his training involved learning how to make rapid decisions while operating under difficult circumstances. Standing there alone with the eyes of everyone in the room lasered onto him, he could hardly imagine a more difficult set of circumstances. By now it had struck home that he had not been summoned to receive an award. The assembly, however, had indeed been called for him.

He was on trial.

All right. If they expected him to break under the pressure, to falter and whimper, they'd picked on the wrong cadet. He would stand tall and answer straight, bolstered by the certainty that he had done nothing wrong. Let the whole council have at him, if that was their wish. And he knew exactly how to begin.

"Yes, sir, I do. I believe I have the right under the same code of conduct to face my accuser directly."

The commandant conferred briefly with the administrator on his right, then looked back. Not at Kirk but toward someone in the audience. A figure rose. It was humanoid but not human. At least, not entirely human. Kirk gazed venomously at his accuser. His accuser gazed right back. They had never met before.

The admiral continued. "Cadet Kirk, this is Commander Spock, one of our most distinguished graduates. He's programmed the *Kobayashi Maru* test for the last four years. And improved it considerably in the process. At least, it was regarded as improved until your last run-through threw many of the modifications into question."

"Cadet Kirk." The Vulcan's voice was deceptively controlled. "Much time was spent assessing relevant information following your recent taking of the test in question. Upon careful review it became clear that you activated a subroutine that had been embedded in the programming code, an insertion that somehow succeeded in evading all protective firewalls and resets, thereby changing the conditions of the test."

Kirk forced himself not to sneer, knowing that was one stance that would not go down at all well with the council. "Your point being?" he responded austerely.

"In academic vernacular," Admiral Barnett elucidated coolly, "you cheated."

At such moments there are two kinds of silence: dead quiet, and quieter than dead. The latter now gripped the entire assembly hall.

"Respectfully," Kirk shot back, not the least intimidated

by his accuser's serene confidence, "you wouldn't accuse me of cheating unless you knew something I don't. The test's rigged, isn't it? I pretty much figured that out after I failed it the second time. Follow-up research into four years of preceding failures that I carried out on my own time only confirmed what I already suspected. You programmed it to be unwinnable. Given the available parameters, there's no way of saving the *Kobayashi Maru* and its crew and passengers. So the only way to win is to alter the parameters."

The Vulcan's stare had not shifted, nor had his equanimity. "I fail to see how that is relevant to these proceedings."

"Don't you? Allow me to enlighten you, Commander. If I'm right, if my assumptions and research are correct, then the test *itself* is a cheat."

"Your argument precludes the possibility of a no-win scenario."

Kirk bridled. He wanted to throw more than just words at the Vulcan. But he could not do so here, now, in this place. Another time and place, however . . .

"I don't *believe* in no-win scenarios."

"Then not only have you violated the rules," the commander informed him calmly, "you have failed to understand the principal lesson that is embodied in the test."

Kirk almost bowed. "I abase myself before your superior knowledge. Please, enlighten me."

"Gladly. A captain cannot cheat death. The inevitable must be met with as much skill and resolution as possible. When 'winning' is self-evidently not an attainable goal, the objective must be to preserve and protect as much as one can. That is a captain's task. That is the task of whoever is forced to take the *Kobayashi Maru* test. To achieve what can be achieved when survivability is no longer an option. To achieve—not to evade."

Kirk replied hastily, but he couldn't help himself. As it was, it was all he could do to keep from charging across the aisle and slamming his fist into that smug Vulcan face.

"Maybe you just don't like that I beat your test."

If his response was intended to elicit an emotive reaction from his accuser it did not come close to succeeding. "I am Vulcan. 'Like' is not a verb in our vernacular. I fail to comprehend your indignation," the Vulcan confessed. "I've simply made the logical deduction that when considering your recent performance and your rationalization for the actions you took, that you're a liar."

Kirk feigned astonishment. "What an idiot I am for taking that personally."

"At last: something on which we are agreed. Management of a crisis situation depends on a captain's certainty that the crew can and will follow orders no matter how desperate or seemingly hopeless the circumstances in which they find themselves. By artificially altering those circumstances you introduced an element that was outside the given parameters of the test. As a consequence those cadets under your 'command' had their own responses compromised. To satisfy your own base need to win at all costs, you were willing to sacrifice their performance ratings."

A murmur rose from some among the assembled. Its tone was not complimentary. Feeling the argument slipping away from him, Kirk tried to counter the Vulcan's analysis.

"A crisis is by definition a surprise. And a surprise by definition has no parameters. It is whatever it is at the moment it announces itself. Consequently any action taken to counter it is self-evidently valid. Which justifies *my* actions. In a real-life crisis situation it's often the actions taken outside accepted rules, regulations, and *parameters* that result in success. Following the rules—going by the book, if you'll excuse the cliché—is frequently the quickest path to disaster. Surprise needs to be met with surprise—not predictability. Not by a ship, not by its crew, and not by its captain. Evidently we espouse different approaches to crisis management, Commander. 'Crisis management'—taken at face value, there's no rule book for *that.*"

The Vulcan did not lack for a response to the accused's diatribe. "Given that your experience in space travel is limited to the day of your birth and a modest subsequent travel interval, you lack the experience necessary to make that judgment. You advocate a methodology based on assumption and emotion, not familiarity and knowledge."

"Have *you* taken the test, Commander Spork?"

"*Spock.* As a Vulcan, I require no additional training to control my narcissism when making command decisions. They are and will always be invariably based on reason, logic, and the *facts as they exist in reality.* Not as we might *wish* them to be in order to conveniently fit some private notion of how the universe is supposed to operate."

Another round of murmuring drifted through the assembled cadets, and for the second time Kirk was aware that he had lost a point in the ongoing debate. At this rate he would not have to worry about being appointed valedictorian. Several additional exchanges like the most recent one and he would find himself cashiered right out of the Academy and on his way back to Iowa.

That scenario frightened him far more than anything the council might do to him.

Despite the Vulcan's seemingly unassailable rhetorical brilliance Kirk was not lacking for a comeback. He was about to propound it when an officer unexpectedly appeared and marched smartly up to the dais. Handing a hard copy to the commandant, he leaned over and whispered something in the admiral's ear. This was followed by a short, tense exchange of words. As the intruding officer stepped back, Admiral Barnett rose from his chair. The eyes of the other council members as well as those of every cadet in the amphitheater locked on the commandant.

"This is a Red Alert—all officers are to report to duty stations. All graduating cadets, report to your barracks' officers in hangar one for immediate assignment. This is not a drill. I repeat—this is not a drill."

There was doubtless more, a lot more, but it was forestalled by the Academy commandant as he rose to his feet. His gaze swept quickly over the assembled anxious faces—all of which, he reflected, were far too young for what he was about to tell them.

"This hearing is at recess until further notice. Assembly dismissed, attendees to comply with all applicable alert regulations." Turning and moving fast, he exited out the back of the amphitheater. The rest of the council was close on his heels, talking animatedly among themselves.

A sea of brightly colored uniforms was set in motion as cadets hurried, under control but moving fast, toward the exits. Some conversed loudly and excitedly with friends. Others broke into a run to beat the rush. No one lingered, wanting to be the last out.

Except Kirk. The center of attention a moment earlier, he had been completely forgotten. Abandoned to himself between assembly and council dais, he gazed as if paralyzed at his rapidly emptying surroundings. As he stood there, a familiar figure passed quickly. Unlike during some of their previous encounters, this time Captain Christopher Pike was all business. He spoke tersely in passing.

"Cheating isn't winning."

Left alone with that, Kirk stood in silent contemplation of what had so unexpectedly and shockingly befallen him. A hand on his shoulder brought him out of his reverie.

"Come on, Jim. You heard the order."

He shook himself. "Yes. But the accusation?"

McCoy smiled. "Didn't you hear the commandant? Recessed. School recess, but not the kind you remember. Let's move."

Nodding, Kirk followed his friend out into the corridor. There they quickly found themselves caught up in the flow of uniforms. The atmosphere was thick with excitement and tension. Not with fear; not yet. No one knew why the alarm had been sounded. "This is not a drill." Which was not conclusive proof they were *not* embarked on a drill. Starfleet could be infuriatingly fickle about such matters, particularly when a graduating class was involved. Still, they had no choice but to proceed as if the announcement had been based on an unknown reality instead of some bureaucrat's idea of a clever test. Any cadet who reacted by treating the broadcast as fake would likely wind up a candidate for quick dismissal from the service.

Just as Kirk had been on the verge of becoming. Talk

about the hand of Fate. First it had smacked him across the face and knocked him for a loop. Now it was dusting him off and sending him on his way. At least, it was for as long as his trial was in recess, he reminded himself. *His trial.* His expression darkened as he glanced over at McCoy.

"Who *was* that pointy-eared bastard?"

McCoy shook his head. "I don't know—but I like him."

To a visitor it might have looked as if the main hangar was consumed by panic. What an outsider took for chaos was in fact organized frenzy. Everyone was in motion, no one was standing still. Cadets and other personnel were reporting to stations as their assignments were delivered and occasional conflicts sorted out. Maintenance personnel ignored them all as they proceeded with preparations for launching several dozen shuttles. Support teams checked out ships and loaded equipment. Everyone knew their job, everyone knew where they were supposed to go—if only, in the case of the anxious cadets, to learn their eventual destination.

The commandant's voice boomed over the swirling mass of Starfleet personnel, not all of whom were human or even humanoid.

"We have a crisis situation. We have received a distress call from Vulcan. Further details will be forthcoming, but as of this moment you are no longer cadets, you are Starfleet officers. I'm afraid that for this year's class the usual graduation ceremonies will have to be postponed. Your official certifications will be placed in your files, which may be inspected at your leisure— once you are in space. I apologize in advance for any omissions. All complaints due to oversights will be duly reviewed. In any

event, you will not have time to monitor their progress. Listen for your assignments. If you do not hear your name called, check with the nearest senior officer."

As they hurried along one line of shuttles searching for a particular craft, names rang out around Kirk and McCoy as different squad leaders bellowed names and assignments.

"Blake—*Newton*...Burke—Starbase Three...Counter—*Odyssey*...Fugeman—Regula One...Gerace—*Farragut*...Korax—*Drake*...McCoy—*Enterprise.*"

There, that was the one they were looking for. Both men turned, heading for the thickset officer standing outside one of numerous identical shuttles. But his destination was not the same as the others', an excited Kirk knew. Not by a long warp. Around them the litany of assignments continued to ring out.

"...McGrath—*Potemkin*...Tel'Peh—*Bradbury*...Davis—*Kongo*..."

The two cadets halted before the officer who had called McCoy's name. Behind the busy lieutenant, cadets and other personnel were filing into a waiting shuttle. Trying hard to restrain himself, Kirk confronted the officer.

"Excuse me—you didn't call my name. *Kirk,* James T."

The man looked down at the thin sheet of continuously changing electrophoretic plastic he was holding. "That's because it's faded out. You're on academic probation, Kirk. Pending the result of your hearing, you're grounded until the council rules on your case."

When he was nine, Kirk had missed a step, fallen into a creek, and hit his head on a protruding rock. His brother George had jumped in and pulled him out. When he came to, he had looked up and seen the terror in his brother's face. Now he understood how George felt, since that was exactly how he felt right now.

"But it's an emergency situation. A general alarm, Red Alert. Starfleet needs every available hand and tentacle!"

The disembarking officer was adamant. "Sorry, Kirk— without authorization I can't let you on board. You know the regs. Be my neck if I let you pass." With that he turned and walked away, studying his readout.

A dazed Kirk stumbled away from the shuttle. He wasn't on the *Enterprise*. He wasn't on *anything*. He would be stuck here on Earth, in an Academy populated by underclassfolk, while every one of his friends and acquaintances soared outsystem, having been flash-promoted in the service of a still-unknown emergency. They would all return as full officers while he . . . while he . . .

That same hand returned to his shoulder, comforting this time.

"Jim," McCoy murmured encouragingly, "they'll rule in your favor. You had 'em on the ropes. Just drawing out the deliberations the way you did when I bet everyone expected you to roll over and play dead . . . They've got to reinstate you, if only so you can verify the truth of your argument." He looked behind him. Kirk was his friend, but other imperatives were calling. "Look, Jim—I gotta go."

Kirk didn't, couldn't, look at his friend. He barely managed to mumble, "Yeah—yeah, go . . ." He forced his face into a half smile.

Torn between friend and future, McCoy pulled away and hurried off. Behind him Kirk had to lean against a nearby pillar to keep from collapsing. There was no reason why he should make the effort, he told himself. Not when everything else he had worked for, everything else he had ever wanted, was falling to pieces around him. Though surrounded by hundreds of cadets, soldiers, support personnel, and others, he was all alone.

Maybe not quite alone.

McCoy was halfway back to his assigned shuttle when a thought hit him. Not as hard or incapacitatingly as the river rock that had knocked out nine-year-old Jim Kirk, but powerfully enough to make him pull up short. A couple of noncoms glanced curiously in his direction as the senior cadet single-mindedly pushed past them, but they made no move to confront him. A Red Alert situation was not the time to be a stickler for military protocol. Besides, the cadet's insignia identified him as a doctor. Doubtless he had a good reason for ignoring them.

They had no idea.

VII

Kirk spun around angrily as the hand grabbed him. Ready to hit out at anything, he was drawing back a fistful of frustration when he recognized McCoy. Shock at his situation gave way to incomprehension as he stared at his friend.

"What— Bones, what're you doing?" He nodded past the doctor. "Your shuttle's waiting. I thought you'd be . . ."

McCoy was tugging at him. "Shut up and come with me."

Too numbed by the circumstances that had befallen him to object, Kirk allowed himself to be dragged along. He was so bewildered that he failed to notice Uhura among a group of waiting cadets as McCoy pulled him forward.

". . . Jaxa—*Endeavor*," an assignments officer was declaiming. ". . . T'nag—*Antares* . . . Uhura—*Farragut* . . ."

Farragut? she thought. She'd heard right, but that didn't make it right. Straining to see over the heads of her fellow cadets, she finally found who she was looking for and broke from the crowd. Noting the look in her eyes, more than one person hurried to get out of her way.

Spock was conferring with several other officers and did not notice her approach. She waited impatiently for the conference to finish. Waited, in fact, exactly one minute. No doubt the Vulcan would have appreciated the precision, but Uhura had no intention of alluding to it.

"Commander—a word? If you can spare me some time?"

Their eyes met and he favored his fellow officers with a slight nod. "Gentlemen, if you'll excuse me for a moment." Commander and cadet moved off to one side. Spock's stance was wholly professional.

"Yes, Lieutenant?"

Her tone was even and controlled, but there was fire in her eyes. "Was I not one of your top students?"

"Indeed you were," he replied without hesitation.

"Did I not receive a gold rating for xenolinguistic skills in all categories, from constructive verbalizations to click, whistle, and atmospheric manipulations of all kinds, giving the Academy first place over Kyoto *and* MIT at the Oxford Linguistics Invitational?"

"An exceptional achievement, to be su—"

Heedless of his superior rank, she interrupted him without so much as a raised hand. "And did I *not,* on *multiple* occasions, make it clear that my dream and the reason behind four years of hard work was to serve on the *Enterprise*?"

"Vociferously and repeatedly, perhaps even to the point of obsession," he admitted. "Your ability to communicate in that regard was the equal of any of your classroom efforts."

Uhura took a step forward. Anyone other than Spock

might have found the movement threatening. *"And yet I was assigned to the* Farragut?"

Time hung suspended between them. Viewing the confrontation from afar, a neutral observer might reasonably have expected the Vulcan commander to upbraid the aggressive cadet, not only for her increasingly aggressive tone but for perceptibly intruding on a superior officer's personal space. The actual consequences were rather different.

Spock looked away. It was impossible to tell if he did so to avoid the cadet's laser-like stare—or to see if anyone was watching. His voice also changed, its tenor becoming a touch less professional, a tad less . . . Vulcan. His reply clearly indicated concern for the agitated young woman standing before him. Concern—and possibly, just possibly, something more. One couldn't tell from the actual words he spoke, of course.

"I was simply," he murmured low enough so that no one else could possibly overhear, "trying to avoid the appearance of favoritism."

She advanced another step, which put her not quite inside his uniform, but close. "Uh-*huh.*" Fiery eyes dropped to the readout sheet he was holding. The gap remaining between them was barely wide enough for him to hold the thin sheet of radiant plastic without crumpling. "A simple entry mistake by Personnel. Happens all the time. Anyone would understand. I'm *on* the *Enterprise.*"

Their eyes held for a long moment. Without further comment he let his gaze drop to his readout. One finger moved against the touch-sensitive material.

"Yes, I believe you are."

A thin smile crossed her face as she nodded, pivoted

smartly on one heel, and stalked off to see to the transfer of her personal effects. Commander Spock watched her go, his gaze following her for longer than was necessary before returning to the essential work at hand.

It took McCoy no time at all to locate the section of hangar he sought. Deemed critical material, the sizable stock of medical gear had been curtained off from less vital supplies. With his still bemused friend in tow, the doctor waited until a worker departed pushing a pallet piled high with stores. Quickly he scanned the contents of several small refrigerated satchels until he found the one he was looking for. Actually it was not the one he was looking for, but given that they had no time to work their way through the considerable stock of equipment, it would have to do. That was what a physician operating under time constraints and in an emergency situation was trained to do, he told himself as he unsealed the container and sorted through its contents.

　　Kirk's attention shifted back and forth between his friend's frenetic searching and the bustle of men and machines on the other side of the translucent shielding curtain. "Bones, what are we doing here? What're you after?"

　　"I'm looking for a solution to a problem in a solution. I couldn't just leave you there, looking all pitiful. Ah—this'll do!" Pulling a cartridge out of the container he had opened, he gripped it between his teeth as he ripped the packaging off a hypospray and shoved the tiny cylinder into the open breech. The delivery mechanism automatically activated the contents of the cartridge—which he promptly jammed against his friend's neck.

"OW!—what the hell was that?" Kirk grabbed at the hypo but McCoy had already pulled it back and was in the process of disposing of it.

"You're gonna start to lose vision in your left eye."

Almost before the doctor finished the explanation, Kirk found himself leaning forward and repeatedly blinking the indicated orb. "Yeah, I already am—have." Abruptly he stood up straight, arched his back, and then bent forward anew. "What'd you *do* to me?"

"You're gonna get a really bad headache," McCoy informed him.

On cue Kirk grabbed at his head with both hands and cringed, closing his eyes tight. "God, what's *happening*!" Straightening, he tried to turn and nearly fell. Anticipating his friend's loss of balance—along with the loss of sight in one eye, fading cerebral capacity, and a delightfully varied assortment of other incapacitating ailments—McCoy grabbed him to keep him from falling.

"I just shot you with a vaccine designed to prevent the viral infection caused by the bite of the Melvarian mud flea. The fact that there aren't any Melvarian mud fleas within a hundred light-years of here is irrelevant. It's the side effects that are important. Since the vaccine is derived from an emulsion made from the internal organs of the flea itself, a mild but easily treatable case of the infection is the unavoidable result. Without getting further into the xenobiological specifics, the short version is that you'll be feeling the symptoms of the disease for about an hour."

Consciously deranged, Kirk gazed openmouthed at his friend even as he had to lean on him for support. "You injected me with an alien *mud flea virus*?"

Getting his body under one of his friend's arms, McCoy started to haul him away from the medical storage site, straining with the effort required to keep them both moving forward.

"Yeah—you owe me one."

They barely made it in time. Whether it would be enough remained to be seen. A Klaxon was sounding and lights on the side of the shuttle indicated it was running through final countdown procedures prior to liftoff. Exerting himself to the utmost, McCoy heaved them both toward the boarding ramp.

The junior officer who intercepted them had been working without a break ever since the Red Alert had been sounded. He was in no mood for argument and had no intention of delaying the small ship's departure. The irate comment he had prepared, however, died on his lips as soon as he got a look at Kirk's face. He had seen some hungover cadets in his time, and some sick cadets, and even a few cadets who had survived classes in advanced Klingon hand-to-hand combat styles.

But he had never seen anyone who looked as bad as James T. Kirk did at that moment.

"Good Lord—what happened to *him*?" The boarding officer's gaze dropped to the cadet's hands. Both had swollen to a degree that suggested an advanced case of highly localized elephantiasis.

Struggling to keep his friend vertical, McCoy spoke without hesitation. "He's suffering from an inflamed epididymis complicated by excessive swelling of the ego region of the cerebral cortex. Got exposed to gram-negative bacterium in the lab. Was writing out the order to send him to the hospital when the alert sounded."

The officer took a long step backward. "Is it . . . contagious?"

McCoy shook his head. "Wholly internalized, transmittal vector is only via direct fluid exchange, no danger to anyone else. He should come through fine if the fever he's suffering from now doesn't boil his brain."

Kirk's eyes widened as they snapped to the face of the man holding him up. There were several questions he badly wanted to ask. Unfortunately his tongue seemed to have transported out of his body, leaving an empty place in his mouth that matched the expanding one in his head.

Pulling a small cylindrical instrument from a breast pocket, the officer ran it the length of the slumping cadet's body. "Kirk, James T." He quickly checked the boarding manifest for the shuttle behind him. "He's not cleared for duty aboard the *Enterprise.*" Raising his gaze, he confronted McCoy uncertainly. "In fact, according to records, he's not cleared for duty anywhere. It says here that he's—"

McCoy interrupted him. "Look, we're operating under Red Alert conditions and I don't have time to argue. I *am* cleared for duty on the *Enterprise,* and Starfleet Medical Regulations state that the treatment and transport of a patient is to be determined at the discretion of his attending physician, which is *me.* Since I'm assigned to this ship, so's he, even if temporarily. Check your regs: medical evaluation supersedes academic dispensation. It's not like I'm trying to sneak my girlfriend aboard. He may be under temporary suspension, but he's not first-year—he's a qualified junior officer, and they'll find something for him to do once he's recovered. But as the physician providing treatment, I can't abandon him. He comes with me." The doctor paused for emphasis.

"Or would *you* like to explain to Captain Pike why the *Enterprise* warped into a crisis situation without one of its senior medical officers?" He glanced pointedly at the other man's ident badge.

The officer hesitated, snuck another look at his manifest. A new alarm began to sound behind him indicating that departure was imminent. He had half a dozen other shuttles to check and he was already running behind. There would doubtless be an evaluation at the end of the emergency period and . . .

Lowering his head, he jerked the stylus he was holding toward the open shuttle portal. "As you were."

"As *you* were." McCoy started lugging his friend up the ramp.

"Been eating more than usual lately, cadet?"

Kirk's cheeks bulged. "I'd appreciate it, Bones, if you didn't mention food for a while."

"Don't worry—any inclination to general nausea is muted by the inflammation of your . . . ," he lowered his voice to a whisper as he continued. Kirk's eyes widened.

"Inflammation of my *what*?"

"Shut up," McCoy hissed as they neared the top of the ramp, "and keep walking. Try to help me, Jim. Make your legs work."

Head lolling, Kirk goggled up at him. "I have legs?"

As soon as they were on board, they had no difficulty finding seats despite the lateness of their arrival. One look in Kirk's direction and everyone gave them plenty of room. A final alarm sounded as the shuttle lifted off and the pilot guided it out of the hangar. Once they were outside and climbing, clean sunlight flooded the interior through the self-polarizing ports. A mumbling Kirk leaned toward his friend.

"One more thing, Bones."

"What's that?" McCoy was pressed back into his launch seat, the usual sweat beginning to bead up on his neck and forehead.

Kirk somehow managed to smile. "I may throw up on you."

Accelerating steadily, the compact craft climbed through the atmosphere. Dark blue sky gave way to violet and then to black. Below, the curve of the Earth stood out like a piece of engraved turquoise in an onyx setting. Advance shuttles preceded Kirk and McCoy's while others trailed behind. The distances between them were sufficient to make those on board feel as if they were utterly alone in the universe.

Until Starbase 1 came into view.

A city in space, the base thrust out enormous transverse arms that terminated in dock and repair facilities for starships. Unusually, every one of them was presently occupied. Resembling irregular snowflakes drifting in an absence of gravity, a storm of servicing craft were swarming around the neatly docked ships, readying them for departure. Despite similar schematics, each vessel featured its own unique, individual design characteristics. All were beautiful and each had something to recommend it. None of which mattered to an enraptured Kirk as he gazed out the nearest port. He only had eyes for one of them. Its markings stood out clear and sharp against the ivory-hued metal and composite skin.

U.S.S. ENTERPRISE NCC–1701

He remembered the first time he had set eyes on her. Unfinished, skeletal, with gaping holes in her sides where her multiple outer hull had yet to be completed. She had been striking then, awkwardly balanced within a web of construction scaffolding on the hard cold plain of central Iowa. Incomplete and out of her element, she had appeared ungainly and graceless—an adolescent starship. Finished and sitting in her service dock, she was a thing of beauty. He couldn't wait to embrace her.

Hopefully by not heaving his guts all over one of her nice, new, spotlessly clean decks.

Describing a smooth arc toward its destination, the shuttle curved into the plane of the base and slowed as it neared the great ship's stern. Greeted by an open, waiting port, the shuttle pilot brought his craft to a smooth touchdown inside the ship's docking bay. Airlock doors closed behind it as he cut impulse power to the shuttle's drive. The taxi craft rocked slightly as a gush of atmosphere pressurized the bay. As soon as the all-clear sounded, the passengers disembarked. Kirk and McCoy were the last to leave.

Fortunately for the struggling doctor, his patient was rapidly regaining his strength.

"Bones," Kirk muttered weakly, "thanks for getting me on board. But I don't feel right. I feel like I'm *leaking*."

McCoy still had alertness and energy enough to see

Spock heading in their direction. "Oh, look—the pointy-eared bastard."

Engrossed in the readout he was holding, the commander did not look up at them. By the time the Vulcan's gaze lifted, McCoy had managed to wrestle Kirk into a side corridor.

A lift deposited the preoccupied commander onto the gleaming new bridge. Unmarred and as yet unused, it sparkled from the proud exertions of the final commissioning crew. No console had been left unpolished, no monitor left uncleaned. In a respectful nod to history, a small plaque featuring an engraving of an ancient aircraft carrier had been affixed to one wall, immensely meaningful despite the fact that it had been placed virtually out of sight. In another corner an unknown technician had left a miniature mop and bucket in deference to the time when such decks would have been swabbed instead of coated with an impact-resistant chemical coating.

All of this registered on the ship's new science officer as he sat down at his station. Whereas other crew members might admire the shine of newly installed instruments or the unvarying multihued glow of projection monitors, the commander was pleased to see that everything fit together as intended and functioned properly at first touch. After running through an initial check of the new ship's systems he turned toward the command chair.

"All decks report ready for launch, Captain." His nonchalant bearing suggested that the science officer had uttered those words a thousand times previously. As indeed he had, if only in elaborate simulations.

"Very well." Shifting slightly in the command chair,

Captain Christopher Pike looked toward the helm. "Set course for Vulcan."

"Course laid in," the lieutenant at the helm controls replied.

"Maximum warp," Pike ordered. *"Punch it."*

Though still in his twenties, Hikaru Sulu was already regarded by many as one of the best pilots in the Federation. Having grown up on oceangoing fishing boats, he had graduated to small hover vehicles and was flying aircraft before he was in his teens. When performing their duties, many of his colleagues appeared to be under stress or laboring to carry out their assignments satisfactorily. Not Sulu. No matter how difficult the situations or simulations, he forever seemed to be smiling at some secret, private joke. This infectious good humor helped to deflect a good deal of the jealousy that might otherwise have attended his rapid rise through the fleet.

The lieutenant's fingers slid deftly over the helm controls and . . . nothing happened.

Uncertain faces began to turn in the direction of the helm. Pike frowned ever so slightly.

"Something the matter, Lieutenant?"

"I'm not sure, Captain. I . . ."

"Where's Helmsman McKenna?"

"Uh, he has lungworms, sir," the lieutenant explained uneasily. "He'll be fine but was unable to report for duty. I'm Hikaru Sulu."

Pike pursed his lips. "And you are a pilot, yes?"

The lieutenant stiffened visibly. "Very much so, sir." Sulu's eyes roved worriedly over the helm console. "I'm not sure what's wrong here . . ."

"Is the parking brake on?"

"No, I'll figure it out, just . . ."

A voice spoke up from the vicinity of the science station. "Have you checked to ensure that all subsidiary connections to starbase have been disengaged?"

As he tried to hide his rising anxiety, the helmsman's gaze flicked to a small readout on one side of the main monitor. His fingers moved. Suitably abashed, he returned his attention forward.

"Ready for warp . . . sir." As he checked another readout he struggled to look anywhere but at the command chair or the science station. "Dock control reports ready for our exit."

Pike nodded. "The external inertial dampener. That's . . . the parking brake." Having dealt suitably with his new helmsman, he let his gaze rove the bridge as he strove to make eye contact with each member of his crew.

"Many of you have served with me before. To those who are new to duty I extend a hearty welcome and my apologies for the haste with which you have been called into active service. Circumstances dictate speed. Stars and galaxies whirl through space at sometimes unimaginable velocities. On such an occasion Starfleet can do no less.

"Certainly the maiden voyage of our newest flagship deserves more pomp and circumstance than we can afford today. Its christening will have to be our reward for a safe return. I know that every man, woman, and other will do their duty." Pride filled his voice. "You are the best that the Academy and Starfleet can produce. I am proud to serve with you and I hope you will not find me wanting in command."

Someone let out a mild "Yea!" This was followed by muted laughter that quickly faded as all eyes focused on the captain. Pike held a stern visage for a moment, then smiled. Everyone relaxed, but only emotionally. Hands and minds remained wholly focused on the tasks at hand. Leaning forward, Pike activated the ship's intercom.

"All decks, this is Captain Pike. Final preparations should be completed and all hands at flight stations. Prepare for immediate departure."

He looked once more toward the helm.

"Now then, Mister Sulu, let's—punch it."

In the wake of the other ships, the *Enterprise* flashed into warp space.

In the main medical bay, technicians and support personnel were completing last-minute setups. There was always something to be stowed, a report to be forwarded, instruments to be placed in readiness for emergencies that hopefully would not materialize.

In Kirk's case it was a matter of waiting for his bloated hands to shrink back to normal size so that he could stow, forward, or place in readiness something smaller than a chair. With his blunt, sausage-size fingers he couldn't even adjust his own tunic.

"Bones, when's this gonna stop, it's *killing* me . . ."

"What is?" McCoy replied phlegmatically. "Pain, or the fact that you're not looking as perfect as you usually think you are? It'll all be over in half an hour, tops." Leaning closer, he lowered his voice so that passing personnel could not overhear.

"Now listen: I can't sit around and mollycoddle you. I

have work to do. I have to secure my portion of this bay for departure, check in with my colleagues, see to it that the techs know where their stations are, and a hundred other details. Remember our deal. You're my new candy striper. Stay on the medical deck and out of sight as much as possible till we get back in a couple of days. Got it? Anybody questions your specialty or your 'training,' tell 'em you're an assistant anesthesiologist assigned to work directly with me." He smiled sardonically. "I've seen you put people to sleep just talking about yourself, so I know you can pull this off."

Kirk was uncharacteristically subdued. "Bones, I don't know what to say." He let his gaze and his gradually returning vision take in their immediate surroundings. Despite everything, despite having his world turned upside down in the most unanticipated and numbing fashion, he was in space. On a starship. On the *Enterprise.*

"Thanks."

"That'll do." McCoy's grin widened. "I'll be back to check on you as soon as I can. As I said, the symptoms should all be gone within a little while and you should feel completely like yourself again. Meanwhile try to keep out of sight and out of trouble." He started to leave, stopped himself, and left his friend with one final admonition.

"And Jim?"

"Yes, Bones?"

"Stay away from my nurses." Then McCoy was out the open portal and heading for the main surgery. Kirk could hear him railing and complaining until a closing door finally stifled the doctor's rant. Left alone, he looked down at his swollen hands.

As if he could do anything even if he felt like it.

VIII

"**E**ngines at maximum warp, Captain." Sulu allowed himself to relax. In the course of their departure from Starbase 1, Pike had not made an issue of what had been a novice's oversight, something for which the helmsman was more than moderately grateful. In any case they were now under way and everything was functioning normally.

"Thank you, Mister Sulu." Pike turned to his left. "Mister Spock, see that all departments receive the full details of the Vulcan transmission so that they can organize their sections accordingly. Let's give them a condensed version first." He thought a moment. "It'll have more impact if it comes from tactical. What's the name of that whiz kid? Chanko? Cherpov?"

A slim hand went up from another of the bridge's occupied stations. The face beneath it was even more unlined than that of the starship's other new officers.

"*Chekov*, sir. Pavel Andreievich."

Uhura glanced over from her station. The ensign had not been part of her group from the Academy. Judging from his thick Urals accent, he had probably been recruited straight from the venerable Star City Conservatory outside Moscow.

"Right—Chekov." Pike acknowledged the identification. "You are familiar with the details of the Vulcan transmission, Mister Chekov?"

"Yes, sir, I have it memorized completely."

The captain was indulgent. "Very commendable, Mister Chekov. Can you please provide a verbal summary for the crew?"

"Certainly, sir." Turning back to his console, he addressed himself to the integrated pickup. "Chekov, Pavel A. Ensign, authorization code nine-five-wiktor-wiktor-two."

The computer responded promptly. *"Authorization not recognized—please try again. Speak clearly and distinctly."*

"I *am* speaking clearly and distinctly. Agh, this is the twenty-third century. What good is voice recognition that doesn't recognize your *voice*?" Since the rhetorical question failed to make the slightest impression on the computer's programming, he was compelled to try again.

"Nine-five-*v*ictor-*v*ictor-two."

"Access granted. Ensign Chekov, you are recognized."

"Oh thank you so wery, wery much," he responded mockingly. "Actiwate—activate intraship communications. All channels."

Throughout the ship the ensign's face appeared on every active monitor, his youthful visage replacing everything from engineering readouts to entertaining fancies. In engineering, technicians and supervisors paused what they were doing to look and listen. Around them inconceivable amounts of energy roared within their containment fields as they worked to twist space around the ship.

"*Your attention, please,*" the young officer on the screens was saying. "*This is Ensign Pavel Chekov speaking to you from the bridge. The keptin has asked me to brief you on our rescue mission.*"

In the main tactical bay, weapons masters looked up from their work at the nearest screen. Around them was concentrated enough destructive power to level a fair segment of a small continent. Since its proximity did not disturb them, they were unlikely to be unsettled by anything the ensign had to say. But their interest was the equal of anyone else's on board.

"*At twenty-two hundred hours GMT,*" Chekov broadcast, "*long-range sensors detected an energy surge of astronomical proportions in the Vulcan quadrant of Federation space. It was described as 'a lightning storm in space.' As there were and still are no known stellar phenomena in the area capable of producing such a surge on such short notice, this eruption immediately attracted the attention of a broad spectrum of Federation scientists. Soon after, Starfleet Command decoded a distress signal from the Vulcan High Council declaring that seismic sensors situated across the entire surface of the planet were predicting massive tectonic shifts within the planetary crust that could trigger immense earthquakes and unprecedented volcanic activity.*" He cleared his throat.

"*Our mission is to confirm the tectonic shifts with an eye toward possible interdiction of dangerous continental plate mow—plate movement, and to be prepared to assist in evacuations should the need arise.*"

In the main medical bay, staff were putting the final touches on a triage setup while paying close attention to the transmission from the bridge. No one was paying closer attention than Kirk, who lay there listening to the remainder of the ensign's briefing.

"Please review all report details thoroughly before our arrival," Chekov concluded. *"Thank you for your attention."*

Behind Kirk two of the medical technicians returned to their labors. "Wonder what could be causing an energy surge like that? Sounds like Starfleet thinks it's connected to the trouble they're having on Vulcan."

His colleague nodded meaningfully. "Mighty strange coincidence if it's not. Spatial consequences of unpredicted gravitational distortions aren't a specialty of mine. If they are linked, let's hope the phenomenon is a transitory one."

"If it is," her associate observed, "there won't be much for us to do when we get to Vulcan—which would suit me just fine."

"Not to mention the Vulcans." The other tech's comment was heartfelt. She had never met a Vulcan and had yet to encounter the newly commissioned *Enterprise*'s celebrated science officer. His kind were reputed to be a cold, distant people—but they were Federation, just like humans.

Kirk's thought processes were recovering along with the rest of him. Lying there silently off to one side, he had made the same connections as the two techs, as doubtless had everyone else on board who had even a passing interest in geoscience. The ensign's broadcast had instructed all departments to familiarize themselves with the complete body of information that had been transmitted from Vulcan. Swinging his legs off the gurney on which he had been resting, he wandered over to an unoccupied console and pulled up the extensive file.

It seemed reasonably straightforward. The energy anomaly, the consequent tectonic disruptions on Vulcan, the related forces involved—all what one would expect given the urgency of the message. It was all there in cold electronic print. According to the interleaved explication it had been translated from the Vulcan prior to transmission. A caveat he had committed to heart during his first year at the Academy flashed through his mind.

"To be certain of accuracy when drawing conclusions, whether in the lab or in combat, always take care to refer at least once to the original information."

A lightning storm in space. Where had he read a description of an energy surge like that before?

No, it couldn't be, could it? Kirk sat up fast, too fast, his head pounding. He hurt so much he wondered why it was so important . . . wondered why the room had suddenly gotten so bright.

Ever the solicitous doctor, and hoping that he could divert the med tech's attention away from his "patient," McCoy stepped over. "Oh good, Jim, you're awake. How 'ya feel?" Kirk's moaning in pain ensured everyone would remember him, but before McCoy could berate his friend for overreacting, he noticed the size of his hands. "Good God, man!"

"What?" Kirk knew something was wrong. He felt it, he just couldn't see it. He lifted his hands up; they had swollen to elephantine proportions. "What the hell's this?"

"A reaction to the vaccine, dammit."

What he was looking at was a translated electronic file. If he entered the appropriate command, the monitor would provide a hard copy—but it would still be the same translated electronic file. What about the original transmission? Not that he was in a position to do anything about it one way or the other, but . . .

Ever since he had once memorized, just for fun, the instruction manual for a certain antique automobile, he had always been a firm believer in acting on *original* information.

It took only a second to pull up the actual broadcast. Unusually, there was no accompanying visual and the words were distorted due to distance and having been relayed several times prior to decoding. He listened intently, and the longer he listened the more he could sense the hairs on the back of his neck starting to rise. His lips parted in disbelief.

"Holy . . . !"

Now he remembered where he had heard of "a lightning storm in space."

McCoy was furiously scanning Kirk. The readings were not good; now his friend had become his patient.

"We gotta stop the ship!"

Kirk whirled, and managed a stride and a half before nearly knocking down McCoy. The doctor glared at him, started to say something, then changed tack as he saw the look on his friend's face.

"What the hell are you d—?"

"Something's not right," Kirk shot back at him. "In fact, if I'm right, it's real wrong. *Serious* wrong." He grabbed at McCoy's arm. "Come with me, Bones—hurry!"

"*What*?" The doctor jerked free of the younger man's grasp. "Jim, I said *low* profile! That means you should . . . "

But Kirk was already out the door and moving fast, leaving him behind. Flustered and fearing for his friend, McCoy rushed after him.

"Jim—slow down! Wait a goddamn minute! Jim, I'm not kidding—we need to keep your heart rate down."

Kirk located a computer interface; he found his fingers had gotten larger. There followed an impressive string of words not exclusively but most emphatically of the four-letter kind. Only when the long exclamation finally concluded did he bark an order at the console.

"Computer, locate crew member and communications specialist Uhura!"

"As an officer Lieutenant Uhura's location is privatized unless . . ."

"DO IT!" He forced himself to take a deep breath. "Analyze urgency in request tone and calibrate accordingly!"

The ship responded without hesitation. *"Intimations of exigency have been analyzed and their source has been noted for the record. Lieutenant Uhura is presently at communications monitoring station twelve, deck four."*

"I haven't seen a reaction this severe since med school."

"We're flying into a trap!"

Fumbling in his medkit for the correct medication, the doctor looked up and noticed that his patient was gone.

Racing down the corridor, McCoy rounded a turn just in time to see the lift doors sliding shut in front of Kirk. The doctor caught up in time to meet the younger man's eyes, but not in time to make it into the lift with him. He took a step back, forced to wait for another lift to arrive.

"Dammit, Jim!"

You try to help someone, McCoy thought. *But if the patient won't listen to his doctor, then he sure as hell is unlikely to listen to himself.*

Communications twelve was occupied by a mix of junior officers and ensigns, all preoccupied with their current assignments. That did not prevent several of them from looking up curiously as Kirk burst in.

Nearly out of breath, McCoy arrived in the entryway. Spotting Kirk racing to Uhura's station, the doctor caught up with him.

"Are you out of your *mind*? What's going on here?" Reaching out, he wrapped his fingers around Kirk's upper right arm. "Maybe, just maybe, if we can get you back to sickbay without being intercepted, I can . . ."

Kirk met his friend's gaze. "Bones, trust me."

McCoy didn't hear him. "Are you trying to get us both discharged from the service? On *our first day on duty*? I don't mind my name going into the books, but not attached to a record like that!"

"I'm trying to save your ass."

McCoy stiffened, and regarded his friend. "Dammit, Jim, stand still!" He injected Kirk and released him.

"Ow, stop it."

Racing down the crowded section, Kirk kept looking for the one person he knew would confirm his conclusion. Finally, he located Uhura. Any other time he would have found amusing the shock that registered on her face as she recognized him.

"Sorry. Listen, I need to talk to you."

She gaped at him in astonishment. "No *way.*"

"You *gotta* listen to me." Couldn't she hear the desperation in his voice? Was there no communication in communications?

"No!" she shot back. "I don't 'gotta' listen to you, James Kirk. You—you can't even *be* on this ship! How *did* you get on?"

"Later." He moved as close to her as he dared. His voice rose to a shout. Now everyone in the room was looking at him. Leaning to the side, one of the officers had begun whispering urgently into a pickup. Kirk knew he didn't have much time. They would haul him back to medical, and if not McCoy, some other doctor would then pump him full of sedative.

"The transmission from the Klingon prison planet—what exactly . . ."

Kirk might be insane, but he wasn't kidding. She shook her head. She stared hard at him. "Oh my God! What happened to your hands?"

He had to get her to understand *now.* "Who?"

"Your hands . . . "

Behind him, McCoy was dividing his attention between his friend, the communications officer he was badgering, his medical scanner, and the portal that somehow still remained devoid of a security detail.

Kirk knew his time was running out. "Who is responsible for the Klingon attack?" He leaned toward her, heedless of how she might react. He didn't care if she punched him out so long as she concentrated.

"Was the ship woluam?"

Uhura was shaking her head slowly and frowning; she

could tell from his inflections that Kirk was deadly serious. "Was the ship what?"

"What's happening to my mouth?"

"You got numb tongue?" the doctor asked.

Horrified that something so stupid could stop Uhura from understanding, Kirk asked, "Numb tongue?"

"I can fix that," McCoy promised.

"Was the ship what?" Uhura asked, concerned that she would never understand Kirk.

Trying to form the word slowly and clearly, Kirk asked, "Wolumn?"

"What?"

"Wolmun?"

This time the communications specialist looked at his lips, seeing how he was forming the word. "Romulan?"

He nodded urgently. "Yea."

"Yes."

"Yes!"

It was not the earthquake itself that drew Amanda Grayson from the interior of her home out onto the porch. It was the realization that whatever was causing the ground to shake was not a normal seismic tremor. It neither rolled nor heaved in the manner of a natural disturbance. Instead, the trembling mounted to a certain level and held there, steady and unvarying. Ignoring toppling sculptures, trembling furniture, and the cracks that the walls strove to automatically repair, she hurried outside.

Across the desert landscape rocks were tumbling and bouncing down hillsides of brown and ochre. Cliffs cracked away as the inspirational pinnacles and spires she had known for most of her adult life began to crumble like columns of stale cake. And all the while the ground beneath her feet continued to quake with a terrifying constancy.

All of that she could have dealt with. All of that she could have handled—there could be some natural law to explain it. But she could find nothing in her store of knowledge to account for the gigantic pillar of swirling energy that was visible in the distance. Fire and fury, it appeared to be drilling into the ground as if the rocky surface of Vulcan were made of nothing more substantial than the Viennese *schlag* of which Sarek was so fond.

Tilting back her head, she traced the colossal column of energy upward into the clear sky. It appeared to be descending from a metal disk whose proportions and details she was unable to discern. The disk in turn dangled from an irregular metallic thread that must have been of considerable diameter in order to be viewable at such a distance. As for the suspending cables, they vanished into high clouds and distance, their terminus invisible from where she was standing outside her home.

Had she been able to track it to its source, she would have seen that the massive control and support line from which the plasma drill was suspended hung beneath a gargantuan ship of half-mad design. Equally unstable was its captain, who at present was standing in the most secure compartment of the entire enormous vessel, looking on as his chief science officer supervised the extraction process.

Suspended and held within a small yet immensely powerful magnetic field were a number of tiny red spheres. The spheres were the visible manifestation of what they

themselves in turn kept in check within their own individual containment fields—minuscule specks of the most unstable material known to galactic science. As an isolation
needle penetrated the surrounding dampening fluid to extract the material from its inner containment sphere, a sub-
officer appeared and saluted.

"Captain Nero, drilling has begun."

The captain of the *Narada* evinced no sign of satisfaction. He had long since given up hope of experiencing again
that particular emotion. Ignoring the sub-officer, he addressed himself to the ship's science chief.

"I want the Red Matter injected into a core pod." Implacable and expectant, he turned to the waiting officer.
"Let me know when we reach core depth."

McCoy and Uhura both tried to catch up to Kirk, but the
cadet was moving too fast for them—mentally as well as
physically. By the time they succeeded in closing the gap
between them, he was already bursting out of a lift. Crew
members stationed on the bridge who did not know him
looked up in confusion at the unexpected arrival. Those
who did recognize the intruder gazed across at him in horror. Unauthorized entry onto the bridge was by itself a
court-martial–worthy offense.

None of which was on Kirk's mind as he rushed toward
the command chair. "Captain Pike! The energy surge near
Vulcan . . . !"

A startled Pike stared at him in disbelief. "Cadet Kirk?
How did you . . . ?"

The lift disgorged McCoy and Uhura. "It's my fault,
sir." In the race from communications twelve to the bridge,

the doctor had resigned himself to one of the shortest careers in the history of Starfleet Medical. "I brought him aboard. At the time I felt it would be a harmless and unnoticed subterfuge. Given the Red Alert situation I thought Starfleet could use every available hand. I gave him a—"

Pike broke in tellingly. "I don't want to know *how,* I want to know *why."* His gaze bored into Kirk, and it was evident the cadet would have one fleeting chance to explain himself before being assigned to the brig for the duration of the voyage. "Not why you're on board, but why you're standing here in front of me right now, looking like someone who just met himself coming. And," he added in a low, dangerous voice, "it better be good."

Kirk steadied himself. "I checked the *complete* available scientific description of the energy surge that was reported near Vulcan prior to Starfleet's reception of the request for assistance. The parameters are almost identical to a similar surge that was detected just before the *Kelvin* was attacked by a Romulan ship more than twenty years ago—the day I was born, sir. Furthermore, that was also described as a 'lightning storm in space.' You know that, sir. I read your dissertation. That ship, which had formidable and advanced weaponry, was never seen or heard from again. The *Kelvin* attack took place on the edge of Klingon space. And at twenty-three hours last night, there was an attack; forty-seven Klingon warbirds were destroyed by Romulans, sir. And it was reported that the Romulans were in one ship, one massive ship."

Pike's expression darkened to match his tone. "And you know of the Klingon attack how?"

All eyes turned immediately to the heretofore silent

communications officer. "Sir, I intercepted and translated the message myself. Kirk's report is accurate."

Kirk stepped forward. Off to one side, a lieutenant moved his hand toward a cabinet that held his sidearm. From looking and listening to the excited, slightly wild-eyed cadet, there was no telling what he might do—or what he might be on.

Kirk held his position, and the lieutenant stayed his hand—for the moment. "We're warping into a trap, sir. The Romulans are waiting for us, I promise you that."

A troubled Pike digested this, then switched his attention to his science officer, who, despite Kirk's startling appearance on the bridge, had remained remarkably restrained and silent.

"The cadet's logic is sound. Lieutenant Uhura's record in xenolinguistics is unmatched in recent records, Captain. We would be wise to accept her conclusion."

Pike considered Spock's counsel. Turning, he ordered the communications officer, "Scan Vulcan space. Check for any transmissions in Romulan."

"Sir, I'm not sure I can distinguish the Romulan language from Vulcan."

"What about you?" Pike asked. "Can you speak Romulan, Cadet . . ."

"Uhura. All three dialects, sir."

". . . Uhura, relieve the lieutenant."

"Yes, sir."

Silence enveloped the bridge as Pike deliberated. Coming to a decision, he turned toward the helm. "Mister Sulu, hail Captain Alexander aboard the *Newton*."

As the helmsman complied, the ship's science officer shot the attentive Kirk another look. It was less than affectionate.

Sulu's eventual response was confused—and ominous. "Sir, our hail's not getting through. We're being blocked by some kind of subspace interference." His hands whipped over the console in front of him. "I can try to analyze the—"

"Never mind that now." Pike was sitting up straight in the command chair. "Try the *Excelsior*."

Sulu complied, and on his own tried several other routings before sitting back slightly. "Nothing, sir. In fact, I can't make contact with any of the fleet."

"'Subspace interference' my ass," Kirk muttered. "Given the reality of what's likely a fake planetary distress call, I'd hardly be surprised to discover that someone or something is deliberately interfering with Starfleet communications. Sounds to me like our signal is being blocked."

Pike deliberated. "We need to refine communications power in order to be able to warn the other ships of what we've discovered."

"Sir," Sulu said unnecessarily, "for that we'd have to drop out of warp so that our signal incurs no distortion from post-lightspeed motion."

Emerge in the Vulcan system in concert with the rest of the armada or fall from warp in order to talk to them: not a choice Pike wanted to make. Try as he might, however, he could not come up with another option. Meanwhile, time was looking over his shoulder.

"Understood," he declared finally. "Emergency stop."

Sulu leaned toward his console. "Emergency stop, aye!"

The six lines of subspace stretching from Sol to Vulcan

abruptly became five as the *Enterprise* dropped out of warp. No stars burned in its immediate vicinity and no planets gleamed nearby. The ship was very much alone.

Pike turned to Uhura, who, following a brief but intense discussion with the lieutenant who had been manning communications, had now relinquished that position to her.

"Hail those ships, Cadet. *Now.*"

"Attenuating relevant frequencies in order to increase power, Captain." Her hands were delicate but their movements were assured as she worked the pertinent instrumentation.

An unusual quiet descended on the bridge as, lost in their own thoughts, everyone waited for a response. When it finally came it was neither what was hoped for nor what was expected. Unrecognizable pings and strange electronic stutters, as if somewhere a transmitter was crying in emptiness.

Interference, an edgy Kirk thought. He stared at Uhura, silently trying to encourage a response that was not forthcoming. "Come on, come on, come on."

She waved a hand in his direction. "Kirk, *quiet*! I've channeled all communications strength into a narrow stream of encrypted information, and the ship is working to send it now." Her other hand worked the console in front of her. "Opening a channel." There was a stir on the bridge as everyone seemed to lean in her direction. At last she announced, "Channel open, sir. If you would like to try and make conta—"

Pike was speaking before she could finish. "This is Captain Christopher Pike of the *U.S.S. Enterprise*. All ships be advised: possibility of hostile Romulan presence in vicinity of Vulcan. Until presumed emergency situation is further clarified, recommend full shields and weapons systems at standby."

"Message sent, sir," Uhura reported.

They waited for a response. And waited. Possibly it was being blocked by whatever was interfering with their communications.

No one wanted to dwell on certain other possibilities.

"No response, sir," Sulu eventually felt compelled to report aloud for the official record. "From . . . any ship."

The fingers of Pike's right hand drummed fretfully on the armrest of the command chair. "What's the fleet's ETA to Vulcan orbit?"

Spock checked his readouts. "They should be preparing to drop out of warp now, Captain."

Pike nodded. "Tactical on screen. Display their automated transponder signals. Those, at least, should be strong and clear enough to penetrate any two-way interference."

Once more the science officer manipulated instrumentation. In response a quintet of glowing blue dots appeared on the forward main viewscreen. Each was accompanied by a name—*Armstrong* . . . *Defiant* . . . *Newton* . . . *Mayflower* . . . *Excelsior* . . . The attention of everyone on the bridge followed the dots as they moved into the Vulcan system.

Spock continued to monitor his instruments. "The fleet has dropped out of warp."

As he watched the monitor, Pike tried not to show his unease. A moment passed, then another, and another. The dots had slowed enormously, but remained exactly as they should. The tension that had gripped the bridge began to subside. McCoy had moved to stand beside Kirk. Both men regarded the screen.

"See?" Leaning close to his friend, the doctor dropped his voice to a whisper. "They're *there*. They've arrived. I shouldn't have just given you a dose of mud flea vaccine—I should've put you under general anesthetic. It would have been better than . . ."

"Bones." Kirk had not taken his eyes from the forward monitor. "*Wait.*"

One of the blue dots had vanished from the screen.

As a communications officer, Uhura had been trained to render reports straightforwardly and without elaboration, but at her age it was difficult to banish every trace of emotion from her voice.

"Captain, we're receiving a transmission on the distress frequency." She worked her console. "I can't get— Wait, something's coming through. I'm acquiring only intermittent bits of contact, nothing complete."

"Let me hear whatever you've got," Pike replied grimly.

She transferred all incoming transmissions to the bridge speakers. None of it was clean, but there was no mistaking the gist of what they were hearing: bursts of screaming voices, cries of despair, orders underscored by hopelessness. The crackling, static-marred bursts of discontinuous distress were accompanied by the quiet disappearance of another blue dot from the viewscreen.

"There are only four ships remaining," a somehow dispassionate Spock declared. "Now three . . ."

Pike's voice reverberated throughout the bridge. "*Red*

Alert! Ready all weapons. Mister Sulu, get us to Vulcan *now*—maximum warp!"

There was no sense of forward motion. One moment the *Enterprise* was alone in the vastness of interstellar space—and then it had dropped into that subsidiary realm where reality was deformed by mathematics into a class of physics that would have delighted Charles Dodgson.

"Arrival at Vulcan in five seconds," Sulu reported calmly. "Four, three, two . . ."

"EVASIVE!" Pike roared.

"ON IT, SIR!" was Sulu's immediate response.

The captain's command was unnecessary. Having dropped out of warp directly in front of the flaring, disintegrating remains of the *Defiant,* Sulu had responded instantly and reflexively to avoid the impending collision. Wrenched sideways on impulse power at the command of her helmsman, the *Enterprise* shuddered but quickly steadied herself.

Chaos was in orbit around Vulcan.

The two remaining ships of the fleet were engaged in a desperate and losing battle against a gargantuan craft the likes of which was as unfamiliar to those on board the *Enterprise* as it was startling in its unprecedented dimensions. Nothing they fired appeared able to penetrate the enormous defensive field that surrounded the hostile intruder. Meanwhile, an unending stream of torpedoes and similar deadly devices continued to detonate against the smaller ships, hammering away at their defenses.

Spock's voice was controlled as ever, but he was speaking faster than usual. "No identifiable registry on the ship.

It's massive. Energy signatures, deployed weapons systems, design—all unknown."

"Get Starfleet Command on subspace!" Pike demanded. Uhura's response was immediate and disheartening.

"Negative! All outsystem transmissions are subject to severe interruption emanating from the vicinity of Vulcan. And there's something else, sir. I think I've located the source of the general interference. I detect the signature— very advanced, but identifiable—of a plasma drill operating in the atmosphere."

IX

On board the *Narada* an alarm was sounding. There was no panic. Between its size, superior technology, and advanced automation its crew felt confident they were in little danger. Nevertheless, the newest intrusion had to be reported to the captain.

"Captain," Ayel informed his commander, "a new Federation ship has dropped out of warp."

Nero acknowledged the information as he watched the continuing but rapidly fading battle on the main viewscreen. His response was succinct as always.

"Destroy it also. Like the others. Waste nothing, including time."

The first officer acknowledged the command. It was exactly what he had expected, but chain-of-command formalities had to be adhered to. Romulus deserved no less.

Images and information collided on Spock's console, and he whirled to face the command chair. "Captain, they're locking weapons systems onto us."

"Continue evasive, come about ninety degrees! Mister Sulu, try to get us underneath them—if their shields are indicative of the ship's design, they may be weaker along the ventral longitudinal axis. Prepare to fire all weapons!"

The stream of torpedoes from the hostile vessel was unending. As the *Enterprise* shifted position, one of the lethal tracking explosives passed directly between her engine nacelles. A second detonated nearby. Overwhelmed shields buckled beneath the unprecedented power.

Secondary explosions tore throughout the impacted decks. Crew members were thrown into the walls, the floor, and the ceiling as artificial gravity was temporarily distorted. In sickbay McCoy was slammed into a wall and pinned there until gravity was stabilized. When he dropped back to his feet he noted with professional detachment that a gash had been opened above one eye. Flames leaped from a rip in one wall. That would not be allowed to continue consuming precious atmosphere. Either the section's fire suppressors would put it out, or it would be snuffed when the area was sealed and remaining air was evacuated. He stumbled toward the exit.

A dazed department technician was standing by the edge of the blaze and staring off into the distance. Grabbing him, McCoy looked into the man's face and talked to him until the tech finally responded. Then the doctor spun him around and shoved hard.

"Get outta here before the compartment is sealed! You want to die unbreathing?"

As comprehension dawned, the man nodded, whirled, and ran. In the wrong direction. Cursing under his breath McCoy started after him, only to find himself cut off as a translucent section of emergency response barrier slammed downward, its base forming a permanent seal with the deck. Halting and turning back, the tech stared in wide-eyed realization at McCoy. Then the severely damaged wall behind him crumpled like foil, shattering into pieces as it was sucked away into the vacuum of space—along with the doomed technician.

There was nothing McCoy could do. He had glimpsed that look of terror before, but only in training vids. Seeing it in person . . .

Mouth set, he turned away. The ship continued to shudder and tremble around him. There would be other casualties, other wounded. As someone whose skills were needed elsewhere, he could not linger to mourn. The crewman he had tried to help was already dead. The doctor hurried off in search of an intact sickbay.

On the bridge isolated flares of combustion continued to be extinguished one after another as her crew struggled to survive and fight back.

"Shields at thirty-three percent," Sulu reported. "Their weapons are more powerful than anything I've ever seen, Captain! Delivery mechanism is not unfamiliar but the explosive force is unprecedented. None of our torpedoes have that kind of focused energy and we don't seem to be able to penetrate their shields with our own weapons." He looked apprehensively toward the command chair. "We can't take another hit like that!"

"Get me Starfleet Command!" Pike ordered.

Spock spoke up before Uhura could reply.

"Captain, the Romulan ship has lowered some kind of enormous high-energy-pulse device into the Vulcan atmosphere. Its output appears to be blocking our communications and transporter abilities."

"All power to forward shields!" Pike commanded. "Continue evasive, Mister Sulu! Prepare to fire all weapons anew. They have to have a weak spot!" *If they don't,* he told himself worriedly . . .

As his ship shook around him, he refused to allow himself to dwell on the possibility.

On board the *Narada* the tactical officer was reveling in the contest with the new target. Its evasive maneuvers were more elegant than those of the Federation ships he had already destroyed and its return fire more incisive, if equally fruitless. Already it had suffered serious damage from a couple of near misses. As soon as the *Narada's* full weapons systems locked on the newest arrival, it would go the way of its annihilated cousins. Another moment and—

"We have them! Preparing to fire terminating torpedo cluster . . ."

His gaze never having strayed from the forward view since the uneven battle had been joined, Nero suddenly leaned forward and thrust out a restraining arm in the direction of tactical.

"WAIT!"

Baffled but obedient, the tactical officer's hand hovered over the control that would expel a final flurry of advanced torpedoes from the *Narada's* bottomless armory. His captain was gazing fixedly at the image on the screen with an intensity he had not displayed even at the height of the battle with the other Federation vessels.

"The enemy hull—give me visual, full magnification."

At the requested resolution the image was unsteady as the *Narada*'s sensors sought to track the fast-moving Federation ship. The vessel slid continuously in and out of view as well as focus, but one brief glimpse was all Nero needed to distinguish her identification: *U.S.S. Enterprise NCC-1701.* For the first time in a very long while his mouth curved upward in a slight smile, this time one of recognition. Nearby, his hand poised over the release element, the tactical officer waited for the order to fire the final, fatal burst.

It never came.

Uhura did not need to translate the incoming signal. Astonishingly, it was perfectly comprehensible as transmitted.

"Captain, the commander of the hostile ship is hailing us!"

At his station Chekov was staring at his instruments and shaking his head. "How are they cutting through the blanketing interference?"

"How are they drilling through the *planet*?" Kirk muttered aloud.

Pike had no time for casual speculation. No matter what the circumstances or the conditions, given the shape they were in, every minute they were not under attack was another minute the crew on devastated decks could use to make repairs and tend to the wounded. Another minute engineering could use to try and restore the ship's defenses. In the current state of affairs, any exchange of communication was to their benefit.

"On-screen," he told his communications officer.

Uhura complied and the forward monitor cleared instantly. Almost as if, Pike realized, the hailing vessel was intimately familiar with Starfleet communications protocols. The image that coalesced was by itself enough to resolve any remaining uncertainty as to whom they were dealing with. The humanoid was visibly Romulan. Furthermore, the enemy commander did not look as if he had been recently engaged in a battle to the death with five Federation starships. His demeanor was relaxed, cool, and his tone was almost . . . cordial.

"Your valor does you great honor, Captain, and the skill of your crew surpasses, however uselessly, any that has preceded it."

Pike was less inclined to be convivial. "To whom am I speaking?"

"My formal designation is Ŏ'ṛên, with an accent and syllabic stress that is difficult for the human larynx to deal with. As is not uncommon, reversing and softening the entire process yields a name you can pronounce. Address me as Nero."

Kirk's sudden intake of breath was not dramatic enough to draw anyone's attention from the gimlet-eyed figure on-screen. Unless there were multiple iterations of this "Nero," he was looking at the same alien who had been responsible for the death of his father. If the connection had also been made by Pike, the captain chose not to make reference to that particular bit of Starfleet history.

"By your actions you've declared war against the entire Federation. Withdraw without further hostilities, and I'll agree to arrange a conference with the Romulan leadership at a neutral loca—"

The alien's reaction to Pike's reasoned offer was unexpectedly violent. *"I do not speak for the Empire! We stand apart."* His gaze wandered while he utilized the *Enterprise*'s transmission to scan the enemy's bridge. *"As does your*

Vulcan crew member, who would appear to bear the rank of first officer, science division. Isn't that right—Spock?"

Every member of the bridge complement except those responsible for tactical and defense turned to look in the direction of the ship's science station. The unruffled individual seated there glanced at his superior officer seeking permission to respond. Pike nodded his approval.

"Pardon me, but I don't believe you and I are acquainted," the *Enterprise*'s science officer responded coolly.

An unexpected but welcome development, Nero mused. Truly the Fates did balance the good with the bad if only one could survive long enough.

"No, we're not—not yet. First I want you to see something. Tell me—Spock. At what price did the Federation turn you from your people? Where does your true loyalty lie? Do you even know yet the meaning of loyalty, or of the responsibility that goes with power?"

The *Enterprise*'s science officer responded with his usual calm. "I'll say what you wish if it will save lives."

The Romulan's gaze narrowed. He had hoped to elicit a more . . . emotional response, even though he knew he was dealing with a Vulcan. He was disappointed, but philosophical. Along the path to the End one inevitably encountered disappointments. In the roll call of regrets, his inability to provoke the Vulcan would have to rank as a minor one. As abruptly as he had singled out the science officer, he altered both his attention and his tone.

"Captain, if you are not already aware of the fact, your transporter capability is disabled along with your communications. You can neither beam off your ship nor communicate

with anyone else. You will man a shuttle and board our ship for negotiations." The smile returned. *"By yourself."*

Pike thought hard and fast. How much time would this Nero allocate for talk when his vessel was so clearly the superior one? How long could the *Enterprise*'s captain stall the enemy? Pike sat in the command chair, pretending to be pondering the demand, until he could see that his opposite number was starting to tense.

"As a sentient being who values honor," he finally said, "give me your word you won't harm my ship if I come aboard yours."

Kirk was not the only one on the bridge who gaped at their captain, but he *was* the only one who spoke up. "Sir, with all due respect—what're you *doing*?"

Pike looked back sharply in the cadet's direction. Concealed from the alien's view, the captain's expression was more than adequate to silence even James T. Kirk.

Indifferent to the nonverbal exchange among the humans, Nero replied genially.

"As sentient beings of honor, we have agreement. You will be allowed sufficient time to depart and arrive. Any delay perceived as excessive on your part will result in the immediate destruction of your vessel." The predatory smile reappeared. *"I would recommend, Captain, that you do not loiter over inconsequentialities."*

"I'll be there as fast as a shuttle can be readied," Pike told him. But the connection was terminated before his reply could be transmitted.

Kirk took a step toward the command chair. "Sir, he'll kill you when he's finished with you—you *know* that. He's already caused the death of hundreds. He won't show you any special dispensation just because you're a senior officer."

From the other side of the bridge Spock added his own equally fervent if less expressive opinion.

"It would be highly illogical to trust the word of—"

"I *understand that.*" Pike rose from his seat. "I need an officer who has been trained in advanced hand-to-hand combat—with all humanoid species."

Sulu's hand shot up immediately. "I have the necessary qualifications, sir!"

Pike nodded. "Then you come with me. Mister Spock, also. Kirk, you too—you're not supposed to be here anyway." As he headed for the main lift he looked toward the bridge's youngest crew member. "Chekov, contact engineering and have Chief Engineer Olson meet us at the shuttlebay."

"Aye, Keptin." The ensign moved to convey the captain's request as the lift doors parted and the four men entered.

They had to change lifts twice more to avoid internal damage and ongoing repairs and make it all the way back to the shuttlebay. Once out in the access corridor Kirk stepped up alongside the captain.

"I have to reiterate: what're you doing—*sir*? Pardon me for saying so, but based on what we know of this individual and his actions so far I'd say we gain nothing by diplomacy. If he wanted to arrange a cease-fire he would have done so with the commanders of . . . the other ships. He just wants to extract any information he can from you. Sure, he can pressure you by threatening to continue the battle, but maybe his vessel has been damaged, too, if not visibly, and he needs time for his crew to make repairs. Meanwhile, he'll have you as a hostage while we have nothing. And if you think his word as a 'sentient being of honor' means anything, I suggest you tell it to the captains of the . . ."

Halting so abruptly that Kirk nearly ran into him, Pike got right in the younger man's face. Speaking through clenched teeth and fighting to restrain himself, the captain proceeded to explain his reasoning.

"If you can look past your initial animal response, *Cadet,* and for a moment think about conditions outside your immediate surroundings, you'll recognize that without transporter capability not only can we not leave this ship, *we cannot assist Vulcan or anyone on its surface.* Additionally, with communications blocked we cannot notify Starfleet of what's happening here, either to request reinforcements, seek information, or simply warn the rest of the Federation." Turning away smartly, he resumed his stride toward the shuttlebay.

"So I'm creating an opportunity to get an away team on that drill and disable it. I hope you're right about this Nero wanting to extract information from me. I pray that he tries. While he's preoccupied with me, it is to be hoped he'll keep his word at least that long and will leave the *Enterprise* alone. Every moment of time I can buy while I'm engaging his attention on his ship is another minute that can be utilized to restore our defensive capabilities and rebuild our fighting potential. Not to mention tending to the wounded and reassigning personnel."

Kirk heard everything the captain said, but a part of him had been brought to a halt by what Pike had mentioned earlier.

"Excuse me, sir—I'm not sure I heard you right. Did you say *onto* the drill? Meaning what?"

Pike turned down the last corridor leading to the shuttlebay. "Meaning you, Mister Sulu—who has advanced combat training—and Chief Engineer Olson will do a space-jump from the shuttle onto the drill, get inside, disable it, and as soon as communications and transporter capability is restored, beam back to the *Enterprise*. I'll get you as close as I can but I can't descend too far toward atmosphere without running the risk of that kind of detour making someone on the Romulan vessel suspicious. And obviously you can't use personal transport pods or any other kind of powered drop gear because they'll be watching my shuttle and would likely pick up the engine signatures. But a trio of driveless free-falling humans ought to go undetected."

Kirk carefully considered the scenario his captain had laid out. "Ohh-kaaayy . . ."

He and Sulu exchanged a meaningful look. It was the first time they had done so. Though they had not been formally introduced to each other previously, preparing to embark on a joint suicide mission has a way of forging bonds between the participants on the spot.

Pike turned his attention to his science officer. "Mister Spock, I'm leaving you in command of the ship. Once transporter capability and communications have been restored, reach out to Starfleet and tell them what the hell's happening here."

One eyebrow arched as Spock regarded his superior. "What *is* happening here, Captain? Beyond the obvious fact that serious hostilities have occurred between Federation forces and a most peculiar representative of Romulus."

"Something you've only precious few minutes to figure out, Commander. If all else fails, fall back and rendezvous with the rest of the fleet in the Laurentian system." He turned to his left. "Kirk, I'm promoting you to first officer."

Kirk gaped at him. "Excuse me, sir, but—what?"

Pike's smile was grim. "While I'm gone we need to maintain the chain of command." He nodded toward Spock. "And you two make a swell team."

If Kirk was stunned, Spock was almost beyond words.

"Captain. Please. I apologize, but the complexities of human pranks escape me. Especially those that are perpetrated at times plainly devoid of anything resembling humor."

Pike lost his smile. "This isn't a prank, Mister Spock. And I'm not the captain—you are."

"If we knock off—" Kirk stopped himself, started again. "*When* we knock off the drill—sir, what happens to you? You'll be stuck on the Romulan ship and they won't be any too happy about what we've done."

By way of reply Pike offered a wry grin. "I guess you'll have to come get me." Focusing especially on Spock he moved out in advance of them to check on the shuttle preparations. "Careful with the ship while I'm gone—she's new."

Exactly the kind of comment a soldier in the field would make, Kirk thought admiringly. No wonder everyone in the fleet had wanted to be assigned to the *Enterprise*. The opportunity to serve under a captain like Christopher Pike was as much a reason for desiring a transfer as was the newness of the ship. If he ever found himself in command in a similar situation, would he have the balls to respond like that?

At the rate he was progressing, he told himself, a command was the last thing he was ever likely to have to worry about. Almost as likely as making an accurate space drop to a thin metal disk hanging by a thread from the enemy ship. A continent—now *that* he knew he could hit successfully. He regarded his fellow drop-mates. It would be hard to imagine better companions for such an undertaking than a ship's chief engineer and her helmsman. Though he had pulled off such jumps in simulations, Kirk decided his best option was to stick as close to Sulu as possible. If anyone could angle an accurate drop, it would be a ship's helmsman.

Pike called back to them. "Suit up, gentlemen. I hope none of you has a particular fear of heights."

"Yes, sir," Kirk responded. If any of his companions did suffer from acrophobia, a free-fall space drop would either cure the affliction or finish off the afflicted.

This time when Spock entered the bridge he was aware that the stares directed his way were backed by a new respect. He had neither the time nor the inclination to revel in his temporary promotion. Such time-wasting vanity was the province of humans, and he had no time to spare. Taking the command chair, he activated the intercom for medical.

"Doctor Puri, this is Acting Captain Spock. Report."

Shaking slightly, the hand of Leonard McCoy slapped down on a wall panel to acknowledge the call. Around him swirled a sea of blood, confusion, protruding bones, exposed organs, tendons dangling like dark strings, and a dedicated but overwhelmed coterie of medical personnel struggling to put it all back into its proper place despite missing supplies and dysfunctional equipment.

"McCoy here. Doctor Puri's dead. In lieu of orders I've been doing what I can."

Spock's expression tightened ever so imperceptibly. "Then you have just inherited his responsibilities as Chief Medical Officer, Doctor McCoy. Prepare all bays for mass triage."

"Aye, sir—I've already instigated procedures on all decks to—"

The science officer interrupted him. "I am not concerned with internal operations, Doctor, as I am confident you by now have them well in hand. We must prepare ourselves for a possible influx of refugees from Vulcan."

McCoy hesitated before replying. "Our facilities are stretched to the limit right now, Commander."

"Get the less seriously wounded back on duty as quickly as possible, Doctor. Try to make some room."

McCoy ground his teeth. Behind him, the unsedated were moaning and occasionally screaming. "I'll do the best I can—*sir.*" Though it was the acting captain's place to terminate the transmission, the doctor was the one who cut it off. There were lives to be saved and bodies to be made whole again and he had no time to debate the logic of what he needed to do. If "Acting Captain" Spock objected, he could file a formal complaint with Starfleet Medical Operations when they got back to Earth.

The Vulcan had called for mass triage. McCoy was fine with that. He had every intention of prioritizing.

• • •

With the aid of shuttlebay technicians, the three men struggled into the semiflexible dropsuits. Lightweight and fashioned of special composites nearly impervious to heat, the suits would keep them from turning into slender human-shaped cinders as they made the plunge into Vulcan's atmosphere.

At least, Kirk told himself as he waited for a tech to hand him his helmet, that was how it worked in Academy simulations.

Where a suitable planetary surface was available and shuttle or transporter was not, space drop was designed to provide a final opportunity to escape a fatally crippled ship. It was strictly a last-gasp maneuver, akin to jumping off a sinking watercraft with nothing more than an antique life preserver. Everything they would need to survive the drop was integrated into the suits. A gleeful Olson took responsibility for the powerful charges that would be used to destroy the drill housing once they landed on it.

Kirk found the engineer's excitement incomprehensible. He himself could be jaunty on occasion, but not when embarking on an outing where there was a very good chance they were all going to die. He did not voice his concerns, however.

He couldn't help but wonder: if they were successful, would he be allowed to continue to serve on the *Enterprise*?

Survive first, he told himself. *Worry about commendations later.*

The techs worked fast. Final checkout was hasty but thorough. Coolant control—on. Intersuit communications

activated—check. Chute deployment and adjustment systems—they would find out real soon. Carrying their helmets, they hurried to board the waiting shuttle.

As they took their seats, Kirk could see that Olson was
grinning as if he was going on a ski trip.

"This is great!" the engineer declared ecstatically. "Isn't
this great?"

"Yes—great." Sulu did not smile as he leaned back into
the padding of his launch seat. His expression was in complete denial of his words.

"I am pumped," Olson continued, "to kick some Romulan *ass*!"

Kirk did manage a smile. It was just as well the engineer, chief or not, was unable to see what he was thinking.
Turning away from the engineer, Kirk turned to his other
companion.

"So—what kind of advanced combat training do you
have?"

"Fencing," Sulu informed him proudly.

Kirk nodded slowly to himself. "Uh-huh, right—fencing. That's—great."

Up in the cockpit and away from his passengers, Pike
was running through departure procedures. He had delayed
as long as he felt able. In fact, he was more than a little surprised that this Nero had not already contacted the *Enterprise* or fired a warning shot.

He must want to interview me really badly, Pike thought
to himself. With luck, the conversation would not be entirely one-sided. He stole a glance at a small monitor. It
showed the three dropsuited men seated in the shuttle's pas-

senger compartment. His men. He wanted—he *needed*—
them to succeed. But that wasn't all.

He also wanted them to come back.

"Hold on. Preparing for departure." His hands worked
the instruments. It had been a long time since he had flown
a shuttle. Usually one was provided for him, together with
an escort and a pilot. As the small craft rose from the deck
and atmosphere was exhausted from the bay, Pike was
pleased at how quickly the necessary command and maneuvering instructions came back to him. Being a starship captain was all very well and good, but you never really got to
"fly" a ship. The helmsman did that, and the science officer,
and the ship's computer and advanced instrumentation.

The shuttlebay doors opened in front of him. He
leaned on the appropriate instruments and the little vessel
darted obediently forward. It was good to be in control of
flight again.

Even if the circumstances that had provided the opportunity were less than promising.

Trying to be as unobtrusive as possible in the course he
had chosen, Pike sent the shuttle speeding toward the enormous alien vessel in as wide an arc as he dared. Minutes
ticked away without any response or comment from the
Narada. If he was not challenged he would be able to strike
the bottom of an arc above the optimum drop point. The
men undertaking the incredibly tricky mission would have
one chance and one only to hit the drop precisely. Once
clear of the shuttle their commitment would be irrevocable.

Ahead he could see multiple metallic threads twining
into one. An enormous spiny cable descended from the
belly of the alien craft toward the yellow-brown world

below. Far below he could just make out the white-hot whirlwind of plasma being emitted by the drill platform. The captain had set out on as inconspicuous a parabolic course as possible and thus far the Romulans had not reacted negatively. Would the arc he had plotted be deep enough? He made minute adjustments to course and speed, trying to slow as much as possible without attracting undue attention. Delicately he trimmed attitude to rotate the shuttle so that its fuselage would be aligned between the *Narada* and the preselected drop angle.

Within the aft bay a Klaxon sounded. Helmets were donned and twisted into place, each man checking his neighbor's seal. As soon as they were locked each suit automatically pressurized. Internal instrumentation would preserve proper atmosphere, humidity, and pressure as long as suit integrity remained intact. If any one of those critical life-support components failed, Kirk knew, it probably wouldn't matter because the suit's occupant would be dead before he realized it.

As they rose from their seats, they checked each other's joints for leaks or unsecured gear. In front of them a port revealed the panorama outside. Beyond lay star field and, below, the surface of Vulcan. Kirk found himself wishing for the brilliant blue and white gleam of Earth. He could see at a glance how such a stark landscape could give rise to a personality as cold as that of the ship's overbearing science officer. A moment later there was no more time for sightseeing.

"Disabling gravity on one," announced the captain perfunctorily. Along with his companions Kirk reached for the nearest handhold. "Three, two—*one.*"

All three men rose slightly from the floor. Having undergone countless pertinent training exercises, they had no difficulty coping with the rapid loss of gravity, though Kirk felt slightly sick to his stomach at the sudden absence of weight. Or perhaps the nausea was due to something else.

"Good luck, men." Pike hit another control.

Below the trio the shuttle's doors snapped open. Instant compartment depressurization kicked them out as forcefully as if they had been shot from a catapult. Beneath and between them and the planetary surface lay thousands of kilometers of mostly nothing. Using their suits' tiny individual, mechanical thrusters, they adjusted their descent attitude until they were rocketing along head-downward and in parallel.

It was the silence that struck Kirk. Free-falling in emptiness, he noticed there was no sound except the familiar pounding of his own heart and the bellows that were his lungs. Vulcan was rushing toward them at incredible speed, its desert surface threatening to rise up and smash them flat. Falling back on the special breathing exercises he had learned at the Academy, he fought to regulate his respiration and heart rate. Despite his best efforts they remained high. Had he been on board, with McCoy in attendance and privy to the relevant readings, the doctor would probably have rushed him to emergency without a second's thought.

There was no emergency bay to go to here, he told himself. He glanced over at his plummeting companions.

They *were* the emergency.

Seconds after drop release they found themselves shooting groundward alongside the mammoth tether that connected the plasma drill to the Romulan vessel. Though they were plummeting toward the surface far too fast to make out many details, Kirk saw enough to convince him that the drill and its tether constituted yet another example of Romulan technology that represented a considerable leap over what was available to the Federation. How had so many scientific and military developments gone unnoticed and unreported upon? Didn't the Federation have reliable contacts within the Romulan Empire?

He had other things to worry about. Descending at numbing velocity toward the planet below, he knew that just as they'd had one chance to hit the drop point, they would have one chance to land on the drill platform. Assuming their suits functioned flawlessly. Powerless, they could not reverse course. Shoot past, and the next stop would be one of Vulcan's extensive desert plains.

At the appropriate instant, and guided by his suit's instrumentation, Sulu deployed his chute. Fashioned of a superthin and superstrong nanocarbonweave variant even more remarkable than the one that comprised the outer shell of their dropsuits, it began to slow his descent immediately. Kirk opened his own chute at almost exactly the same instant.

A gleaming red blur shot past him, heading directly for the looming drill platform. Heedless of the fact that by saying anything he was upbraiding the actions of a superior officer, Kirk barely had time to shout a warning into his helmet pickup.

"Olson, pull now, now!"

Utterly lost in the moment, the chief engineer continued to hold back. He intended to show the two junior officers how it should be done. He was going to land on the platform ahead of them and commence its destruction even before they touched down. The drop had been exhilarating and had gone entirely according to plan. He almost laughed at the anguish in the younger man's voice that was screaming in his ears.

"No problem, Cadet. Another second, another two, three . . ." The chief engineer finally deployed his chute. *"See? Slow, slowing . . ."*

Not slow enough.

Olson hit the platform hard but intact. The impact knocked the wind out of him and sent him slewing sideways across the curved metal shell. Stunned, he scrambled for a handhold on the slightly sloping surface as he slid toward the edge. Still deployed, his chute had caught air and was dragging him backward. Reaching out, he hit the control to retract the fabric. As he did so, he lost what grip he had and tumbled off the edge.

Fingers fumbled for the appropriate contact. He had failed in his attempt to land on the drill platform. Frustrated and angry at himself, all he could do now was redeploy the chute to descend safely to the surface below and . . .

His angle of descent sent him spinning toward the tornadic column of downward-driving plasma. Before he could reopen his chute, he made the slightest contact with its white-hot periphery.

Incineration was instantaneous.

X

A determined Kirk likewise came in rigidly, but the hard touchdown did not disable him or send him tumbling over the side, unlike the unfortunate and foolish Olson. As air pulled him sideways he quickly hit the retract control on his suit. Slits immediately materialized in his chute to virtually eliminate drag just before it retracted cleanly back into its compact storage compartment. As he scrambled to his feet he realized they had caught another break: even at this altitude the air was still and there was virtually no wind.

A shout in his helmet drew his attention to the far side of the platform. Having deployed his chute just a second or so before Kirk had caused Sulu to become entangled in the support strand and its main subsidiary cables. Now he was hanging upside down as the wind blew him back and forth. Strong as they were, his chute cables began to abrade against several metal strands. Unsealing his helmet and putting it aside, Kirk rushed to help his companion.

"Hang on! I'm coming for you!" he shouted upward.

As his chute cables started to part, one by one, Sulu

struggled to climb up them in search of a stable perch. As he worked to right himself, movement near Kirk drew his attention.

"Behind you!"

Kirk spun just in time to see a startled Romulan rising from a hatch in the previously unbroken surface. Having detected the intruder, the guard started to raise the heavy rifle he was carrying. With less time to remove his own sidearm from its sealed compartment in his dropsuit, all Kirk could do was charge and hope. As he tackled the bigger humanoid, they both went down, grappling, punching, and kicking at each other atop the disk-shaped metal platform thousands of kilometers above the ground. There was no railing, nothing to keep either or both of them from sliding off into oblivion. Still wearing his suit, Kirk would probably survive the fall, but that would leave only Sulu to try and complete the mission on his own.

As they fought, a second guard emerged from another hatch and started to take aim with his own weapon. Desperately Kirk fought to keep the body of the Romulan with whom he was wrestling between himself and the newcomer. At the same time, his opponent was intent on doing the opposite: trying to present the human's back to his cohort.

He was on the verge of doing so when Sulu landed atop the second guard and knocked his weapon out of his hands. Instead of rushing to try and recover it, thereby exposing his back to his assailant, the guard drew a *vrelnac* from its scabbard. The ceremonial sword would make slower but more satisfying work of the intruder. Keeping his eyes on the weapon, Sulu backed away warily. There was little space in which to retreat.

Reaching around his stymied adversary, Kirk managed to pull the Romulan's own *vrelnac* and skim it across the platform. Seeing it sliding toward the standing human, the Romulan confronting Sulu tried to cut short both the fight and his opponent. He never did quite figure out how the helmsman managed to avoid the strike he leveled, get around him, roll, and return to a standing position with the other guard's sword held in one hand.

He was not the first foe to find himself taken aback by Sulu's unexpected fighting prowess.

While the two exchanged blows, Kirk found himself tiring under the weight of his adversary. Struggling to break free, he caught first one punch and then another. Rocked by the impacts, he staggered backward, slipped—and went over the edge. At the last instant he managed to deploy his suit chute, only to see it snag on a projection. Reaching up desperately he managed to catch the edge of the platform.

He was caught between a fall of thousands of kilometers and one triumphant Romulan.

He only just managed to avoid the booted foot that descended toward one hand. Amused and relaxed now, the guard took his time raising the other foot before bringing it down. Guessing correctly, Kirk shifted his other hand to one side just in time to avoid the crunch. His adversary frowned. A short game to begin with, it was already growing tiresome. Next time he wouldn't miss.

A most peculiar expression came over his face. Lowering his gaze, he was startled to see the business end of his own *vrelnac* protruding from his chest. As Sulu drew it back out, the dying guard tumbled forward past Kirk on the start of his journey toward the planetary surface far below, trailed by a few choice words from the human he had nearly killed. While Sulu whirled to deal with the remaining guard, Kirk hit a control on his suit. Retracting into its compartment, the jammed chute dragged him back up onto the platform. A short burst from his own sidearm finished the second guard.

Alone and alive together on the platform with the drill roaring away beneath them, they examined their surroundings anxiously.

"What now?" Sulu wondered aloud. "Olson had all of the explosives."

As soon as the Romulan's tractor beam locked onto the shuttle, Pike eased back in the pilot's seat. It was out of his hands now. Any chance of flight or of changing his mind at the last possible second was gone. In a way it was a relief. From now on he did not have to issue orders: he had only to react. As the shuttle was drawn into the *Narada's* enormous docking bay, he took time to marvel at the immense construction. While some of it was clearly far in advance of anything in the Federation, other sections looked unfinished, as if the ship's builders had begun in one area only to cease work in the middle of construction and start an entirely new project somewhere else. There was also a noticeable lack of internal movement: something that hinted at a minimal crew that was supported by a great deal of automation.

Knowing all this would do nothing to improve his chances of success, but Pike had the kind of inquisitive mind that could not simply accept his surroundings at face value. He wanted—he needed—to understand. As he had been told on more than one occasion, he would have made a good research scientist. He doubted that opinion would carry much weight with his opposite number.

Drawn into the nearly empty hangar bay, the shuttle was positioned above the deck and restrained until the airlock behind it had shut tight. Only then did his hosts set it down alongside another vessel, one of modest size and a design Pike did not recognize. For a brief moment before the Romulans' tractor had locked onto him he had considered accelerating to maximum and crashing into the giant ship. It was an emotionally gratifying but impractical scenario. The shuttle was far too small and its drive far too weak to do any real damage to such a giant. His task was not to strike a futile blow against their assailant but to try and buy time, both for the drop team and for the rest of the crew back on the *Enterprise.*

Flanked by a pair of guards, the being called Ayel was waiting for him as the shuttle's ramp deployed. Pike lingered in the open portal, peering down at the individual he had previously known only from terse transmissions. In person the Romulan spokesman was less physically impressive but just as unyielding. A hand beckoned impatiently, and Pike made his way down the ramp. At the bottom he did not bother to snap to attention.

"Captain Christopher Pike presents himself. Starfleet identification number—"

Driven to his knees by the blow that acknowledged his greeting, Pike wiped a trickle of blood from his mouth as he gazed angrily up at his attacker.

"So much for diplomacy."

• • •

Kirk considered Sulu's query for about a second before moving to pick up one of the dropped Romulan weapons. Since it had been designed and manufactured to accommodate humanoid, if not human, limbs and hands, it was simple enough to figure out what made it go bang.

"Look what I found." Turning, he aimed the rifle at the junction of support cables and platform and pulled the trigger. A blast of energy tore into the structure. "The 'off' switch."

A grinning Sulu recovered the other rifle and joined in. Together the two men methodically began to pick apart and blow to pieces every corner of the platform that looked as if it might have anything whatsoever to do with the actual operation of the drill. After the strain of hand-to-hand combat that had nearly resulted in his death, Kirk was not surprised to discover that he was enjoying himself. He only hoped that the destruction he and Sulu were wreaking was enough to put a stop to whatever the Romulans had been up to.

A few minutes of continual and conscientious fire from the heavy rifles was enough to start fires raging within the platform. Another couple of minutes and the mammoth device stopped vibrating altogether. A glance over the side revealed that the downthrusting column of ravening, penetrating energy had ceased.

On board the *Enterprise* telltales on the main communications console as well as throughout the bridge and relevant portions of the rest of the ship unexpectedly sprang to life. Uhura checked them out one at a time. With everything at her station having gone from dead to back online in an instant, it was easy enough to draw conclusions without having to check with the science officer.

"Interference has vanished—the energy disruption that was blocking communications is gone. Full communications capability reestablished."

"Transporter controls active and reengaged," Chekov announced from his position.

Intent on his own set of readouts, Spock was less enthused than the rest of the bridge complement by the sudden change in their fortunes. A good deal of his interest had been and still was directed elsewhere. When assigned to be chief science officer to the *Enterprise,* he had not anticipated having to make use of his studies in geology on its maiden voyage.

"Telemetry and remote instrument readings indicate the enemy has bored at least as far as Vulcan's core. Ensign Chekov, direct all gravitational sensors to the affected area—I want to know what they're doing."

"Aye, Commander—Keptin. Sorry, Keptin."

The Romulan science officer eyed his console in surprise, then ran a hasty check of backup instruments. Given what he was seeing on his readouts the latter was hardly necessary, but woe betide the officer who reported bad news to the *Narada*'s commander without making absolutely certain of his information. In this case there was no question what had happened. Too many readings had dropped to zero without rational explanation. The continuing silence of the guards posted to the disk itself who would ordinarily be available to confirm or deny any query from the ship only further confirmed the science officer's suppositions.

"Captain, the drill's been sabotaged! I cannot reactivate, nor can I raise the maintenance personnel. Multiple indicators point to sudden and extensive damage." He indicated his console. "In order to effect necessary repairs the machinery will have to be brought back aboard."

How? Nero wondered. The remaining Federation vessel had been completely disabled by the *Narada*'s superior weaponry. No disturbance or intrusion had been detected in the vicinity of the drill. What artifice had the cursed enemy employed? Moving to stand behind the science officer, the commander of the *Narada* peered over his subordinate's shoulder and examined the available information for himself. Depth at so and so, bore diameter at such and such, temperature at maximum depth achieved so many degrees. Satisfied, he stepped back.

"Whatever happened to the drill is of no consequence now. We're deep enough. Launch the Red Matter!"

The science officer looked back at his captain. "We haven't reached the preselected core depth." He checked one especially crucial readout. "Temperature may not be high enough to trigger the necessary reaction."

"I—don't—care." Nero's eyes locked on the officer's. It was not a gaze any sentient being wished to endure for long, not even members of his own crew. "Launch the delivery pod *now*!"

Infinitesimally tiny compared to the sweeping, angular mass of the great warship, a small, self-powered pod was ejected from its underside. Pausing a moment to allow its internal guidance system to orient its engine, it then plunged swiftly toward the brown world below. Much smaller than a zero-g torpedo or virtually any weapon of significance contained in the arsenals of known space-traversing species, it was potentially far more deadly. Within its internally generated magnetic containment field it held a diminutive red sphere. Within the sphere, itself a secondary containment field, floated a fragment of one of the most volatile substances known to galactic science.

It was not the substance itself that was lethal but the disruption it could engender when sufficient heat and pressure were applied to it. Ordinarily it existed in a free state in open space, its unique destructive properties cold and harmless unless it came in contact with the surface of a star.

Or, by some unnatural means, with the molten core of a planet.

As he and Sulu waited to be beamed back aboard the *Enterprise,* a sound caused Kirk to look up and squint at the sky. A high-pitched whine that rapidly became a shriek, it trailed behind a small solid object that was plunging toward them. For one nerve-racking instant he feared it was going to hit the drill platform. Could the Romulans have divined their presence on the disk? But even if they had, he told himself, it was unlikely they would destroy such a complex piece of equipment just to get rid of two human interlopers. Sulu also saw the descending object and raised a hand to point.

Plunging planetward at high velocity, it shot past them. Moving carefully to the edge of the platform, both men followed its trajectory downward. At their present altitude it was difficult to make out fine details on the planet's surface, but both agreed that had the falling object struck the surface, there would have been a visible impact. Instead, moments passed without any indication that there had been contact at all.

Nothing traveling at that speed from this altitude could possibly make a soft landing, Kirk told himself.

Even as the realization struck him, far below a puff of gas billowed upward. It marked the spot, which both men had noted earlier, where the plasma drill had been piercing the planet's crust. *Some kind of bomb?* Kirk wondered.

Then the shock wave struck, knocking both men off their feet and forcing them to struggle to stay on the platform. The wave's effects did not last long, but to feel something so powerful at this altitude, on a platform rigged to remain steady in the strongest winds, suggested that something far more intense than a simple thermonuclear device had been sent rocketing into the borehole far below.

Having disabled the drill and thereby terminated the interference it had been generating, he fully expected his communicator to work. He was more than slightly relieved when it made a connection.

"Kirk to *Enterprise*! They just launched something into the planet." He glanced over at his companion, who nodded confirmation. "Helmsman Sulu validates. Whatever it was, it went right down the borehole they've been drilling. Time delay was followed by severe atmospheric shock wave. Size and composition of subsurface discharge unknown. There was no visible flash, so it must have detonated at considerable depth."

Sulu was now leaning over the side of the platform and beckoning. "Jim, get over here. You've got to see this."

Scrambling on hands and knees, Kirk joined the helmsman in gazing at the terrain far below.

Beneath them, Vulcan was starting to break up.

Huge fissures opened across the desert landscape. Mountains began to crumple in upon themselves. Light flared in multiple locations as previously inert summits were transformed into active volcanoes. The threatening yellow-red glow of fresh lava appeared as magma boiled to the surface.

The true scope of the rapidly escalating cataclysm was far more visible from the *Enterprise*.

Chekov stared at his instrumentation in disbelief. He did not want to accept the readouts and he especially did not want to report them to the ship's current commanding officer, but he had no choice.

"Keptin, gravitational sensors have gone off the scale. The components of what the Romulan vessel launched remain unknown, but if my calculations are correct, the contents of the pod they dispatched has generated a singularity in the vicinity of the core that will consume the planet."

Even for a Vulcan, even for one as accomplished and highly trained as Spock, it must have been nigh impossible to remain unmoved by the ensign's report. Yet the science officer betrayed no sense of what he surely must be feeling. He barely acknowledged Chekov's account.

Uhura labored under no such emotive restraints. "You're saying their device is opening a *black hole* at the center of Vulcan?"

Glancing back at her, the ensign nodded, while trying hard not to look in the direction of the science station.

"An oversimplification of the physics that have been set in motion, but the consequences cannot be overstated. A re-action has been started that will surely cause the planet to collapse in on itself." He swallowed with difficulty. "Once initiated, such a reaction cannot possibly be stopped. De-pending on the extent of the singularity, it will consume all matter in its vicinity. Including us, if we remain in this orbit at this altitude."

Silence followed the ensign's evaluation. Everyone tried not to look at the science officer and acting captain. Every-one failed. When Spock finally responded, it was in a tone and manner that anyone who knew him would have ex-pected.

"My own calculations confirm your readings, Mister Chekov. How long?" he finished simply.

The ensign fought back the tears that threatened. "Minutes—Keptin."

The science officer and acting captain turned back to his console. *To work?* Uhura wondered. Or so that no one could see his face?

"Signal a planetwide evacuation." Spock's voice was a monotone. "All channels, all frequencies. Transmit con-densed version of available geophysical information. Alert Vulcan High Command that traditional shelters are not safe. Anyone who can get to a ship must do so and initiate maximum escape velocity as quickly as possible." Rising from the chair, he whirled and started toward the lift.

Leaving her station, Uhura rushed after him. "Spock, wait—where are you going?"

He paused in front of the turbolift. "To evacuate the Vulcan High Council. Those tasked with protecting and preserving our cultural history. My parents will be among them."

She stared at him. "Do you have to go yourself? Can't we beam them out?"

"It's not possible. They'll be in the *katric* arc. The shelter was built to withstand not only conventional disruption but all varieties of radiation. Transporter waveforms will not penetrate. It is not possible to get a beam lock through its shielding. I must get them myself." He paused only for an instant. "Given the scale and rapid escalation of tectonic disruption I suspect they will already have moved deep into the main shelter." He stared at her, looked for a moment as if he was about to say something else, and finally did so.

"Lieutenant Uhura," he declared with astounding calm as he moved quickly toward the lift, "you have the conn."

Mouth set, she acknowledged the change of command. "Yes, *sir.*" There was more she wanted to say, much more, but there was no time. There never seemed to be enough time.

Then he was gone, the lift doors closing behind him.

The *Enterprise* was not the only ship in the vicinity that was suffering convulsions, but in the case of the *Narada* they were of the atmospheric rather than emotional variety. Hovering at a lower altitude, even the enormous bulk of the Romulan warship was being buffeted by repeated concussions from below. His expression and attitude one of alarm, her chief science officer conferred with the ship's second-in-command until Ayel broke off the conversation and moved quickly toward the command chair. While less panicked than that of the science officer, his own expression was fully reflective of his cohort's rising concern.

"We must withdraw! The drilling has left us too close. If we remain in this orbit we risk being drawn into the expanding singularity."

Nero nodded absently. While he was thoroughly engrossed in monitoring the destruction of the hated world below, that did not mean he wished to share its fate. Romulus too had its version of the Pyrrhic victory. He had no intention of adding to that particular lore.

The officer in charge of tactical spoke up. "What of the *Enterprise*? Their present orbit is borderline relative to the projected singularity."

"Leave it," Nero replied curtly. He looked to his left. "Retract the drill and fall back. Set course for our next target. Our work here is done." Settling himself in the command chair, he leaned forward to rest his chin against one hand.

"The rest of our work has just begun."

XI

*N*either man was prepared when the drill platform lurched sharply and unexpectedly upward. Leaning over the side of the disk as they studied the planetary surface, they were completely engrossed in the catastrophe that continued to escalate below them. Knocked sideways, Kirk managed to keep his balance. As he steadied himself, he looked in his companion's direction. There was the briefest instant of eye contact.

Then the helmsman was gone over the side.

"SULU!"

If Kirk had thought about it, he might have acted differently. Instead, he simply reacted. Crew—in danger—death. Without hesitating, he leaped after the rapidly plummeting helmsman.

Sulu's training had been no less thorough than Kirk's. Though extinction was rushing toward him at well over a hundred kilometers an hour, his task as a trained crewman and as a human being was to postpone that apparent inevitability for as long as possible. Spreading his arms and legs wide and keeping parallel to the ground, he did what little he could to slow his plunge as much as possible.

Above him, Kirk was doing exactly the opposite. Legs held together, face forward into the shrieking wind, and hands pressed to his sides, he dropped like a stone. Even as he closed on the helmsman, he knew he would have only one shot at what he was going to try. Streak past Sulu and it was unlikely they would have enough time to try the midair maneuver again.

Left arm out slightly to adjust his angle of descent, head up and chest out to slow as much as possible—*wham!* It was not a gentle rendezvous, but Sulu did not complain. With his arms locked around the helmsman, Kirk screamed into the other man's face.

"I GOTCHA—PULL MY CHUTE!"

Nodding vigorously to show that he had heard and understood, his left arm wrapped around Kirk's waist, Sulu reached down and fumbled until his fingers made contact with the requisite control. A firm touch was all it took to cause Kirk's chute to snap out of its container. Billowing, it expanded above, jerking them to a momentary halt.

Momentary, because an instant later their combined weight coupled with the inertia acquired during their plunge proved too much for the chute to handle. While the fabric remained largely intact, the cords that connected it to Kirk's suit, already stressed from the demand that had been put on them by the space drop, snapped. Direction, velocity, and plunging toward imminent death resumed straightaway.

At least, Sulu thought, *I won't die alone.* Better if Kirk had let him go.

Too busy for philosophical reflection, Kirk was yelling into his suit's pickup. *"Enterprise,* we're falling without a chute! Beam us up or we're dead!"

On board the *Enterprise,* his cry resounded over the newly restored communications. Springing to another console, Chekov let his fingers fly over the instrumentation. He had done this sort of thing dozens, hundreds of times previously—in simulations. As he worked frantically he was shouting toward the console communicator.

"Transporter room, come in! This is Ensign Chekov on the bridge. Emergency command override, transfer full control to the forward console!"

At her station Uhura was also hurriedly requesting, manipulating, and entering information. "Preparing intercept coordinates—stand by for transfer!"

The officer who had assumed the responsibilities of the science station when Spock had departed now looked up anxiously. "The singularity's expanding. We won't reach minimum safe distance if we don't *leave!*"

"SHUT UP!" Uhura and Chekov responded simultaneously. Their reaction was not regulation, but it had the desired effect. Grim-faced, the replacement science officer turned back to his console. Sweat was beginning to stream down his face as he confronted numbers that implacably recognized an escalating sequence of physical events that were no less lethal for their mounting improbability.

At the forward transporter console an increasingly fretful Chekov was desperately manipulating the manual targeting control. It was not quite like doing it during a simulation. For one thing, there was no one to back him up. For another, knowing that real lives were at stake instead of career points was having a deleterious effect on his blood pressure.

"I can't get a target lock on their pattern signatures! They're falling too fast!"

Far below, Kirk noted with interest that they had now dropped farther than the peak of a nearby mountain. He chose this method of estimating their present position because the alternative would have been to look groundward. This he preferred not to do, having decided that when the impact came he would rather it arrive unexpectedly.

"Enterprise, *now, now, now!*"

"Boost the waveform on the gain stream!" Uhura was shouting. "I need more signal in order to lock!"

"Trying!" Chekov yelled back. An instant later, "Got 'em—*toopik!*" His free hand slammed down on a large control disk.

On the other side of the bridge one junior officer frowned at another. "Did he just say 'toothpick'?"

His companion ran a terrestrial language quick-check through his own console, then glanced up. "Russian's his ancestral language. *Toopik*—it means 'dead end.'"

His expression one of deep concern, the other officer looked in the tactical officer's direction. "I hope he meant that in a *good* way."

In the *Enterprise*'s main transporter room, several technicians glanced up apprehensively from the consoles and instruments they were monitoring. The sensitive curved chamber before them still stood empty. According to their readouts, entanglement had been successful. Far below the ship, two falling bodies supposedly had vanished. If that information was accurate, then their exact duplicates ought to be . . .

It was not a neat rematerialization. Not at all regulation, no. Instead of arriving in upright stances, faces forward, hands behind back, the two bodies slammed into the deck with considerable force.

But not, if the pained grunts that issued from each man were to be believed, lethal force.

Though the tech crew was stunned by the manner of arrival, they were not nearly as stunned as the two officers. Both men slowly peeled themselves off the transporter deck. Holding himself, Sulu blinked in Kirk's direction.

"Th-thanks."

"Uh-huh," his colleague replied weakly. Starting at his head and working his way downward, Kirk checked himself, not overlooking a single bone. By the time his examining fingers had traveled as far as his thighs he was becoming convinced he had somehow made it intact. "I swear we were so close I could smell the dirt."

Sulu was formulating a reply when the transporter room portal parted to admit the ship's science officer. Kirk gaped as the Vulcan strode purposefully past him, turned, and positioned himself for departure.

"Step—or roll—aside. I'm going to the surface." Without waiting to see if the men on the floor were complying, Spock addressed himself to the transporter's chief engineer. "You should already have received coordinates for a specific disaster shelter located near the city of Shi'Kahr. While physical design constraints prevent putting me down inside, get me as close to the entrance as you can."

"I'll do my best, sir." The transporter chief bent to work.

Drawing himself into an upright position as he staggered away from the transporter platform, Kirk could only gape at the self-possessed figure standing in the exact center of one of the modules.

"The surface of *what*? You're going *down* there? Are you *nuts*?"

As was his wont, the science officer was not prone to acknowledging rhetorical questions. His attention remained focused on the transporter engineer.

"Energize."

In an instant he was gone, leaving in his wake a grim team of transporter techs, an exhausted and seriously woozy helmsman, and one disbelieving junior officer.

Spock nearly lost his balance and fell as he rematerialized on the surface of his homeworld. It was not he who was unstable but the ground underfoot. While they varied considerably in strength, the quakes that were shaking the surface to pieces were continuous now. Floating atop the planet's upper mantle, the continents were temporarily buffered from the complete destruction that had commenced farther below.

The transporter team had fulfilled its instructions with precision. Directly in front of him the entrance to the shelter beckoned. Running lightly to keep his feet, avoiding chunks of collapsing construction material and stone, he raced toward the opening.

Deep within the sanctuary as their world crumbled around them, six sets of hands rested on the *katric* ark. Vulcan's single most sacred object, it purportedly held the *katra* or soul of the ancient known as Surak. Together with its contents, the ark represented all that was good and noble and revered in the humanoid species that called the desert planet home. Linked together by mind-meld as they sought to shut out the chaos rising in intensity around them, the six Elders chanted softly among themselves. Among them was Amanda Grayson's husband. Though she could not by herself join the collective mind-meld, it was important to Sarek that she was present.

She was more than a little startled when her son burst out of the entryway, glanced around once, and came quickly toward her.

"Mother, the planet is not safe. A singularity has been ignited in the core. There may be only seconds left." Tilting back his head, he allowed himself a last sweeping look at the sanctuary. It would need to be remembered in something other than recordings. It would need to be remembered in the mind of someone who knew it from life—and remembered in the heart. "We must evacuate this shelter immediately. Nothing is going to remain. Nothing."

Looking up at him and meeting his gaze, she nodded. She did not understand him completely, but she trusted him completely. "Go and tell your father and the others."

He knew they would be reluctant to leave. A comparable group of humans charged with similar spiritual duties would have been adamant in their desire to remain, to perish with their relics and their sanctuary. It was possible that the Elders felt similarly, but the decisions of Vulcan Elders are not made on the basis of how they happen to feel. A runaway singularity would destroy their planet. It must not be allowed to destroy their civilization. Removing the ark from its pedestal, they carried it between them as they rushed to abandon the collapsing sanctuary.

They had barely emerged into the open when they were greeted by a sight none could have envisioned in their wildest dreams or worst nightmares. In all directions, as far as any of them could see, mountains and bluffs and ridges and desert were breaking apart and falling inward. Vulcan was folding in upon itself.

Spock knew that paralysis, whether mental or physical, was not a luxury he could afford. Whipping out his communicator he spoke into the open channel.

"Spock to *Enterprise*. Emergency transport for seven additional in my immediate vicinity together with large object they are carrying—*now.*"

On the bridge of the orbiting starship Chekov strained to simultaneously and accurately lock in a transport room full of strangers along with their cargo. He needed more time. On the other side of the bridge a junior helmsman was staring fixedly at his instrumentation.

"Thirty seconds before we *must leave*—or we never will."

"Locking signatures," Chekov announced. *"Transport in five, four, three . . ."*

As her world—their world—crumbled around them, Amanda Grayson looked at her son and almost smiled.

"It's okay," she told him quietly, "to be scared."

Behind the assembled Elders the wall of the sanctuary ripped free from the stabilizing pylons that had been driven into solid rock. The latter had become an oxymoron: there no longer was any solid rock on Vulcan. It was all crumbling, contracting, collapsing in upon itself. As the first stages of transport coalesced around them and they began to dematerialize, the ground beneath Amanda Grayson's feet vanished and she began to fall, to drop away. A few meters was all that separated her from the last transporter signature lock—all that separated her from her son.

"MOTHER!"

The eight vanished, their signatures to reappear elsewhere. Seven rematerialized on board the *Starship Enterprise.* The eighth . . .

The eighth had become one with the compacted body of Vulcan.

In the main transporter bay technicians worked furiously to finalize the progression. Seven shapes began to take form. One of them emerged in an awkward, ungainly position, body bent forward with an arm extended as if reaching for something. Sarek and the other Elders gazed around them and took stock of their new surroundings. Only Spock continued to stare into the distance, searching for something that was not there. A moment ago she had been barely an arm's length away, directly in front of him. Now—she was gone. Forever. There was no *Restore* control for a human being.

On the bridge an agonized Chekov spun around to bellow at the acting helmsman. He had tried, desperately, to bring eight signatures on board. *"Transport complete!"*

He knew he had managed only seven.

It was the report the junior officer had been waiting to hear. Without pausing for confirmation—there was no more *time* for confirmation, or anything else—he swept a hand over glowing controls.

"Maximum warp—engaging emergency power!" Engineering would scream in protest at that, he knew. He was not worried. At least they would be able to scream.

As the starship bolted in the general direction of the center of the Milky Way, its rear-facing sensors recorded a disruption that was insignificant on the galactic scale but terrifying in human terms. Soundlessly, crumpling in upon itself like a candy wrapper in a child's hand, Vulcan imploded. Deserts, atmosphere, oceans—all the familiar geological features that combined to give the surface of a world its character—vanished, along with cities and infrastructure and the people who had built them. In their place a brief blaze of intense light lingered on the retinas of those looking on—the last glow of the planet's molten core. Then it, too, was gone. Only a very small black hole remained at the interstellar coordinates where once a high civilization had thrived. Despite having swallowed an entire world, the perpetrator was visible only to those astronomical instruments capable of recording its occultation of a few background stars.

The incredible gravitational strength of the indiscernible monster that was the singularity reached out in all directions. It licked at the fleeing *Enterprise,* but the range of its all-consuming grasp extended only to a zone from which the starship had already fled. Behind lay the rest of the Vulcan system—and memories of a world that was no more.

While the other Elders murmured among themselves, father and son embraced. From the expression on their faces, it was impossible to tell what Sarek and Spock were thinking. Impossible to tell, but easy enough to imagine.

Kirk found himself moving toward them. One small part of Academy training dealt with the ways in which a senior officer could personally comfort family members on the loss of a loved one in battle or on general duty. There was nothing in the manuals that he could recall that dealt with how to console survivors on the loss of their entire world. Spock had just lost both. In lieu of precedent, Kirk spoke as he would have if he had been trying to comfort a neighbor back in Iowa.

"Spock—I'm sorry."

The ship's chief science officer did not respond. Perhaps, Kirk thought, he was finding comfort in his own thoughts. Or more likely, in the Vulcan way of responding to tragedy—by retreating into logic. Spock's first comment on being brought back aboard more or less confirmed Kirk's supposition as the science officer removed his recorder and spoke into it.

"Acting captain's log, stardate twenty-two fifty-eight—point forty-three. In the absence of Captain Christopher Pike, and pursuant to the relevant Starfleet regulations, I have assumed command of the *Enterprise*. We've received no word from Captain Pike since he was taken aboard the atypical Romulan vessel known as the *Narada*. I have therefore classified him as a hostage of the war criminal known as Nero.

"Based on readings taken as the enemy vessel departed and in consultation with the *Enterprise*'s computational facilities, it is hypothesized that its next destination may be the Sol system—and, presumably, Earth. Further updates will be forthcoming as new information becomes available."

Clicking off the recorder, he stepped down from the transporter platform. He did not look in Kirk's direction as he departed, nor did Kirk try to intercept him.

For one of the very few times in his life, the younger officer could think of nothing to say.

Every sickbay including medical central was full to overflowing. In addition to the Elders a number of other citizens of Vulcan had managed to survive the catastrophe that had eradicated their homeworld. Most had been working in bases on T'Khul, the Vulcan system's third world, and had been beamed aboard the *Enterprise* subsequent to Vulcan's destruction. Bewildered and ignorant of the details that had orphaned them, many were traumatized in ways that humans could not understand. It was left to the Elders to mind-meld where possible and see to their treatment with appropriate medications when mind-to-mind contact proved insufficient.

Many had been brought aboard in haste and had suffered injuries as a consequence. In addition to the new arrivals most sickbays were already crowded with injured crew members who had survived the *Narada*'s original devastating attack. As more and more patients were treated and discharged, living quarters on the ship became crowded and her life-support facilities increasingly strained. No one complained. When a request was put out for those willing to share their living space with survivors, every member of the crew promptly volunteered. Where possible, healthy crew members moved in with friends and turned their private quarters over to dazed Vulcans. While it was clear to everyone that the Vulcans were handling the tragedy far better than would a comparable group of humans, there were still far too many cases of mind-shock.

As he wandered through the main sickbay, Spock tried to take stock of the survivors. Their total number was pitiful. There were Vulcans elsewhere, of course. In missions and embassies on other worlds, operating by themselves within distant scientific outposts or in conjunction with humans and other sentient species, traveling on other starships. His people would go on, albeit enormously reduced in number and influence. He delineated as much as he murmured into his recorder.

"While the essence of our culture has been preserved in, among other aspects, the Elders, including my father, who now reside upon this ship, Nero has destroyed my home planet. Of its six billion inhabitants, I estimate that no more than ten thousand survived. An additional number yet to be determined are safely scattered elsewhere throughout the Federation and its allied systems." Without a hint of irony in his voice he concluded, "I am now a member of an endangered species."

As he continued to inspect the progress that was being made by the ship's medical teams, he happened upon the stowaway Kirk. Having disabled the Romulan plasma drill, albeit too late to save Vulcan, the junior officer would have been more than within his rights to have retired to quarters. Instead he was here in the bay. At the moment he was tending to a Vulcan girl, murmuring to her sweetly and smiling as he wrapped a slender arm stained with green blood in a self-sealing bandage. Noticing Spock standing nearby and watching, Kirk sent a look of regret toward the science officer. Regret, and sympathy. Their eyes met.

Turning without speaking or responding in any fashion to the junior officer's expression of empathy, the acting captain exited the sickbay.

Uhura was heading down the main corridor when she saw him prepare to enter a lift. She managed to slip in before the doors closed and the internal transport headed for the bridge.

They were alone in the lift. As had everyone else on board, she tried to think of something to say. And as happened to everyone else on board, she could not find words to express how she felt. Surely any words, she thought, no matter how well-meaning, would constitute an intrusion. Yet as the lift continued on its way she felt—she knew—that she had to say something.

"I only wish I'd listened to that distress call more closely and sooner."

How banal, she thought angrily as soon as she had spoken. *How utterly, utterly inadequate. And stupid.* Seeing her expression twist and deducing the reason, he peered down at her sympathetically. He, who had just lost his homeworld and the vast majority of his kind, had room enough within himself to feel compassion for her.

"Without you, none of us would have survived. What has happened is hardly your fault. Based on what knowledge and information is available I do not see how it could have been prevented." He sounded almost wistful. "Perhaps in another universe, another chain of cosmic links, a small change in this or that sequence of events might have made a difference. But not in the here and now. You must not blame yourself. What happens to us, how our lives and that of all around us progresses, hinges on very small decisions."

They stood like that for a moment, until Uhura did something any other member of the crew would have found odd—but not out of character. Reaching out, she thumbed the *Stop* on the lift. It immediately came to a halt between decks. Then she leaned forward, put both arms around him, and pressed her lips against his. Though mixed with sorrow and regret, no one would have mistaken it for a platonic kiss. In a manner plainly half-human, half-Vulcan, Spock responded. In a fashion sufficiently straightforward to indicate that he had done so before.

Eventually she pulled back. "I'm so sorry. I can't do anything about what's happened, about your world and your people. All I can do is try to do something for you."

He looked away, bewildered, lost, uncertain. Nothing he had learned in his long course of education prepared him to reply. Nothing except what lay within him could conceivably conjure an appropriate response.

"What can I do?" she pressed him. "Tell me what you need."

What I need? How to respond logically and rationally to the human woman so close to him? How to respond logically and rationally to such a question from anyone?

"I—need."

Almost, he responded emotionally. Almost, he let himself go. But the time he had spent on Earth and among humans did not begin to equal the time he had spent maturing on Vulcan. He was his father's son and his mother's son, but in the end he could only be *him*.

Whatever that might turn out to be. With a start, he realized that despite all his certainty about himself, despite all the knowledge he had so assiduously cultivated, that was one question to which he still had no resolution.

In lieu of an answer he could only continue to be what he had become thus far. Reaching toward the control panel, he restarted the turbolift.

"I need for us all to continue performing admirably in the face of the terrible calamity that now confronts my people, our fellow Starfleet personnel, and the entire Federation."

The doors parted and he stepped out. Uhura's gaze followed him until they closed once more.

XII

It was easier when she was on station. Not because she didn't think of him or of what had passed between them but because attending to ship's communications required nearly all of her attention. No matter what happened, she told herself firmly, she was not going to overlook another potentially critical signal or transmission regardless of its nature or its content, or where it happened to be directed.

As Uhura listened to the ether, searching among the background hiss of stars and nebulae for anything of potential import, a conference laden with grim significance was taking place elsewhere on the bridge.

"As it stands," Spock was saying, "we've not yet received any kind of orders or recommendations from Starfleet on how to respond to what has happened here, which suggests that even our emergency transmissions are still being jammed, deflected, or otherwise prevented from reaching the nearest relay."

Kirk nodded in agreement. "We have to assume that every Federation planet's a target. Since we still have no idea what's motivating this Nero and his crew, we have no way of predicting for *certain* where or how he'll strike next, other than a best-guess estimate that he may be heading for Earth." His gaze met Spock's. "If only we knew the 'why' of the carnage he's causing."

"Agreed," added Chekov, "but why didn't they destroy us? Why all the other ships and not the *Enterprise*? They have demonstrated without a doubt that they have the capability to do so."

Sulu shrugged. "Why waste a weapon? We were seriously damaged and no longer a threat. Especially if they have greater goals in mind."

"That's not it. He said he wanted me to see something. The destruction of my homeworld." The ship's acting captain turned toward communications. "If, insofar as we have been able to determine, they are indeed heading for Earth, then their ambition and intent suggests the destruction of a single remaining starship is no longer high on their agenda."

Standing, as usual, slightly off to one side, Leonard McCoy was, as usual, finally unable to contain himself. "And how the hell did they do that, by the way? When did they jump so far ahead in the arms race? While my specialty doesn't require me to be familiar with the technological details of alien arms and armaments, I do have to have some knowledge of the damage they can inflict because I'm expected to repair it, at least on the personal level. I've never heard or read anything about a Romulan vessel the size of this *Narada* or the kind of destructive abilities it just displayed."

Spock nodded imperceptibly. "It is a question, Doctor,

that I have been mulling over with deep concern ever since our initial encounter. It is self-evident that such a technological leap as we have recently witnessed does not take place overnight, nor even over a period of several years. The exact time frame required to accomplish such feats can at this time only be speculated upon. The engineering and technological knowledge necessary to artificially generate a black hole such as was utilized to destroy my homeworld may point toward a possible answer.

"Such technology could, in theory, be manipulated for a purpose other than destruction. It could hypothetically be manipulated to create a tunnel through space-time, though from what we know of the possibilities, such a voyage would be extraordinarily risky for anyone attempting it." He did not quite smile. "Of course, such conjecture is based on models that rely on current physical and mathematical knowledge. We know nothing of future possibilities."

"Dammit, man—I'm a doctor, not a physicist," McCoy snapped. "Are you suggesting they're from the future?"

Kirk stared at the acting captain. "That *is* what he's suggesting, and I don't buy it."

Spock eyed him evenly. "If you eliminate the impossible, whatever remains—however improbable—must be the truth. Process of elimination does not automatically disregard what has not yet been mathematically proven. Recall the words of Saint Clarke: 'Any sufficiently advanced technology is indistinguishable from magic.' "

"How poetic," McCoy commented sardonically.

"For some, Doctor, the possibility of time travel is nothing less than magic. Or poetry, if you prefer. For the enemy we now find ourselves facing, it may simply be a matter of sufficiently advanced technology."

"If their technology is so advanced," Kirk wondered aloud, "then what would *an angry future Romulan* want with Captain Pike?"

"Simply because their technology is exceptionally advanced in one or several areas does not mean they are dominant in all," Spock pointed out. "Perversely, it is a good sign."

McCoy's gaze narrowed. "How can their taking Captain Pike as a captive be a 'good sign'?"

"It suggests," Spock explained calmly, "that while their technology is superior to us in many ways, they are not omnipotent."

Sulu was nodding vigorously. "Captain Pike knows as much as any admiral about Starfleet's defenses. If their next target *is* Earth and they felt certain of being able to penetrate its defenses, why else would they want him except to extort information?"

"We have to get him off that ship," Kirk growled.

Spock turned immediately. "That is not an option. He left us with standing orders that in the event of his failure to return, we should rendezvous with the rest of the fleet on the other side of the quadrant. It was a sensible command, clearly thought out and only reinforced by subsequent events. As has been amply demonstrated, we're technologically outmatched in every way and are fortunate the *Enterprise* is still functional. A rescue attempt would be illogical."

Fighting to keep calm, Kirk struggled to reply in kind. He did not entirely succeed. "With all due respect, what about loyalty to one's commanding officer?" He nodded sharply in the helmsman's direction. "If Mister Sulu's correct, then if Pike's not dead he's likely being tortured to give up what he knows about Earth's defenses."

The science officer was not moved. "The captain's committed *our* loyalty to *his* sacrifice. He would be the first to repeat and to emphasize that we carry out his final order. He understands that the needs of the many outweigh the danger to the one." Spock's voice tightened slightly. "It is the kind of decision one is required to make when one assumes the responsibilities of a starship captain."

"He also," Kirk shot back, "believes officers shouldn't blindly follow orders without looking for alternative ways of doing things. I can speak to that from personal experience. As his crew, we owe him the effort to explore alternative possibilities."

That much, Spock was willing to bend. "As stated, I am always open to suggestions."

"All right, then. I *suggest* we find a way to *catch up*, get on that ship, and get him *back*. Again, if Mister Sulu's observation is accurate, then time is of the essence. We already know they command means of destruction far beyond our own capabilities. We can only assume that they have access to methods of persuasion we can't imagine. Captain Pike is a resilient officer, but he's only—if you'll pardon the expression—human. We have to get him back and we have to do it *now*."

"Fantastic," McCoy muttered. "I'm in."

"Even though we think we know their destination, they would have to drop out of warp for us to overtake them," Spock pointed out inexorably. "And that is assuming that their technological advances do not include the ability to travel faster than our own vessel."

Kirk was not so easily thwarted. "What about assigning engineering's best people to try and find a way to boost our warp yield, if only for a short period of time? As you'll remember, we were required to consider such possibilities as part of courses dealing with emergency situations."

"I also recall," the implacable acting captain responded, "that they remained nothing more than possibilities. Several of which, *you* might remember, risked complete destruction of any vessel daring to attempt such extreme manipulation of its warp field. Anyway, even if such an adjustment could be tried in time, engineering is fully occupied restoring our drive capability and helping to repair damage, without which we cannot communicate with Starfleet. They do not have time to spend it on wishful fantasies."

Yet again Kirk found himself deterred by logic. "Okay, okayokayokay—there's gotta be *some* way . . ."

"When thoroughly analyzed, the information we've gathered about the enemy warship may point the way toward some method of defeating them—but *only* if we assemble the fleet to balance the terms of our next engagement. As already inferred, they are clearly not omnipotent. It may be that by bringing sufficient firepower, even if it is inferior firepower, to bear, it may be possible to destroy their advanced vessel through sheer force of numbers. If such were not the case, they would not take the time and trouble to counter our attacks so energetically."

Kirk took a step forward. "*Spock*. By the time the fleet is redeployed, it'll be too late. Too late for Captain Pike and too late for Earth. You know how Starfleet operates. A decision of such magnitude will require conferences, discussions—by the time Command appoints a committee, reaches a conclusion, decides on a strategy, and issues orders to move against Nero, he'll be finished with Earth and on his way to still another doomed system. How many planets are you willing to risk?" Seeing that his appeal was having no effect on the ship's acting captain, an increasingly irate and desperate Kirk tried another tack.

"You wanna be logical? Then do what this Nero doesn't expect you to do. Respond *illogically.* Be unpredictable. It's the last thing he'll expect from you." A smile cut across the younger man's face. "I can guarantee it."

As usual, the sarcasm had no effect whatsoever on the Vulcan officer. "You're assuming Nero knows how events are predicted to unfold, and that by acting in an illogical manner we could somehow disrupt his intentions."

"You just suggested he's from the future," Kirk pointed out.

Spock nodded agreement. "In which case his intent in traveling to this point in the past would appear to be to significantly alter it. If he had no intention of doing so, then there would, logically, be no point in making such a dangerous attempt simply to observe what he already expects to happen. It is clear that his purpose in making the time traverse is to change the past. Insofar as we know, his actions since entering this time plane have been unremittingly hostile to the Federation. We may safely assume they shall continue to be so.

"Through his actions subsequent to his entry into our time he has altered the flow of history, beginning with the

attack on your father's ship twenty-five years ago and culmi-
nating in the horrific events of today. These actions have
created a new chain of events that cannot be anticipated by
either party. At least, not by those living and functioning in
the present. As we have no knowledge of additional alternate timelines, it is useless to speculate upon them. We can
only influence our own, and I am required to make decisions based on our knowledge of what and where we are at
the present time."

McCoy wore the expression of someone who had accidentally sat down on one of his own sedative hypos. "Does
anyone understand him?"

Uhura murmured softly in amazement. "An alternate
reality. An alternative past."

Spock nodded. "Precisely. There may be a thousand
others, a million, or only this one. Certainly, Nero is acting
as though this is the only one that matters." He scanned the
faces around him. "Whatever lives we might have lived if he
had not appeared here to alter the time continuum of this
reality have now been permanently altered. Our destinies,
whatever they were, have changed."

Chekov's mind was churning. "Even if we somehow
manage to stop this Nero, what's to prevent him from reen-
tering his time portal, however he achieves that, and simply going back in time a little farther to stop us all over
again? For that matter, if his objective is the destruction of
the Federation, why didn't he go back to an even earlier
date when our defensive technology was even more primitive?"

"It may be," Spock surmised, "that the method of time
travel employed is not perfect, or is fraught with limitations

we cannot imagine, and that twenty-five years ago was the optimum time for him to attempt to send his vessel into the past." He hesitated, thoughtful. "It may also be that he is subject to other motivations of which we as yet have no knowledge. We could speculate on an infinity of possibilities, any one of which might prove fruitful but none of which exist at the moment. And at the moment, I am charged with carrying out Captain Pike's last order." He met the helmsman's gaze.

"Mister Sulu, plot a course for the Laurentian system, warp factor three."

Kirk stood nearby, shaking his head vigorously. "Commander, I disagree, because—"

"*Captain,*" Spock corrected him, sharply this time. "Your opinion is duly noted, Mister Kirk—but my *order* stands."

They locked eyes. The other officers on the bridge looked on uneasily. This was no time for a confrontation. Whatever actions they next embarked upon had to be carried out with some degree of unanimity. Those who knew something of Kirk expected him to explode—or at least to raise his voice in an attempt to dominate verbally, if not logically. He did not.

"Captain. *Spock.* We've all been through a lot the last couple of days. You more than anyone. But I ask that you separate your feelings from—"

"I have," Spock broke in. "You may rest assured on that point. Were I not to do so, I could not reasonably remain in command. And as you and I have both lost a parent to this creature, we must assure that our mission does not become a personal vendetta. Must I point out that while I have lost the bulk of my species I have acted and continue to act in a wholly rational and logical manner, whereas you—"

It was Kirk's turn to interrupt. "We don't have time for debate-team niceties! Every second we spend discussing alternatives, Nero's getting closer to his next target and probably closer to extracting what he wants to know from Captain Pike!"

"Then we are in agreement," Spock replied tightly. "No more time should be spent discussing alternatives. Therefore, I'm instructing you to accept that I alone am in command and that I alone am the one responsible for making the decisions that govern the actions and response of this vessel."

Kirk responded with an entirely different argument. It bore all the hallmarks of rationality—but not of common sense.

"Not if the ship's chief medical officer says you aren't."

McCoy stepped back in horror. "Oh crap—Jim, don't do that."

Spock's gaze turned as hard as his voice. "Your attempt at subterfuge is insufficiently subtle to disguise your true intentions, Lieutenant. What you're proposing is nothing less than mutiny. You will cease this course of action or suffer the consequen—"

"Under Regulation One-twenty-one," Kirk declaimed coldly, "I'm citing you as being emotionally compromised and therefore unfit for continuing in the position of captain of a Federation vessel. As a replacement I propose . . ."

This time it was Spock who stepped forward. "Yet you're the one acting emotionally, as I am certainly willing to have a board of inquiry determine. As of now you are relieved of duty—and now that I think of it, I am not at all certain you were ever formally *placed* on duty.

"Lieutenant Kirk," Spock declared in the no-nonsense tones of command, "I gave you a *direct order.* Failure to comply is a court-martial offense!"

"Jim, please!" McCoy struggled to mollify as well as mediate. "He's the *captain!*"

Kirk froze, staring blankly at the doctor. From the time they had met at school, McCoy had been his best friend. Maybe his only real friend. And now, when it mattered most, his closest friend wasn't with him. He let his gaze sweep around the bridge. There was some sympathy in the eyes of his fellow officers, maybe even some understanding—but no support. He had chosen to cross a very dangerous line, and it was now clear that he had crossed it by himself.

He had chosen his own Rubicon but, unlike Caesar, had fallen off his horse and was rapidly being swept downstream.

Spock wasn't finished. "If I confine you to the brig, you'll likely escape. The very resourcefulness that makes you potentially a good officer now marks you as a threat, not only to this ship and to its continuing mission but to yourself. I can't allow you to remain on this ship, where your zealous insubordination poses a danger and where your admitted powers of persuasion might inveigle the less secure into additional unwise actions." He turned to his left.

"Mister Chekov, signal the bay to prepare transport for Mister Kirk. He will be transferred to a venue where he can utilize his talents to whatever degree he desires, but where he will not be able to adversely impact this vessel's assignment. Mister Sulu, Mister Chekov—escort him out."

Stepping forward, Sulu took Kirk's elbow and pushed gently but firmly. The regret in his voice was genuine. "Sorry, man."

"Yeah." Kirk appeared to shrug it off. "Don't worry abou—"

Whirling, he swung hard. Sulu ducked back, spun, and grabbed the wrist of the other man's striking hand. Kirk hit Sulu with an elbow as Chekov reached for his sidearm. Wrenching forward, Kirk slammed into the younger man and sent the phaser spinning to the deck. The sidearm lay there, tempting the first fingers that could close around it. Kirk lunged in its direction—and collapsed, unconscious.

As swiftly and precisely as he had administered the nerve pinch, Spock stepped back. His expression had not changed and he was not breathing hard.

What had just occurred was merely one more in a series of disagreeable incidents that he had recently been compelled to deal with.

Under other circumstances, and in the presence of a good deal more illumination, Pike might have found his watery surroundings pleasant. The straps that held him in place atop the semisubmerged platform likewise contributed to a general sense of ill-being. The Romulans who were working to make certain he was secured and unable to move went about their business with the determined efficiency he had by now decided was a product of fanaticism and not fear. They respected their captain, were even in awe of him, but they were not afraid of him.

Nero watched attentively as his crew concluded the process. When they had finished their work, he approached the tightly bound prisoner and spent a moment staring down at him. Pike did his best to ignore the examination. Instead, he filled his mind with Mozart, though he doubted the anti-interrogation technique would be sufficient to save him from whatever was coming.

Expecting a blow, contemptuous spittle, or at least a tongue-lashing, he was taken aback by his captor's almost apologetic tone.

"Captain Christopher Pike. An honor. Truly. I regret that the circumstances must be as they are."

"Likewise." Pike gazed determinedly at the dark ceiling as he played back the last movement of the *Jupiter Symphony* in his head. "Romulan."

Nero sighed. "Centuries ago, before the Vulcan High Council decided to reveal themselves to the people of Earth in order to inform them that they were not alone in the universe, and to invite them into the Federation, we would occasionally observe your species from a distance." He paused. "You are a more noble race than our deplorable fallen cousins."

Pike let out a snort. "If that's an attempt to drive a wedge between us, it's a pretty feeble one."

Nero smiled. "An understandable presumption on your part, but such is not my intent. I speak truly when I say that I feel that humankind is a more decent species than the Vulcans—the great majority of whom are now, thankfully, no more. Humans can feel, can suffer, can be aware of their surroundings on a level the forever 'logical' Vulcans cannot. In this you are closer to my kind than to them."

"You'll excuse me," Pike muttered, "if at the moment I don't feel any special kinship."

Nero stiffened slightly. "I'll take no pleasure in humanity's extinction."

"Your attempts to draw a link between our different species are growing progressively more feeble. Pardon me if I don't feel reassured."

"It's not your fault," Nero went on, "that Starfleet chose Earth for its headquarters and the Federation for its center, nor do I chastise you for your allegiance to your own. I find both it and you admirable. But despite this there is something I require from you and will obtain by whatever means necessary, in spite of my avowed admiration."

"Let me guess," Pike posited. "You want to know how to pick up females."

Nero's tone darkened. "Your impertinence does not serve you well, Captain. I expect that in a short while such attempts at humor will be halfhearted at best." He leaned toward the pinioned prisoner. "You must have so many questions for me. I have only one for you. I need the subspace frequencies that alert Starfleet to hostile intrusion. Specifically those surrounding Earth."

Pike's voice grew faint and his expression distant. "It— it's strange, but I—I find myself . . ." Nero and a couple of other attending officers leaned closer.

". . . not remembering," the *Enterprise*'s captain concluded. Fastened athwart the platform, he managed to smile. "Recent events must have affected my memory. I'm afraid the information you're asking for has completely and permanently fled my mind."

Stepping back, the commander of the *Narada* gestured. Two crew members who had been standing in the shadows now advanced toward the platform and its pool. One of them was carrying a container; his companion, instruments. Pike tried not to look in their direction.

"Ambushing your opponent isn't very noble," he told Nero accusingly.

"True." The Romulan nodded in agreement. "In this case it's an act of mercy. I give you one last chance to recall the information I require." He smiled thinly. "I strongly suggest you look hard into your 'deteriorating' memory."

Pike turned away. "Christopher Pike, Captain, *U.S.S. Enterprise.* Registration NCC-1701."

Nero's tone hardened. "Christopher. Answer my question."

"No. *You* answer for the genocide you just committed on a peaceful planet."

"I prevented genocide." Calming himself, the commander of the *Narada* continued. "Christopher, I chose a life of honest labor to provide for myself—and the wife who was carrying my child. I sit here now, knowing you as an enemy. Not just of today, but of tomorrow. I watched helplessly as your *Federation,*" he spat the word, "did nothing. They let us die, to the last man, woman, and child."

Pike suddenly found himself more confused than fearful. "Then Nero, you're mistaken. Romulus has not been destroyed. How can you blame the Federation for something that hasn't happened?"

"It *did* happen. I remember it. I—felt it. When I lost her, I promised myself I would not speak another word until the day of my retribution. In twenty-five years I forgot the sound of my own voice. But I didn't forget the pain. That feeling cannot be erased." Unrepentant anger crept back into his voice. "A feeling that every surviving Vulcan now shares."

"If what you say is true," Pike hurried on, "you can save Romulus. You have a second chance to . . ."

"Yes." Nero overrode him. "Which is a gift I won't waste on mercy. My *purpose,* Christopher, is not simply to avoid the destruction of the home I love, but to create a Romulus that can exist free of the Federation. Only then can her future be assured."

Pike turned away and half closed his eyes. "Then we have nothing more to discuss."

The commander of the *Narada* sighed anew. "As you wish. Given the determination you have displayed thus far it is, while time-wasting as well as disappointing, no less than I expected of you. I regret the discomfort that is to come."

In addition to the newcomers, a brace of attending crew moved forward to close in around Pike. One handed Nero a pair of gleaming metal tongs, the other a sealed box.

"The frequencies, please."

"Christopher Pike, Captain, *U.S.S. Enterprise.* Registration NCC-1701."

"As you wish."

Pike braced himself, but the instrument was not directed at him. Instead, Nero inserted the tongs into the container and probed inside briefly before withdrawing them carefully. Clasped firmly between the metal tips was an alien arthropod of a body type and configuration unknown to Pike. A pair of long tentacles extended from the head while the abdomen squirmed in a futile attempt to gain freedom.

Nero regarded it thoughtfully. "This is a—well, no matter. We're not here to discuss Romulan entomology. I can tell you that it likes neither the light nor cold. What it prefers is a warm, dark place safely inside another creature where it can estivate in peace until it is ready to emerge and spawn. As the bulk of its favored host creatures have an understandable dislike of its presence, it seeks to prevent being ejected from various bodily orifices by clamping itself securely around a portion of its host's spinal cord. This ensures that it cannot easily be dislodged and expelled." As he spoke he was bringing the metal tongs and their writhing carapaced prisoner closer to Pike's face.

"When thus settled it secretes a fluid to ensure that it does not damage its host's nervous system nor prevent it from functioning properly. When released within sentient beings, however, the fluid has an interesting side effect. It blocks deception. When asked a question, someone hosting one of our migratory little friends invariably responds with a truthful answer." He nodded at the crew surrounding the prisoner.

Pike struggled violently, to no avail. His mouth was forced open, the squirming arthropod dropped into it, and his mouth closed tight. He was forced to swallow. He could feel the intruder kicking and writhing as it went down his throat.

He did not expect it would be pleasant when it forced its way out of his stomach and went hunting for his spinal cord.

Nero seemed to read his thoughts. "Don't worry, Captain Pike. You'll be given adequate local anesthetics to mute the pain of its passage. We want you healthy and alive when the first secretions start to loosen your memory."

"What—what happens—afterwards?" He fought not to throw up, nor to think about the creature that already must be starting to chew its way through the inner lining of his stomach.

"Afterwards?" Nero looked thoughtful. "Why, afterwards you will be invited to watch the annihilation of your own home planet and its entire resident population. After which, you will be permitted to join them."

XIII

*L*ately it seemed to Kirk as if all he was destined to do was to endure painful falls from very high places.

Vision and consciousness returned simultaneously, though not efficiently, as he struggled to free himself from the encumbering safety harness. He had not gone quietly. At least he had departed the *Enterprise* secure in the knowledge that sedation had been administered by someone other than Bones McCoy. The good doctor might have disagreed with him on strategy and chosen to side with that pointy-eared usurper, but he had also opposed the need to ban Kirk from the ship.

"I can keep him quiet and out of trouble while he's on board," McCoy had insisted.

"With all due respect for your medical expertise, Doctor," acting Captain Spock had responded, "from what I have seen and know of Lieutenant James Kirk, short of placing him in permanent stasis it is not possible to do either. And even then I would have my doubts."

· · ·

Groaning, Kirk pushed himself forward out of the deceleration chair and tried to focus on the bank of blinking instrumentation in front of him. Other than insisting that he was alive and more or less intact, which conclusion he had already reached independent of mechanical confirmation, the readouts were not especially informative.

A quick look around indicated that he was in a standard one-person survival pod. He ought to have been flattered that the *Enterprise* had dropped out of warp long enough to deposit him wherever the hell he presently was, but for some reason he was less than thrilled. No doubt the pain in his shoulder had something to do with his lack of appreciation. At least he had been put down somewhere habitable.

When he finally managed to squirm completely free of the couch and peer out the single port, he discovered that while his present venue might be habitable, it was anything but inviting.

Spread out before his gaze was a pale vista of ice, snow, slopes of raw rock, scudding dark clouds, and a lowering sky that loomed over a landscape that was anything but benign.

Welcome to the resort world of Antarctica Twelve, he told himself bitterly. Somewhere far out in space a certain Vulcan commander unexpectedly raised to the rank of captain was no doubt smiling at his younger colleague's predicament.

No, Kirk corrected himself. Spock might be logical to the point of indifference, but he was not vindictive. That would have been un-Vulcan. Whereas he, Kirk, felt completely comfortable raging against the situation in which he currently found himself. Leaning toward the hatch, he winced and caught himself as his shoulder protested.

"Oh—that sonofa*bitch.*" Reaching up, he felt the throbbing joint. A strain suffered on touchdown, he decided. At least nothing was broken.

Turning toward the pod's nearest pickup, he began with the most obvious and necessary question. "Computer, where am I? And don't tell me you're incapable of responding, because I'm just in the mood to pound the circuits out of something."

Ignoring the empty threat, the pleasant synth voice responded with gratifying promptness. *"Current location is Delta Vega, Class-M planet, unsafe. You have been ordered to remain in this pod until retrieval can be arranged by Starfleet authorities. Please acknowledge."*

"Bite me. How's that for acknowledgment?"

Wonderful, he thought. Another glance out the port confirmed what he could recall from studies of the world on which he found himself. Empty, hostile, unpleasant.

Well, it couldn't be any more empty, hostile, or unpleasant over the next hill, and he was damned if he was going to sit in one place and suck survival concentrates until the six-legged cows or whatever organisms dominated this part of the planet came home.

The fact that he was clad in cold-weather gear showed that his marooners had prepared him as best they could for his abandonment. He felt confident that he wouldn't freeze if he took a little hike. Slapping a hand down on the appropriate corner of the console caused the pod's canopy to rise. Frigid atmosphere slapped right back, stinging his face and turning his breath to vapor. It might have reminded a more wistful traveler of the Pacific fogs that still sometimes swept over San Francisco. Kirk was not in a wistful mood.

"Warning," the mechanical voice piped up immediately. *"You have been ordered to remain in your pod until you are retrieved by Starfleet authorities. Your location has been recorded and sufficient supplies are available to sustain you until that occurs. Except in the case of an emergency, unwarranted excursion in this vicinity is not recommended. This area has been deemed unsafe."*

Even though there was no one to see his expression, Kirk smiled. "There is an emergency. If I have to stay here and listen to you, I'll go crackers."

Putting his hands on the sides of the exit, he pulled himself out.

The immediate surrounds of his landing site did not vary much no matter which way he looked. Ice and snow gave way to ice and rock, which occasionally was supplanted by ice and gravel. The lack of variety in the terrain was vast and numbing. Still, he kept walking. For someone of his temperament the thought of squatting in the survival pod until someone came to pick him up and place him under formal arrest was intolerable. Anger at the state of affairs in which he found himself kept him going. Pulling out his tricorder, he muttered into it.

"Lieutenant's log, supplemental. I'm preparing a testimonial for my Starfleet court-martial—assuming there's still a Starfleet left by the time I'm picked up. The circumstances in which I find myself are embarrassing, debilitating, and due entirely to the actions of a certain Acting Captain Spock, whose rationale for marooning me on this dismal snowball I can comprehend but utterly disagree with."

Preoccupied with unburdening himself of his self-righteous anger, he failed to notice that the ground nearby was in motion. Something was traveling beneath the ice and snow parallel to his present path. It was unseen, silent, and quite large. He continued speaking into the tricorder.

"Acting Captain Spock, whose only form of expression is apparently limited to his left goddamn *eyebrow,* has abandoned me on Delta Vega in what I believe to be a violation of Security Protocol Forty-nine-oh-nine, governing the treatment of prisoners aboard a starship. According to the relevant Starfleet regulations, I am entitled, as an officer being kept under detention, to a standard holding cell on board a ship equipped with the minimum of civilized amenities, as opposed to *being dumped on the friggin' icebox of the galaxy!*" He took a deep breath of the frosty air, which helpfully seemed to contain a slightly higher than Earth-normal percentage of oxygen.

"On the plus side," he continued heatedly, "it's really great here—if you like staring at *nothing*! Or if your favorite color is *white.* Even a damn *hospital* isn't this white!"

He halted, swaying slightly. Without knowing how long he had been walking, it was impossible to determine how far he had come. Not that it mattered. Here looked the same as there, and there the same as anywhere. Rock and ice, ice and gravel. His head tilting back slightly, he howled at the uncaring sky.

"*Sonofabitch-bitch-bitch! There's nothing here-here-here! You pinch-faced neck-pinching mother—!*"

"*Nurrrgghhhhh!*"

Uh-oh.

He turned slowly. Though not half the xenolinguist

Uhura was, he had still been required to take and pass the usual minimum of courses in alien languages, and what he had just heard did not sound like a convivial greeting in any of them.

Glaring back at him out of a pair of black orbs that screamed murder was a massive furry shape that resembled the bastard offspring of a polar bear and a gorilla. *How enchanting,* he decided as he took an uneasy step backward. A polarilla. No, that's a . . . *drakoulias.* It snarled again, exposing dentition that had not evolved for masticating vegetables. Painfully aware of his lack of access to any defensive weaponry more advanced than a rock, Kirk continued his studious retreat.

"Um . . . s-stay . . . ?"

The monster took a step toward him, in one stride making up all the distance the diminutive human had thus far managed to put between them.

"Sit?" Kirk opined plaintively.

"RAAURRRRHH!"

Whirling, Kirk bolted.

Though not built for speed, the land leviathan's stride allowed it to keep pace with the fleeing biped as Kirk sprinted for his life. *So this is how it ends,* he told himself as he ran as hard as he could. *As a quick snack for some heartless carnivore on an out-of-the-way planet in a nowhere system.* No one would find his body. There would be nothing to bury, no one to grieve over him, and no honorable career to memorialize. He would end up a single-line footnote in the annals of Starfleet, the least memorable of an otherwise unforgettable class.

It was gaining on him, it was going to eat him alive, it was going to pop his head off his shoulders like a cap on a drink bottle, it was . . .

The ground exploded beneath his pursuer as something massive, crimson-hued, multiarmed, and far more alien in contour than the *drakoulias* enveloped the startled carnivore in its tentacles and proceeded to cram it down an enormous circular gullet. The fur-covered meateater had been almost familiar in shape. The scarlet monstrosity that was now burping it down looked as if hell's own crab had collided with a giant squid. A *hengrauggi*. *Where am I pulling these names from?* Willing himself to all but fly over the icy surface, Kirk somehow managed to increase his pace.

". . . shoulda—stayed—in the pod." He was breathing like a freight train.

A panicky glance behind him showed the monstrosity gaining rapidly. *Too big,* he decided. Too many legs. And him with only two, and short ones at that. He looked back again. Tentacular red terror now filled his gaze.

It was replaced by sky as the ground dropped out from under him.

The slope was long and steep, but as he fell he managed to miss most of the protruding rocks. Snowdrift cushioned the rest of his descent. On the occasions when his head happened to be facing rearward he saw that the creature, after a moment's hesitation, was still coming after him. It was almost as if, by temporarily escaping its clutches, he had enraged it even more. That might be all to the good, he told himself. The angrier it became, the more likely it was to tear him limb from limb quickly instead of taking its time and dismembering him like a plucked chicken.

Hitting bottom, he rolled to his feet and resumed running just as the *hengrauggi* slammed into the ground on the exact spot where he had been lying a moment earlier. Scrambling up onto its multiple legs, it charged off in pursuit, unfortunately none the worse for wear from its fall. A desperate Kirk examined his surroundings. He was out of breath, out of energy, out of ideas.

Off to his left, a dark hollow in the rocks. A cave. Espying it sent a shot of adrenaline surging through him as he made desperately for the opening. Without even slowing down, his pursuer smashed into the too-small breach behind him. Rock and ice went flying as it battered its way forward, enlarging the aperture with each heave of its massive body. Running down its prey had become a matter of determination. It gave every indication of following Kirk all the way to the center of the planet, if necessary.

He was slowing, slowing. The last burst of energy that had enabled him to reach the cave had truly been his last. Slowing to a walk, he sought in vain for a smaller hole, a fissure or crack into which he might wedge himself. As he searched, something like a soft rubber cable wrapped itself around one ankle and jerked him off his feet.

The circular mouth that opened in the center of the creature's forebody was more than wide enough to swallow him whole. Horrified at the prospect of being gobbled alive and slowly assimilated by unknown alien digestive fluids, he hoped that before that happened the muscular orifice would crush his chest or, preferably, snap off his head. Defiant to the end, he scrabbled at the hard ground with his hands, fighting for a purchase on available rocks. He might as well have been trying to resist the pull of a starship. Slowly but inexorably he found himself being dragged toward that waiting, gaping, hungry maw.

It was over. All of it, over. He closed his eyes and waited for the end.

His backward progress halted.

Opening his eyes, he saw that the monster's attention had suddenly been focused elsewhere. An irregular but bright light flashed, causing him to blink. Evidently it caused his gruesome assailant to do more than that, because the tentacle that had been gripping his leg abruptly released him.

Under the press of that flickering luminosity the monster drew back, recoiling reluctantly but inexorably. Now, Kirk saw that the source of the light was a torch, large and possibly fueled by more than just the large chunk of wood from whose tip flames danced. The creature's retreat was understandable. On the frozen world of Delta Vega, fire and heat would be perceived as alien and threatening to an indigenous species unfamiliar with a flame's inexplicable distortion of the atmosphere. Additionally, the high level of oxygen in the atmosphere would make any fire that did start spread dangerously fast.

Advancing on the crimson-skinned monster, the figure wielding the torch continued to move forward until finally the predator gave up and conceded both the cave and the hunt. Tossing the torch aside, the biped turned toward the disbelieving but greatly relieved Kirk. Bundled against the cold beneath heavy furs and related synthetic materials, his savior was definitely humanoid. As his vision cleared and strength returned, Kirk could see that beneath the fringed cloak his savior was a . . . Vulcan. A very old Vulcan but unmistakably a member of that now nearly annihilated race.

Not that the identity of his rescuer mattered. At that moment Kirk would gladly have kissed the feet of a Netronian garbage macerator. He staggered weakly to his feet.

The figure commented evenly, "Notoriously afraid of heat."

"Whoever you are—*thank you.*"

His rescuer continued to stare at him. Was his savior, considering his palpable great age, senile? Kirk hoped not. He badly wanted to ask a number of questions. As he debated how to proceed, the one who had rescued him finally spoke. There was uncertainty in his voice as he squinted at the still exhausted human.

"Jim?"

Kirk's lower jaw dropped. "How—how'd you know my name?"

The Vulcan stared back at him, dark eyes that had seen much searching the human's stunned visage. "How did you *find* me? Does Starfleet know of my presence?"

Kirk hardly heard him. *"How do you know my name?"*

No smile in response, no expression at all—or was that just a slight upturning at the corners of the Vulcan's mouth? A weakening of logic confronted by overwhelming emotion?

"I have been, and always shall be, your friend."

It was a nice sentiment, particularly here and now, but instead of warmth and recognition an aching Kirk felt only bafflement. Maybe the Vulcan confronting him *was* bordering on the senile. For saving him from the predator Kirk's gratitude knew no bounds, but that did not mean he was ready to connive in an old man's fantasies.

"Look, I'm sorry. I don't know you. The only Vulcan I know isn't exactly a *buddy.*"

It was no consolation that this response seemed to render the oldster as confused as the individual he had just rescued. He seemed to retreat into himself, pondering, contemplating, calculating. Or maybe just fading away— Kirk couldn't tell. The oldster's next observation, when it finally came, was worse than confusing. It was frightening.

What made it worse was that the Vulcan recited it all with utter assurance.

"You *are* James T. Kirk. James, after your mother's father. Tiberius, after your father's father. Your father is George, as is your elder brother. Your mother's name is Winona. You were born in the year twenty-two thirty-three on a farm in Iowa . . ."

Kirk just stared back at the specter who had saved him. "I was born on a *ship*. How d'you know these things about me? Who told you about my family, my past? Who *are* you?"

By way of response the Vulcan gestured toward the back of the cave. "We need to get away from the entrance, where it is colder and where our scents can be detected. We have much to discuss . . ."

By the light of a fire and after Kirk had ravenously devoured food provided by his mysterious host, that worthy proceeded to explain himself. Had he told his guest that he was the reincarnation of an ancient Terran deity, Kirk would have been no less flabbergasted than he was by the actual truth.

"Though much of what I am about to tell you will be difficult to accept," the oldster began, "the first thing you need to know is that *I am Spock*. One hundred and twenty-nine years senior to the Vulcan you know from your days at Starfleet Academy."

Kirk considered carefully. His response was, if not eloquent, characteristically terse. Under the circumstances, he could have been excused.

"Bullshit."

"I understand your skepticism." The individual calling himself Spock responded to Kirk's challenge without so much as a hint of a smile. That, at least, accorded with his claim. "The odds of us meeting across space-time are so improbable that at the moment of actual confrontation I too wondered if I was dreaming." Pausing, he looked away. "I have had too much time to dream, and have dreamed too much." He went silent.

As Kirk studied the face of the being seated across from him, dawning realization mixed with rising astonishment. "It's not possible. It's just not. But it *is* you. I'll be damned."

"While it is entirely possible that both of us may be, it is remarkably most pleasing to see you again, old friend. Especially after the events of today."

Kirk was taken aback afresh. "'Old friend,' sir?" He shook his head in disbelief. "I don't know how you know what you know. But I don't know you and if you are Spock we're not friends. You *hate* me. You marooned me here for mutiny." His expression twisted. "Or for what you and you alone decided was mutiny. Or incipient mutiny. Or insubordination or whatever rationalization you concocted in that perpetually rationalizing brain of yours."

Now it was the Vulcan's turn to looked mystified. "Mutiny? You are not the captain of the *Enterprise*?"

Kirk was utterly baffled. "What kind of perverse Vulcan game is this? *You're* the captain. Pike was taken hostage. We have no idea if he's dead or alive."

This information caused something to gel within the Vulcan's thoughts as disparate bits of information came together.

"Nero." Spock's expression tightened ever so slightly. "He is a remarkably—troubled Romulan."

Had a human spoken the name, it would have emerged as a curse. Uttered by the old man in the cave, it was, despite all its menacing connotations, just another name.

"Yes." At least they agreed on *something,* Kirk thought. "We left Vulcan—the Vulcan system—to rejoin Starfleet *yesterday.*"

His host went silent, once more lost in deep thought. Studying him, Kirk was ambivalent. He wanted, he *needed* to know what was going on in that venerable mind. At the same time, the thought of what he might find there unsettled him more than he cared to admit.

What he could not realize was that he was about to get his wish—or realize his fear.

Rising from where he had been sitting by the fire, his unlikely rescuer approached and extended a hand toward Kirk's face. "Please. Allow me. It will be easier, faster, and more articulate than talking."

His reflexes revived by the food, Kirk thrust out a hand

to restrain the reaching fingers. "What're you doing? The last time you came at me like that you put me out cold."

His rescuer paused. "In the wrong hands the mind-meld is potentially lethal. In my culture it's a way of sharing experiences. You—leastwise, another you—already know that. I repeat it to the you of this time frame."

Time frame? Still Kirk hesitated. The memory of the nerve pinch the other Spock (the younger Spock? the alternative Spock?) had delivered on board the bridge was still fresh in his mind.

"You swear you're not going to knock me out and store me for food or something?"

"If I wished to do so, it would already have been done. I promise that you will remain aware throughout the exchange. It is impossible to convey information to the unconscious." Once more the barest suggestion of a smile played around the deeply lined face. "I speak from experience when I say that you would make an especially tough meal for anyone to digest."

Kirk stared back at him. "Damned if I'm not starting to believe you." He readied himself. "All right—go ahead. With whatever it is I'm supposed to be familiar with." He released the oldster's hand.

Gently, the elder Vulcan placed his fingers against Kirk's face, fingers to cheek and temple, seeking particular nerve endings, probing for contact. As he did so, he whispered an ancient mantra of his kind.

"Our minds—one and together."

His eyes snapped shut. At the same time Kirk twitched as if an electric charge had been shot through his entire body.

• • •

Billions of stars. Swaths of nebulae, brilliant and flaring. The cosmos revealed. Infinitely vast—and yet all contained and restrained within the dazed but aware mind of James T. Kirk. And permeating it all, another presence besides his own. Another intelligence, beside him and yet with him, speaking solemnly.

"One hundred and twenty-nine years from now a star will explode and threaten all civilization in this part of the galaxy. That's where I'm from, Jim—the future. I was ambassador to Romulus. The Federation was mining in the vicinity of a nearby star when it unexpectedly went supernova. The consequences were predicted to destroy everything in its vicinity.

"As ambassador, I promised the Romulans I would find a way to save their planet. I returned to Vulcan and asked the Science Academy and the Federation to take immediate action. We outfitted our newest, fastest ship. Utilizing Red Matter, I would attempt to create a black hole that would absorb the exploding star and its expanding field of deadly radiation. I was en route to do so when the unthinkable happened. The rate of propagation from the supernova accelerated suddenly and at a velocity previously unrecorded for that type of exploding star. It destroyed Romulus.

"I could no longer save their homeworld, but I could still stop the expanding supernova. I had little time. Before the first bow wave destroyed my ship I had to extract the Red Matter and shoot it into the supernova. And it worked. The supernova was neutralized by the black hole. All of the radiation and energized particulate matter it was blowing outward fell back and became part of the accretion disk.

"As I began my sad return journey home I was intercepted. He called himself Nero—last of the Romulan Empire. In my attempt to escape from him, both of us were pulled into the black hole. Nero's ship went through first—back through time. So he was the first to arrive in this time frame. Nero and his crew spent the next twenty-five years waiting for my arrival. For my emergence from the wormhole.

"But what was years for Nero was only seconds for me. I went through the black hole. When I arrived here in this day and time, he was waiting for me. He blamed the Federation for not stopping the supernova and held me, who had promised to help, responsible for the loss of his world. He captured my vessel and spared my life for one reason: so that I would know his pain. He beamed me down here so that I could observe his vengeance. As he was helpless to save his planet, so I would be helpless to save mine. Billions of lives lost, Jim—because of me. Because I failed.

"And though the means on Delta Vega exist to contact the Federation, it is intermittent. In the end there was nothing I could do to stop him. The local communications facilities proved inadequate and I was unable to issue a warning in time."

Kirk blinked. The dream he had been dreaming vanished as Spock drew back and lowered his hands. The meld had been terminated. But everything Kirk had experienced remained in his mind, fresh and clear as if he had conceived it for himself.

"Didn't—didn't you try to explain to Nero that if he just left you alone in this time frame you could destroy the unstable star before it went supernova and thereby save Romulus? Wouldn't you then be working to achieve the same purpose, the same ends?"

"I did indeed. But as I said, he would not listen to me. Consumed with rage and regret and anger at the destruction of his world that had already taken place in our own future, he was convinced that if he let me go I would simply disappear and allow the Romulus of this time frame to also eventually be destroyed. He is utterly convinced that, regardless of the time frame, only Romulus will be allowed to suffer destruction and that this has been the real intent of the Vulcan and the galactic councils all along. That they sought and still seek a galactic civilization without Romulus. So he made clear that he would strive, in this time frame, to create a galaxy with Romulus but without the Federation. After utilizing the Red Matter device to destroy Vulcan and the other Federation worlds, only *then* would he use it to annihilate the star that would become the destructive supernova."

"That's," Kirk searched for an appropriate frame of reference, "that's—irrational."

Spock nodded slightly. "Just so. But how many times throughout history have great catastrophes been caused by individuals acting in an irrational manner? I am convinced that even if he once was, Nero is now no longer entirely sane. Having already witnessed the destruction of his entire homeworld once, he is unwilling to rely on the word of a representative of the people he blames for its destruction to now prevent it in the past. From his viewpoint that may be a logical conclusion. He would rather destroy the Federation and ensure the survival of Romulus in this time frame than give me a chance to save both." He broke off, the agony of his loss and his failure having communicated itself whole and entire to the shaken human standing across from him.

"Forgive me—emotional transference is an effect of the mind-meld."

Kirk did not try to hide his surprise. "So you *do* feel."

"*Cthia* is the stricture that binds our emotions, but it is harder to sustain for the few of us who are not wholly Vulcan."

The younger man just stared, still trying to digest all that he had been shown. "Going back in time, you changed all our lives. Because of this, our futures will no longer be what they once were."

Spock nodded solemnly. "Yet remarkably, events within our different timelines—characteristics, people—seem to overlap significantly."

A million questions, Kirk thought to himself. He had at least a million questions. This elder Spock must know of so many things. Not just advances in science, but the future of individuals. In his future he would know, among others, James T. Kirk. *What was his future self like?* Kirk couldn't help but wonder. On initially meeting him here Spock had called him "captain." Captain of the *Enterprise*? The Vulcan elder was quite certain in his tone. At the moment, Kirk felt his future seemed to hold out the promise of a court-martial, not a promotion.

What had happened in the future to change him and the circumstances in which he presently found himself? Now that this time paradox had intervened, would that future still take place? Would someone, sometime, still refer to James Kirk as "captain"? Or would it be "inmate"? Or worse?

It struck him suddenly that this elder Spock's future had already been determined—but that in this time frame the future, including his own, was yet to be made. Future

Kirk's destiny was set. His own was still his to make. And if they did not do something about the other intruder from the future, the Romulan known as Nero, then if Spock was to be believed, all futures would be wiped out. This corner of the cosmos would be left sterile and dead—except for present-day Romulus.

His head was starting to hurt as he struggled to resolve all the potential contradictions. All the possible futures.

Enough about projected tomorrows, he told himself. Right now everything demanded that he focus on the present.

"So Nero has a chance at revenge. And a weapon that can destroy the Federation." He stared at the elder Spock. "Your weapon."

"The device was designed and built to save, not to destroy. Throughout history great power has often been put to uses which its discoverer did not foresee or intend. In this instance, the discoverer was the Vulcan Science Academy. In your own history, consider among other examples what happened to the work of Alfred Nobel." The strain of isolation and the burden of guilt was plainly weighing heavily on the elder Spock.

"But let us pause a moment to consider other things. I cannot restrain my own curiosity. Tell me about the rest of the crew of—I am presuming you were of course on the *Enterprise.* Knowing only their future selves, I wonder if and how they exist in this continuum. What of Chekov, Uhura . . . ?"

"Tactical and communications," Kirk told him.

"Sulu?"

"He's the helmsman, *why?*"

"Doctor McCoy would assert our meeting here is not a matter of coincidence, but rather indication of a higher purpose."

Kirk nodded. "He'd call it a miracle."

"Yes." Spock turned speculative again. "It may represent the time stream's way of attempting to mend itself. We know far too little about the physics of such deviations to determine actualities and can only speculate on how they function in the greater continuum. In both our histories the same crew found its way onto the same ship in a time of ultimate crisis. Therein lies our advantage. It suggests that whatever the future of this present may hold, it does not deviate so radically from mine that ultimate catastrophe cannot be avoided. We must hope that events bear this out. Indeed, we can only proceed on that assumption." He turned and gestured.

"We must go. The future past waits for no man—or Vulcan. There is a largely automated Federation outpost not far from here. It is the location of the inadequate communications facilities to which I referred earlier and which provides me with the minimum of necessities that allow me to sustain my miserable existence. Having no hope of saving my world and not wishing to further inflict the paradox that is myself on this unknowing present, I have taken to dwelling apart from it and its few inhabitants. Paradoxically—if I may continue to employ the term—this very self-isolation has resulted in my encountering you. As I said, perhaps the time stream attempting to heal itself.

"While I can no longer do anything for Vulcan in this time frame, I cannot stand by and watch while Nero destroys *your* future. Possibly between the two of us we can yet do something to stop him." Reaching out, he briefly rested a hand on Kirk's shoulder. "It was so, once. Perhaps it can yet be so again."

Kirk pondered. He was ready to follow this intriguing, curious, and enigmatic being who insisted he came from the future. But that did not mean he was without questions of his own.

"Where you come from—in your future—did I know my father?"

Spock responded without hesitation. "Yes. You often spoke of him as your inspiration for joining Starfleet. Indeed, as the inspiration for everything that you became. He was, I believe, immensely proud of what you accomplished."

"That means—I must have accomplished something besides a spell in prison."

Sharply angled eyebrows drew together. "Prison, Jim?"

Kirk waved it off. "It's nothing. At least, I hope it turns out to be nothing. But that's a matter for the future, isn't it? The future that lies ahead of us and that we're going to try to sway."

"The future that we *must* sway," Spock corrected him. "Otherwise there will not be one. Not for you, not for your father, not for anyone."

Kirk was still trying to imagine what life would be like had his father not perished years ago trying to stop Nero. The sleeve of one arm wiped across his eyes.

"I am responsible for whatever is upsetting you," Spock commented immediately. "That was never my intention. Something you should know: he proudly lived to see you become captain of the *Enterprise.*"

Captain. That was how this Spock had addressed him

when they had first encountered one another. It was still hard to accept.

It would be even harder for this Spock to accept if he knew the current James Kirk's history.

" 'Captain'? Are you *sure*?"

Spock nodded. "Of a ship we must return you to as soon as possible if we are to have any hope of stopping Nero."

XIV

It was quiet on the bridge. Each officer, each refugee, carried out their duties efficiently, silently, and lost in thought. The immediate past had been devastating. What the near future might bring no one could say, but the encounter at Vulcan had left everyone wondering not about careers or promotions but far more elemental matters. Family. Homeworlds. The future of the Federation itself.

In the center of it all stood Acting Captain Spock. Everyone wanted to offer him comfort. Everyone desired to express their condolences. And none of them quite knew how to go about doing so. With one exception, and she had already expressed her empathy in every way she knew how.

From the helm Sulu looked over at the straight-backed figure standing at command. It was a relief to be able to break the silence with something as straightforward as a status report.

"Warp three, Captain. Course one-five-one mark three, for the Laurentian system."

Indicating that he had heard, Spock looked over at Uhura. His tone was perfectly even, as was her response.

"Communications—status report?"

"All decks are functional again, Captain. Remaining damage is gradually being repaired. Hull integrity has been fully restored. We are not at a hundred percent yet, but we're getting there."

"Thank you, Lieutenant."

"You're welcome, Captain."

Something in her reply caused Sulu to glance in Uhura's direction, then across at Spock. But the communications officer was no longer looking in the direction of the command chair, and the Vulcan's gaze was directed straight ahead. Giving a mental shrug, the helmsman forgot all about it as he resumed monitoring his own station.

The turbolift doors parted and the ship's chief medical officer entered. Considering all the wounded on board, he ought to have been preoccupied, but McCoy had the ability to separate professional thoughts from the personal. While one part of him was going over in his mind such matters as forthcoming surgeries and the next series of specific prosthetic replacements he would have to approve, another part focused laser-like on the ramrod-straight figure occupying command.

"You wanted to see me?"

Unexpectedly, the Vulcan gestured for him to come closer. When Spock finally spoke, it was in an atypically discreet tone. He did not exactly whisper, but the steel of command that everyone on board had recently become familiar with was absent from his voice.

"Yes, Doctor. I just wanted to say that I'm aware that

James Kirk is a friend of yours, and that your recent support of me must have been difficult for you. Having to choose between a close friend and cold regulations is never easy."

McCoy blinked uncertainly. For a change, he also kept his own voice down. "Are you thanking me?"

"I'm simply acknowledging awareness of your personal difficulties in the course of an awkward moment."

No direct thanks. Nothing about offering credit where credit was due. No overt expression of gratitude. Merely an observation. McCoy was unsure how to react. On the other hand, he did have something to say.

As his crewmates were finding out, he usually did.

"Permission to speak freely, sir."

Spock didn't hesitate. "I welcome it."

"Are you out of your Vulcan mind? And I don't mean by projecting it. I have to ask: Have you done the logical thing by expelling James Kirk from this ship ? Probably. The right one? Debatable. One thing I know for damn sure: That kid doesn't know *how* to lose. Just isn't in his DNA. No matter how difficult the situation in which he happens to find himself, no matter how seemingly impossible the odds, he's going to find a way to come out on top. You, of all people, should know that."

The acting captain stiffened but withheld any comment. McCoy didn't need to explain the reference, and Spock certainly did not require additional explication.

Unabashed, McCoy continued. "Back home we have a saying. 'If you're gonna ride in the Kentucky Derby, you don't leave your prize stallion in the stable.' "

Spock pursed his lips. "A curious metaphor, Doctor. If I'm not mistaken and my admittedly limited knowledge of the finer points of equine psychology is reasonably accurate, a stallion must first be broken before it can be trained to achieve its full potential. Teaching it that it is not always in full command of a situation is necessary to induce receptivity to directions." His eyes cut in the doctor's direction. "Does this not, in the end, make for a more successful race-horse?"

McCoy stared at him, shaking his head. *Logic, nothing but logic.* Aside from the eloquence with which it had been delivered it was exactly the kind of response he might have expected from a computer.

"My God, man—you could at least *act* like it was a hard decision. You had him *marooned.*"

Spock hesitated only briefly before replying. "Now that we are on course for the Laurentian system, I had intended to return to my lab and consult with my subordinates and assistants in the science department in an effort to break through continuing interference and warn Starfleet. However, if the ship's doctor feels that morale would be better served by my roaming the corridors weeping profusely, I'll gladly defer to your far more extensive medical expertise."

A human might have concluded the brief speech with a four-letter word, or on a rising intonation. Spock punctuated his riposte to the doctor's comment by holding his gaze for a moment longer before turning back to the command chair.

Utterly frustrated and not knowing what else he could say to make his point, McCoy could only stand off to one side and fume quietly.

Fumes of a far different and more pungent kind attended the interior of the outpost where a relieved Kirk had his first welcoming contact with artificial heating since walking away from the transport pod.

"What are we looking for here?"

The elder Spock was leading him down a seemingly endless corridor lined with steaming, occasionally clanking conduits, pipes, and other poorly maintained subsistence paraphernalia. If the outpost's communications equipment existed in a similar state of disrepair, Kirk thought as he walked alongside his guide, it was no wonder that the elder Spock had been unable to deliver any kind of warning to Federation authorities in time to save Vulcan.

"You will see soon enough," the old man assured Kirk in reply to his question. "Though I have been aware of this particular individual's presence here for some time, there was no reason to pursue further contact. Until your arrival. That has clarified for me how the time stream is struggling for resolution. Hopefully we can be of assistance. Sometimes the hand of Fate can use a hand itself."

The younger man didn't try to hide his confusion. "I don't follow you."

"That is quite correct," Spock told him. "You precede me."

Kirk considered how best to reply to this, decided that he was still too cold to think clearly, and held his piece. At least, he did until they turned a corner and found themselves confronting one of the outpost's personnel.

The small, dark alien eyed them uncertainly.

"My name is Keenser. Can I help you?"

"Are you the station chief?" Spock asked him.

The alien looked them over, then came to a decision. "No—this way."

As they followed their diminutive guide, Kirk found himself wishing he was back on the *Enterprise*. Even as a prisoner. Wishing, however, would get him nowhere. The wizened Vulcan who had saved him from becoming an indigenous predator's snack just might. It wouldn't get him back to the ship, of course. They were well and truly stuck on Delta Vega. But having hiked a small portion of this planet, he had already decided that anywhere under cover was a better alternative.

Looking past Spock to scrutinize the young human who accompanied him, the alien chattered a bit more with the Vulcan, then turned and led the way down the huge corridor. Around them the machinery that sustained the outpost and its largely automated functions throbbed away, generating heat, water, and a host of other necessities for the outpost staff.

The rest of that staff appeared to consist of a single individual. Leaning back with his feet propped up on a console, the Starfleet officer was sound asleep. Approaching without hesitation, the alien tapped one boot.

"Hmm," the lanky human mumbled.

Keenser stepped back. "Visitors."

Peering out from beneath his cap, he glared at the pair and essayed a salutation that to his way of thinking, no doubt, constituted a polite greeting.

"You realize how unacceptable this is?"

Kirk swallowed his instinctive reply while he took a moment to identify the raspy terrestrial accent. Initially through globalization and then via stellarization many such locutional variants on standard English had long since withered away. But not all. Some traditional Earth cultures were too fond of their linguistic distinctions to surrender them completely. And a few were too stubborn.

Scottish, Kirk finally decided. *Definitely Highlands Scottish.*

"Excuse me?"

Spock was staring at the clearly annoyed officer. "Fascinating . . ."

Kirk was more than slightly confused. "What?"

Ignoring him, the officer slid out of the chair and straightened. "I'm sure it's nae your fault, and I know ye lads are just doin' your job, but could ye nae have come a wee bit sooner?"

"I beg your pardon?" was all Kirk could think of by way of a reply.

The officer was pacing back and forth in front of them. "I mean, six months I've been livin' on nothing but Starfleet protein nibs and the promise of a real food delivery! It's pretty clear what's going on here, isn't it? Punishment! Ongoing! Without me havin' recourse to so much as an appeal. For something that was clearly an accident."

"You're Montgomery Scott," Spock declared abruptly.

Kirk turned to the elder Spock. "You know him?"

"Aye, that's me," the officer admitted readily. " 'Scotty' to me friends. You've got the right man." He gestured expansively. "Are there any other hardworking and equally starved Starfleet officers around?"

Visibly offended, the alien looked up at him. "Me."

Scott glared down at him. "You eat nothing. A bean, and you're done for a week." His eyes were a little wild now.

"I need *food.*" He turned back to the two visitors. "And now you're here. So—thank you." He tried to see behind them. "Where is it?"

"You *are* in fact the Montgomery Scott who postulated the theory of transwarp beaming." Spock spoke without mentioning anything about food.

The engineer eyed the Vulcan warily. "How d'ya think I ended up *here*? Too smart to waste and too reckless to trust: that's how they described me at the—well, it wasn't a court-martial, exactly. They couldn't find a suitable regulation with which to charge me. So they resorted to callin' it a straight 'transfer.' Woulda been better if they'd 'transferred' me to a jail on Earth. Or at least to some half-civilized world. *Anything'd* be better than this." With a wide sweep of his arms he encompassed his entirely functional and unadorned surroundings.

"Look at this place, willya? A man kinna even deteriorate in the company of his own species!" His eyes fastened on Kirk. "But then, you're too young and innocent to know about anything like that, laddie."

Kirk did not smile. "You'd be surprised at what I know. What *did* you do to get yourself posted to this vacation paradise?"

Scott grew animated. "I got into a debate with my instructor on the issue of relativistic physics as they relate to subspace travel. He seemed to think the range of transporting a, say, roast turkey, was limited to a few hundred kilometers. So I told him not only could I beam a bird from one planet to an adjacent planet in the same system, which is no big deal anyway, but that if I were so inclined I could actually do it with a viable life-form. Long-range transwarp beaming is supposed to be impossible." He snorted. "Difficult maybe, but not impossible."

"Says you," countered Kirk.

"Says I, aye." The engineer glared back at him. "My mistake was in attemptin' a practical demonstration. Unfortunately, for a test subject I chose Admiral Archer's prize beagle." He shook his head sadly. "Shoulda scanned the little mutt's ident implant first, I suppose."

Kirk's expression changed to one of surprise. "I know of the admiral—and his dog. What happened to it?"

Scott looked away. "I'll tell ye when it reappears. I'm convinced it will, one of these days." His voice dropped to a mumble. "Somewhere. Somehow. If I'd known it was the bloody admiral's I would've been more careful." He perked up. "Sweet dog, though. Nice ears. I feel guilty."

Spock moved closer. "What if I told you that your theory was correct? That it is indeed possible to beam from a fixed point onto a ship that is traveling at warp speed? And that you only required the correct field equation for the continuous recrystallization of dilithium while transport is in progress? And availability of sufficient power for the transporter being used, of course."

Scott carefully regarded the Vulcan. "Haven't been out of touch *that* long. If such an equation had been discovered and verified, I'd 'ave heard." He shook his head in disagreement. "Delta Vega's out of the loop, but not completely out of touch. I keep up as best I can. Otherwise I'd go crazy here. And I haven't heard of any such development."

"The reason you haven't heard of it, Mister Scott, is because you haven't discovered it yet."

Surprised yet again, a startled Kirk turned to his rescuer. Simultaneously, the engineer narrowed his gaze as he took a much closer look at the Vulcan he knew only as a hermit and occasional visitor to the outpost in search of supplies. *All those lines in his face—just age lines?* he asked himself. *Or physical manifestations of wisdom?* You never could tell whether a Vulcan was telling you the truth or having you on. They would've made the Federation's best poker players—had they not found the game insufficiently challenging from an intellectual standpoint.

"And how would you know something like that?" he finally inquired. "You said 'yet.' Heard ye plain as day. Come from another time, do ya? From the future? Brilliant! Do they still have sandwiches where ye come from? Piece an' jam? Mince an' tatties? Cockaleekie soup?"

"What's he talking about?" Kirk asked. This time it was Keenser and not Spock who responded.

"Food."

"I'm not gonna believe anything anyone says without something more than their word to back it up," Scott declared challengingly. "Personally I think you're full of month-old haggis, but I'm so bored here that I'm willing to listen to anybody's tale, no matter how tall. So let's see if ye can support your whimsy with something more than talk." He punctuated the challenge with a lopsided grin. "That's 'logical,' ain't it?"

"Indeed it is, Mister Scott." Spock regarded their surroundings. "If you will allow us access to your shuttlepod I will gladly show you what a genius you actually are."

The engineer hesitated. Leaning over, his assistant conversed with him in excited tones. There followed an animated conversation whose exact content Kirk could not decipher but whose gist he could gather from the amount of energy expended. The squat alien was expressing his doubts about the visitor's request in no uncertain terms while Scott continued to vacillate. In the end, curiosity won out. Or maybe, as the engineer had indicated, it was just boredom.

The old shuttle's transporter pod was not exactly primitive, but it was basic. It was also constructed to industrial-strength standards, having been built to handle heavy supplies as well as individuals. Whether it was powerful enough to send a pea, let alone a primate, across the necessary spread of subspace remained to be seen.

What Spock had in mind was considerably larger and more complex than any vegetarian component.

Scott indicated the control console, stepped back, and waved grandly. "Have at it, future man."

Sitting down at the console, Spock accessed the necessary files and began typing, his fingers moving far faster over the controls than should have been possible for someone of his advanced age. Numbers and symbols began to fill the formerly blank monitor. There was no hesitation, no pause in his work. The Vulcan was not composing: he was dictating.

An increasingly serious Scott looked on approvingly. The Vulcan might be full of imploding mind-meld, but he could certainly input. He was at the console for only a minute or so before he rose and stepped aside.

"Rapid," Scott commented quietly. "That's impressive."

"Your equations for achieving long-range transwarp beaming—Mister Scott."

The engineer eyed him doubtfully, then began to study the monitor. He studied it for longer than it had taken the Vulcan to input the information. As he pored over the symbols and figures his expression progressed from confused, to dumbfounded, to one of utter delight.

"Carry the omega—twelve to the fourth—imagine that! Never occurred to me to think of space as the part that's moving. No wonder I could never resolve the central string! I was looking at it from the perspective of the beamer instead of the beamed." He peered down in wonder at the quietly unassuming Vulcan.

"Point of fact," Spock told him forthrightly, "it *did* occur to you." The elderly Vulcan began inputting an entirely different string of queries.

"What're you doing now?" The engineer's voice was still tinged with wonder and disbelief. "Adjunct equations?"

Spock did not turn from his work. "On our way here, Captain—Lieutenant Kirk—you informed me that your current acting captain intended to set a course directly for the Laurentian system with the intention of rendezvousing there with the rest of Starfleet."

Kirk nodded. "That's right. Knowing—him—I doubt that once his mind is set on a course of action he would be unlikely to change it."

Again, Spock did not quite smile. "Yes. He sounds quite fixed in his ways. I can sympathize." His tone turned wholly serious once more. "Prior to departing for that destination he detoured briefly to deposit you here. It is therefore not difficult to extrapolate the *Enterprise*'s logical and

most practical vector between Delta Vega and Laurentia."
His fingers continued to work the console's inputs.

Scott frowned. "'*Enterprise*'?" He looked over at Kirk.
"Had its maiden voyage already, has it? Well, well, ye
must've done something right to be assigned to that ship,
boyo."

Kirk swallowed and looked away. "It's a little complicated."

Scott was daydreaming. "She's a well-endowed lady,
that's for sure. Love to get me hands on her ample nacelles—if you'll pardon the engineering parlance."

"This will be your chance, Mister Scott." Spock continued to work the console.

The engineer stared at the back of the Vulcan's head.
"You're serious about tryin' this, aren't you? What am I
thinking—of course you're serious. Vulcans don't believe in
practical jokes." He shook his head slowly. "Even if I believed ye, that I'm the genius who wrote that code—and
I've plenty o' confidence even in a version of meself that
hasn't happened yet—we're still talking about slingshottin'
onto a ship travelin' at warp speed that by now is a considerable distance from here. And one without a properly activated receiving pad or engineering team awaitin' us. It'll be
like tryin' to intercept a bullet with a smaller bullet. Blind-
folded. While ridin' a horse." He grunted. "No—it'll be like
tryin' to hit a grain of sand with a bullet. While they're both
travelin' at angles to one another. In a tornado. While
they're both—"

Spock interrupted. "Ease off on the similes, Mister
Scott, or you will exhaust your arsenal before you depart."
He sat back from the console and contemplated the com-

plex information he had entered. "I calculate no more than a four-meter margin of error provided transport is energized within the next ten minutes—local time."

"That's all well and good," Scott concurred, "unless you rematerialize four meters outside the ship, or in a solid slab of metal. Not that I'm buyin' this technical twaddle for one minute, you understand."

Spock considered briefly, then returned to working the console's inputs. "Agreed. Therefore I determine that the aft engineering bay is the best option. A large open space, no unpredictable airlocks, located well within the ship in an area with which you will be familiar. And most importantly, one with a remote access point that will allow you to override the helm and redirect the ship's course." For a second time he sat back, satisfied with the work he had done, and turned to regard the engineer.

"Well, Mister Scott? You said you have confidence in yourself as well as in your future selves. Do you have confidence enough to put your abilities to an actual, practical test?"

The engineer considered. Then he broke out in a wide, wild grin. "At the hearin' about the dog they said that unless I straightened up I was going to the dogs. Aye, Mister Pointy-ear, let's do it! What's the worst that can happen? That I spread meself all over a wide corner of the cosmos? Better to go out in a flash than a footnote." He looked over at the younger officer. "And you, Lieutenant—Kirk, was it?"

Kirk nodded. "I don't have any choice, Mister Scott—Scotty." The engineer didn't chastise him for employing the nickname. "There's far more at stake here than you yet realize. And I can't do anything about it if I'm stuck here on this planet." He smiled thinly. "No matter how convivial the company or engaging the surroundings."

Only one of those present protested the chosen course of action. It was clear that the alien did not want his human associate to leave. Excited at the prospect of not only escaping the backwater that was Delta Vega but at the chance to acquire actual proof of a notion with which he had been toying for years, Scott gently reassured his fellow officer that all would be well. Unable to sway his friend, the alien responded understandingly but with obvious regret.

As the Vulcan rose from the console chair, Kirk confronted him uncertainly. His attitude toward his savior was still a confused mix of gratitude, awe, and uncertainty.

"You're coming with us?"

"No, Jim. May I call you Jim?"

"Sure, I guess." Coming from this elder incarnation of Spock it sounded . . . odd. Odd, but nice, Kirk decided.

"My destiny lies along a different path," the Vulcan told him. "You must make your own without me. The situation in which we find ourselves is unprecedented and fraught with potential danger. My presence as you seek to determine your future would present complications whose consequences cannot be foreseen and which, I feel, are best avoided."

It was not the response Kirk had been hoping for. "Your destiny can wait. *He* won't believe me. Only *you* can explain wha—"

The Vulcan cut him off. "Under no circumstances can the one to whom we are referring be made aware of my existence. *You must promise me this.*"

Kirk struggled to keep up with the possible ramifications while simultaneously trying to persuade his rescuer to change his mind.

"You're telling me I can't tell *you* I'm following *your own orders*? Why not? What happens if I do?"

Spock moved closer. "*Trust me,* Jim. Above all, this is the one rule you cannot break. To stop Nero, you alone must take command of your ship."

Kirk's expression was grim. "Over your dead body?"

"Preferably not," the elder Spock replied. "There is, however, Starfleet Regulation Six-nineteen." When Kirk failed to respond, the Vulcan sighed knowingly. "Yes, I forget what little regard you had for such things. Six-nineteen states that any commander who is emotionally compromised by the mission at hand must forthwith resign his command."

Kirk frowned uncertainly. "So I need to emotionally compromise you?"

"Jim," the elder Spock told him gravely, "I just lost my planet, my whole world. I *am* emotionally compromised. What *you* must do is get me to—show it."

Kirk considered this. Quietly, carefully, and intently. "Hmm."

An equally intent but far more ebullient voice sounded behind him. "Aye, then! Live or die, laddie, let's get this over with! The *Enterprise* has decent food service facilities, I'm guessing." Whistling to himself, the engineer headed for the transporter pad.

Kirk started to follow, then looked behind him. "You know, coming back in time, changing history, informing someone in the past about what's happened in the future—

that might be construed by an impartial onlooker as *cheating.*"

"A trick I learned from an old friend." Stepping back, the elder Spock retreated toward the transporter console. Before taking the seat, he raised one hand with the fingers separated into pairs. Kirk took up a stance on the pad beside the whistling engineer.

"Live long, and prosper," the old Vulcan told the young lieutenant.

Then he sat down and activated the transporter. Both men dematerialized. When, where, and whether they would be reconstituted he did not know for a certainty. He knew that Montgomery Scott's equations were valid. Spock could only hope that his own computations were applicable.

If they were not, if they were off by more than the four meters he had calculated, then nothing else would matter. Ever.

XV

There was no one present in the open engineering bay to hear the steady, powerful hum of the ship's engines. Maintenance was busy elsewhere, still battling to repair the last of the serious damage that had been incurred in the fight with the *Narada*. At the moment no technicians were on hand in the vicinity of central cooling and water distribution, a largely automated corner of the ship that required little attention.

So it was that there was no one present to see the twin vertical columns of lambent particulate matter that swiftly solidified into the shapes of two human beings.

One of those figures stumbled, gasping, to look down at itself in amazement. *I am intact,* Kirk realized. His brain and attendant mechanical parts had all survived the impracticable, implausible journey in one piece. As he rose and began to slip out of his cold-weather outer clothing, a quick look around revealed that he was indeed in the engineering section of a starship. While no identification was readily at hand, he had little reason to doubt it was the *Enterprise*. If the elder Spock had managed the transport, surely he had also succeeded in putting them aboard their target vessel. Engineer Scott would confirm it.

Where *was* Engineer Scott?

Looking around anxiously, Kirk searched among the huge tubes and conduits for his enthusiastic if unlikely sub-space traveling companion. He turned only when he heard a faint banging. His eyes went wide as he located the source.

Scott had rematerialized equally intact and energetic—but inside one of the cooling tanks.

As a stunned Kirk looked on, pressure shoved the wide-eyed engineer upward and into a crosswise conduit. Trapped like a worm in a hose, cheeks bulging, Scott was spun sideways with Kirk in pursuit. Fists pounding desperately on the transparent unbreakable composite, the engineer could see Kirk but not reach out to him.

Racing along below, a frantic Kirk looked ahead in search of an access. Instead of a port or sampling cylinder his eyes fell on the main coolant distribution chamber. If the trapped Scott made it that far, he would not have to worry about drowning: the greatly increased pressure in the chamber would crush him and distribute the pieces to different parts of the ship.

If he didn't do something *quick,* the *Enterprise*'s maintenance engineers were going to find some unpleasant clogs in various corners of the ship's hydrologic system.

No tools were at hand—not that the tough, durable synthetic of which the coolant tubes were made would yield to hammering driven by mere human muscles anyway. There, just off to one side—a control panel. But did it offer access to the *right* controls? When only one option presents itself, decision-making becomes easy. He made for it as fast as his feet would carry him.

Beneath his pounding fingers a schematic of the complete cooling system offered itself up for inspection. Which conduit, which direction, which valve . . . ? A sideways glance showed that if he didn't do something fast it would no longer matter—Scott's lungs would fill with water before his body even reached the distribution chamber.

Try *something*, Kirk shouted at himself. His fingers stabbed wildly at the console.

On the bridge a small portion of a usually unimportant display suddenly went from green to red. Chekov frowned at it, fingered a couple of controls, and double-checked before daring to report.

"Keptin, we're detecting unauthorized access to one of the auxiliary cooling tank control boards." He checked his console. "Appropriate retrieval code was not entered."

One eyebrow rose sharply. "Auxiliary cooling?"

Chekov eyed his console again. "Yes, Keptin. Perhaps the technician on site forgot to punch in his identification."

The acting captain considered. "Perhaps. What is the board's current status?"

"Still in use, Keptin. And there is something else. The sequences that are being entered: from an engineering standpoint they seem almost—random."

Spock nodded curtly. "Someone is being derelict in their duty. Or . . ." He paused, pondering. "Send a security team to check it out. Tell them to take sidearms. Set to stun."

"Aye, Keptin." Chekov issued the necessary order.

• • •

Kirk forced himself to take a mental step backward. "Okay-okay—comeoncomeoncomeon—*think*. Pretend you're in the relevant simulator." His fingers moved again; slower and more assured this time. With purpose instead of panic. "Manual control; enabled. Pressure; calculated. Emergency pressure release; located."

Fluttering eyes half shut, Scott was shooting down the final conduit leading to the distribution chamber. All that remained was to see if he died from drowning or being torn apart by the distributor pump. Then . . .

The rush of water ceased as emergency seals fell into place on either side of him and a maintenance access panel in the underside of the conduit abruptly dropped open, unceremoniously dumping onto the deck a couple hundred gallons of water and one severely waterlogged engineer. Kirk rushed to his traveling companion and propped him up as a gasping Scott spasmodically relieved his insides of a liter or so of involuntarily imbibed liquid. Worse, it was water.

"You all right . . . ?"

Taking a deep breath, the engineer wiped at his dripping face, looked up, and recognized his new friend.

"Nice," he coughed up water, "ship. Really."

Kirk helped him to his feet. "Better to be remembered as the inventor of the equations that allow for long-range ship-to-ship transporting than as the first man in history to die from drowning aboard a starship." Still supporting the engineer, he was looking around worriedly. All this commotion in what was normally a tranquil section of the ship was bound to attract attention.

"Come on—let's get to the bridge!"

His prescience was soon proved correct as a security team arrived barely moments after they had departed. Noting the presence of entirely too much water on the deck, an emergency release latch that showed no sign of having accidentally given way, and wet bootprints leading deeper into the ship, the team drew their sidearms as they went on immediate alert.

"Captain," the team leader reported into his communicator, "we appear to have unauthorized access on the engineering level."

Spock responded quickly to the new information. "Seal engineering. All security personnel on high alert." He moved quickly toward the helm station. "Mister Sulu, activate security imaging. Check the entire crew, including the wounded and those still in sickbay. Also all refugees—their vitals should have been entered into records by now. Do we have any unregistered life-forms on board?"

Sulu swiftly entered the request. In response to his query the monitor provided a scalable schematic that showed every deck and every corner of the *Enterprise.* On some decks dozens of green dots glowed, often in small clusters. On other decks only a few green identifiers appeared. On engineering . . .

Two red dots, moving fast and beeping steadily.

"Affirmative, sir." A disbelieving Sulu confirmed what was evident on-screen. "Engineering bay—hydrologics. But—but that's *impossible.* . . ."

Spock leaned forward. "There is visual confirmation. It *could* be a system anomaly."

• • •

The two security guards had their weapons trained directly at Kirk and Scott. With nowhere to go, both men slowed. Bemused but professional, the security team came closer. Then one of them grinned unpleasantly at Kirk.

"Come with me—moonbeam."

Kirk recognized the voice as well as the body. It was the cadet he had bloodied in an Iowa bar in what now seemed like centuries ago . . .

When they entered the bridge the pair were greeted by stunned expressions. From Sulu, Uhura, and Chekov. Only Spock, and his father, who was also present, regarded the arrivals calmly. Scott wisely kept silent and drew little of the attention. He knew none of them anyway and was unaware that the tension on the bridge was due as much to the awkward relationship that existed between its acting captain and Kirk as to the far greater danger that now threatened them all.

Spock straightaway confronted the one prisoner he knew. Flanked by security personnel, Kirk met the Vulcan's probing gaze without flinching. The effects of the stun that had been used to subdue him had already worn off.

"Surprise," Kirk said.

Ignoring him, Spock eyed his companion. "Who are you?"

"He's with me." Kirk's smile widened.

"How did you beam yourself aboard this ship while it is traveling at warp speed?"

Battered and exhausted from what had been a very long day indeed, Kirk still managed to grin. "You're the genius: you figure it out." He nodded toward a particular bridge station. "Why don't you ask the ship's science officer?"

"As captain of this vessel I order you to answer the question." It was not exactly a shout, but much more than a casual request. "You are a prisoner. There is nowhere for you to go. This question impinges on the very security of Starfleet itself. I assure you that I will utilize whatever authorized methods are at my disposal to convince you to respond to my inquiry."

"Well, I'm not telling."

Clearly taken aback, Spock had no rejoinder for that. Relishing the confusion he had engendered, an energized Kirk pushed harder.

"Does that frustrate you? My lack of cooperation? Does that make you angry?"

Turning away from him, Spock studied the stranger who had accompanied him.

"You are not a member of this ship's crew. Under penalty of court-martial, I order you to explain how you beamed aboa—"

"Don't answer him, Scotty."

Spock was not to be denied. "You *will* answer me," he ordered the stranger.

Scott looked from Vulcan to Kirk—and demurred. "I'd rather not take sides, if you dinna mind."

Frustrated beyond measure, Spock nodded to the security guards. "Escort them to the brig."

But Kirk wasn't yet ready to go. In fact, he was just getting warmed up.

"What is it about you, Spock? Your planet was just destroyed. Your whole *civilization* was wiped out. Your mother murdered—and you're not even *upset?*"

Spock stared back at him, hard and unblinking. "Your presumption that these experiences interfere with my abilities to command this ship is inaccurate."

"Ha! I mean, did you see that bastard's ship? Did you see what he did?"

"Yes, of course I . . ."

"So are you angry or aren't you?"

"I will not—allow you to lecture me about the merits of emotion."

Kirk moved closer, before the guards could think about intervening. "Then why don't you stop me?"

Spock's eyes did not waver from the human confronting him. Off to the side, McCoy was watching the growing confrontation nervously. Sarek merely—watched.

"Step away from me, Mister Kirk."

"Tell me, Spock." Kirk didn't move. "What's it like not to feel? *Anger.* Or *heartbreak.* Or the need to stop at *nothing* to avenge the death of the woman who gave *birth* to you?"

A vein had begun to pulse in the Vulcan's neck. His eyes had widened slightly.

"Back away. . . ."

"You must not feel *anything,*" Kirk persisted. "I guess it must not *compute* for you. When it comes down to it, I guess you must not have loved her at *all.* . . ."

"Stop it, you sonofabitch!" Rising from her communications station, Uhura started toward them. A hand caught her arm and held her back. Looking around in surprise she saw that she was being restrained by, of all people, the ship's doctor. McCoy wore an indecipherable, almost speculative expression.

"Let 'em fight."

Spock snapped.

Kirk did his best to fight back, but no human could have moved as fast as the acting captain of the *Enterprise* did at that moment. Spock became a blur, a whirlwind of striking hands and darting fingers. Every blow Kirk struck was blocked, every attempt at defense repulsed as Spock tore into him. Blood—considerably more than a trickle—began to appear on the taunter's face as the Vulcan pounded him relentlessly. A couple of crew members hesitantly tried to intervene. Spock threw them aside as if they were weightless. Bedlam reigned on the bridge as other officers yelled and shouted in an attempt to stop the fight.

Lifting Kirk off the ground, Spock threw him against a far wall. One of the security team charged with guarding the intruder tried to step between the two, only to find himself thrown to the deck. Eyes blazing, Spock caught Kirk before he could spin clear and clamped a hand over the tormenting human's throat. Now even an alarmed Uhura was yelling at the Vulcan to stop. But all the acting captain heard was the uncontrolled raging in his own mind. Nothing could penetrate the white heat that was driving him, no one could make themselves heard above . . .

"SPOCK."

From where he had remained standing near a far wall, Sarek had finally stepped forward.

Spock maintained the death grip for an instant longer. Kirk's eyes fluttered and started to roll back into his head. Then, with the sound of his father's voice echoing throughout his entire being, Spock abruptly released the younger human. His attitude now that of the defeated instead of the victor, he stepped back, stunned by what had transpired. Clutching at his throat and gasping for air, Kirk barely managed to remain on his feet. Though his face was bloody and bruised, there was no hatred there. Only compassion.

No one gave much notice to the visage of the battered lieutenant, however. Their attention was focused solely on their commanding officer. After a moment Spock gathered himself, straightening, and wiped at his eyes as he struggled to regain some semblance of his natural dignity. A condition now fled, he knew. Thoughts elsewhere, his attitude uncharacteristically hesitant, he walked calmly over to where McCoy was standing and staring back at him wide-eyed . . .

"Doctor. By order of Starfleet Regulation Six-nineteen I hereby relinquish my command on the grounds that I have been—emotionally compromised. Please note the time and date in the ship's log." He pushed past the staring physician and exited the bridge.

"I *like* this ship," Scott declared into the ensuing silence. "It's exciting!"

McCoy turned to Kirk. "Congratulations, Jim. Now we've got no captain—and no goddamn first officer to replace him."

Kirk didn't hesitate. "Yeah we do."

If he didn't hesitate, the same could not be said for his shipmates. It was left to Sulu to point—in his direction. That was when it hit them. That was when they remembered.

Pike had made Kirk first officer before leaving the ship.

"What!?" McCoy blurted in disbelief as the same realization struck him.

Kirk offered him a lopsided smile. "Thanks for the support, Doc." As he moved purposefully toward the command chair, he passed Uhura.

"There's a lot I'd like to say—*Captain.*" She all but hissed the title. "But I'll save it for another time. Meanwhile, I sure as hell hope you know what you're doing."

Under the circumstances, he thought, her comment practically amounted to a vote of confidence. He nodded slowly.

"So do I."

Spitting blood that was decidedly not green, he moved painfully toward the command chair. When McCoy stepped forward as if to examine the injuries the younger man had just suffered, Kirk waved him off. There would be time for that later, he knew. If they did not move swiftly and decisively now, there would be no time for anything. Slumping into the chair, he directed his voice to the communications pickup.

"Attention, crew of the *Enterprise.* This is James Kirk. Captain Spock has resigned his commission and advanced me to acting captain." Throughout the ship stunned crew and officers stopped what they were doing to listen to the announcement. Those who knew Spock could not imagine a scenario under which the Vulcan would have resigned as commanding officer.

They had not been witness to the clash on the bridge.

"I know you were all expecting to regroup with the rest of the fleet," Kirk continued, "but I'm ordering a pursuit course of the enemy ship that we believe to be headed for Earth. I want all departments at battle stations and ready for combat in ten minutes. Either we're going down or they are." Ending the transmission, he looked around to regard the bridge crew. Some of them were still in shock. It had all happened so quickly.

Not unexpectedly, it was Uhura who finally broke the stunned silence.

"I want some *answers*. Where the hell did you get transwarp technology?" She jerked her head in the direction of the still silent and unmistakably damp figure who had remained standing inconspicuously off to one side of the lift doors. "Surely not from that vagrant you brought on board with you?"

That drew a response from the subject, who looked wounded. " 'Ere now, lassie, I think that's uncalled for."

Kirk smiled, winced at the pain this induced, and tried to answer. "Lieutenant Uhura, that 'vagrant' is Montgomery Scott, an experienced Starfleet engineer of unexpected mental and technical gifts, if possibly dubious character. As to the definitive source of the actual physics that were employed to get us on board, trust me—it's complicated."

Sulu looked over from his position at the helm. "How about *you* trust *me*? I have a doctorate in astrophysics and a master's certificate in interstellar navigation—not to mention having completed a wide assortment of advanced seminars in subspace theory and related disciplines. Whatever explanation you care to propose, I think I can handle it."

"And I also," declared Chekov. "Between Mister Sulu and myself I doubt there's any account you can provide, Mir . . . Kir—Keptin Kirk—that we will be incapable of dissecting. Or is it that you want us to trust *you* but you won't trust *us*?"

The expressions and attitudes of the rest of the bridge

complement indicated that not only did they agree whole-
heartedly with the two officers but that Kirk was going to
have a hard time getting them to listen to him if he was not
soon more forthcoming on this particular subject. Still, he
hesitated before replying. When he finally did so it was because he knew that when the time came to confront Nero
and the *Narada,* the one thing they could not afford was
uncertainty regarding the top of the chain of command. It
would be critical that everyone respond promptly and to
the best of their ability to whatever orders he might have to
issue. The battlefield was not the place to question the com-
petency—or the honesty—of one's commanding officer. He
had no choice but to respond to Sulu's and Chekov's and
Uhura's probing.

Even if it was likely they wouldn't believe a word he
said.

"Okay, you want answers? The necessary equations to
program a transporter for transwarp beaming came from
Spock." Looks of bewilderment were exchanged among the
bridge crew. They only grew deeper as Kirk continued.

"Not the Spock who just resigned his command of this
ship. Not the Spock who just nearly killed me. They came
from an *older* Spock. A much older Spock. One from the
future who traveled through a wormhole and is currently
residing in our present."

Seated at the helm, Sulu was staring back at him.
"Okay—I find myself having to amend my previous statement: I'm not sure I *can* handle it."

"Do you think we're all crazy, Keptin?" Chekov challenged him.

"No." Kirk found himself growing in confidence the

more he explained. "I *am* asking you to *think*. Consider our opponent, the great Romulan starship, the *Narada*. Bigger by far than any Romulan warship in the catalog. Utilizing weaponry whose basics are familiar but that are far more powerful than anything previously encountered. The unremittingly hostile, even vengeful attitude of its commander and crew. An attitude that to us has no basis in reality. In *this* reality."

Sulu looked at Chekov, who looked back at Uhura. The change in attitude on the bridge was perceptible. Or maybe, Kirk thought, he was just fooling himself. But at least they were listening to him. At least they were *thinking*.

Logic was not the exclusive preserve of Vulcans. Humans too, on those occasions when they calmed down, were capable of rational thought. And when all possible reasonable explanations for a sequence of events had been exhausted, they were frequently willing to consider the impossible. He continued to present it.

"This Nero followed the older Spock back in time because he blames Vulcan and all Vulcans for the destruction in the future of Romulus. He thinks the Federation, and Vulcan in particular as exemplified by a future mission headed by Spock, could have saved his homeworld. He doesn't trust the Federation, Vulcan, or Spock to do it in this time frame. So now he thinks the only way to save Romulus in the future is to destroy the Federation in our present. That's the *truth*. As for transwarp beaming capability . . ." Turning, he nodded in the engineer's direction. "Ask *him*. He's the one who invented it. Spock—the older Spock, the one from the future—just supplied a reminder."

This time it was not just Uhura but everyone on the bridge who looked penetratingly in Scott's direction.

"Is what he says true, Mister—Scott?"

The engineer nodded, his attitude a mixture of pride and embarrassment. "Aye—and me friends call me 'Scotty.'"

The astonishment and uncertainty that had heretofore dominated the bridge now dissolved into excited debate.

"So this changes all our histories, or what?" McCoy began. "Does it change the general thread of history and not personal pasts, or does everything change?" He looked down at himself. "Do we change physically, too? I kind of like the way I am." His gaze narrowed as he regarded the new captain. "If we alter the future so that everyone has to do transwarp beaming, I'm not sure I want to go there."

"Our history is only altered," Sulu was saying, "if you think of time as a single thread."

"Then possibly it's more like we're living out a parallel strand than an alternate one," Uhura speculated aloud. "If you believe that the future is immutable and that it already exists, what we're doing is only changing the past. That same future, or if you prefer, parallel one, will continue on whatever plane it exists. Only ours, only this one here and now, will be altered."

"Parallel?" McCoy stared at her. "How many damn universes *are* there?"

"If this one is changed," Sulu continued, "does it only affect this one, or are all the others affected as well?"

"A ripple effect across the entire continuum." Chekov was clearly excited by the possibilities, however theoretical they might remain. "But can such a ripple affect only parallel existences, or, if it is strong enough, can it also affect a future that has already happened?"

Turning away from the animated and slightly chaotic discussion, McCoy put his hands over his ears. "Kentucky," he told himself solemnly. "Think bluegrass. Quiet caves. Real food. Not parallel food."

Kirk eventually called for silence. *"Look,"* he told them, "I'm not sure what it means or if we can even make things go back to the way they were—the way they're *supposed* to be. Our task *right now* is to try and save Earth and the Federation from someone who doesn't care about the future of either. We have enough to worry about trying to save the present, without tying ourselves in mental knots wondering if we can save the future. One thing I do know for certain— if we don't save the present then there'll *be* no future. At least, not for the Federation." He tried to meet each of their stares in turn.

"Maybe if this ship was crewed by Einstein, Rutherford, Bohr, Planck, Hawking, Ashford, T'mer, and Lal-kang instead of *us* they'd be able to come up with some answers to questions that we can barely formulate. But it isn't. There's just us. And if we want our descendants to have any kind of future, then it's up to us to see that it comes to pass. All I know is, we can't tell Spock—our Spock, the present-day Spock—any of this."

Evidently, McCoy's hands were not pressed tightly enough over his ears, because he turned to frown at the command chair. "Why the hell not?"

"Because I promised him," Kirk explained.

Uhura looked baffled. "Promised *who?*"

"Spock." Kirk struggled for clarity—and feared he was

losing the fight. "The *other* one—the other Spock. The one from the future. I promised him that I wouldn't tell him in the present about him from the future because him from the future made me promise." His voice rose. *"Dammit, are you gonna trust me or not?"*

In response to his manifestly frustrated appeal, silence once more settled over the bridge. But not comprehension.

No one bothered him as he stood in the transporter room, staring at the pad where his mother should have rematerialized. He was unspeakably grateful for the privacy. No one intruded on his personal space to try and comfort him, or to sympathize, or to offer insipid uplifting homilies. He was not in the mood for any such well-meaning platitudes. All he required, all he wished for, was to be left alone. Had anyone come and tried to access his solitude he would have turned them away, politely but firmly. Upon resigning command he had clearly and unequivocally stipulated that he should be left alone. It was a demand no one would rebuff. Save one.

His father.

Sarek, child of Skon, child of Solkar, entered the main transporter room and stared at his son in silence. On the Council of the Vulcan Academy of Sciences he had always known what to say. Acting as an ambassador for his people he had rarely been at a loss for the necessary words to make Vulcan's case before the Federation. As a husband wed to a woman of another species he had never . . . he had never . . .

That was one place too painful now for even Sarek to go. Instead, he concentrated on a destination still within reach. It finally caused him to break the respectful silence that had been in place between them for over an hour now. It had taken that long to settle on the right words.

"You must not punish yourself."

Hands folded in front of him, Spock looked over at his remaining parent. "I require seclusion. I ask that you respect my wishes and leave."

At least, Sarek thought to himself, *he has not retreated permanently into silence.* It was a hopeful sign. "How many times since you were born have I heard those same words, albeit voiced by a child and subsequently an adolescent in command of far less gravity? I remain because I wish you to speak your mind, Spock."

The younger man looked away. "That would be unwise."

"What is necessary is always wise, my son. If I did not feel it necessary for you to speak of what is inside you, then I would not wish for it. It is true that logic is often its own reward—but it is a reward best shared with others. That which is beautiful is magnified by being shared with others. That which is painful is often moderated by being shared. Both approaches are equally logical."

Spock hesitated, then let out a little of what was clearly seething inside him. "I feel as conflicted as I once was. Like a child. Have I made so little progress that I cannot contain myself even when entrusted with the position of starship captain? If that is so, then I am truly not fit for such duty."

"You will always be a child of two worlds, Spock," Sarek replied gently. "As such, you will forever be forced to make decisions that partake of both. You must not castigate yourself for failing to be wholly Vulcan because you cannot be so. Instead of viewing your heritage as potentially embracing the worst of one world or the other, try to extrapolate the best of both. Even if ultimately only made possible by biological manipulation, your birthright, Spock, should be as much a wonderment to you as it is to me. I am grateful for it. And for you." He found himself pausing once more. "And not only because you are all I have left of—her."

As the science officer turned to his father he did not become emotional—but he came undeniably close.

"I feel such—anger. For the one who took her life. Illogical as it may be, I cannot escape it. It troubles me every moment I am awake, like an equation whose components are all present but that still cannot be solved. It is an anger I cannot stop."

Sarek nodded understandingly. "It is not how I would react, of course, but I believe *she* would say—do not try to."

Their eyes met—and this time, held.

"You asked me once," Sarek continued, "why I married your mother. I married her—because I loved her."

Nothing more was said, but for Spock, child of Sarek, child of Grayson, something important had clearly been resolved.

XVI

On the bridge a strategy session was in full swing. Having no particular plan of his own other than to catch up to the homicidal Romulan called Nero and somehow stop him, Kirk was willing to listen to suggestions no matter how outrageous or who their source. Had a coterie of the *Enterprise*'s maintenance crew come before him with an idea, he would have listened to it with as much respect as he gave the thoughts of Chekov and the rest of the ship's tactical team.

But first they had to find some way to resolve the small matter of the distance separating them from the *Narada*.

"Can we catch up?" Kirk finally asked the question that could not be avoided.

Sulu had already run the simulation half a dozen times, each time factoring in different options that represented wishful thinking more than they did solid physics. His response this time was identical to the previous six.

"Not a chance. I've run every option, Captain. They're

going to be in geosynchronous orbit around Earth in eight minutes. We'll never make it."

"Even if we could," McCoy pointed out, "you can't go in with guns blazing."

"The doctor is correct, Keptin." As chief tactical officer it was Chekov's job to anticipate an enemy's moves, to put himself in their position—however distasteful the mental transposition. "First of all, they'll have their own defenses up. They'll be looking for remnants of the fleet as well as local defenses to strike out at them. Ground-based aircraft and missiles won't have a chance of penetrating their shields. Any ship of starship size that drops out of warp near Earth will get pulverized before it has a chance to respond. And we already know that this *Narada* from the future is far more powerful than any Federation vessel." He shook his head dolefully. "The only chance we might have of inflicting any significant damage is to take them completely by surprise." Tactical chief and helmsman exchanged a knowing glance.

"There's no way we can drop out of warp within effective attack range without them detecting our presence and responding," Sulu added. "They'll be scanning everything inside the orbit of Mars. If we emerge outside detection range it's even worse: they'll have plenty of time to see us coming if we try to engage on impulse power."

Kirk considered. "Then we have to find a way to get on that ship and steal the device from under them."

"Don't you mean 'destroy' the device, Keptin?" Chekov asked.

Kirk sighed. "And how do you propose destroying it, Mister Chekov? If you destroy its dual containment fields, then you end up releasing the contents." He smiled thinly. "That's just what we want—a bunch of Red Matter floating around the solar system. We have to capture the device in one piece. Then we can utilize it, dispose of it—whatever Starfleet decides to do."

"As far as getting on board the Romulan vessel, ye can forget transwarp." Scott was emphatic. "Beaming from a fixed point on a planetary surface to a ship travelin' in subspace is one thing. Tryin' to beam from a ship *travelin'* through subspace onto another travelin' through subspace boggles the calculus." He looked at Kirk. "Hittin' a bullet with another bullet is hard enough. Imagine if both guns are in motion."

More hopeful than realistic, Kirk glanced toward communications. "Anything from Captain Pike? At this point I'd be happy to hear him acting as intermediary for terms of surrender—anything to indicate he's still alive."

"I'm sorry, sir," Uhura reported gravely. "I've been monitoring all channels including the original reception frequency from the *Narada*. There's been nothing."

"Keptin Kirk?"

Attention on the bridge shifted to the young tactical officer. "Yes, Chekov?" Kirk prompted him.

"We can't drop out of warp close enough to the *Narada* to fight her or to transport an assault team aboard without alerting her defenses. To be sure of avoiding their detectors yet achieving your aim, we have to come out of warp somewhere close enough for our transporter system to be able to lock onto the Romulan ship without activating her defensive system."

McCoy stared at him. "What would you suggest?

Coming out of warp behind the moon? If we come out of warp and there's a solid body between us and the *Narada*, then we can't use our transporters. If we come out of warp behind the moon and move out to where we *can* use our transporters, then they'll spot us. And if we emerge far enough out so that they don't detect us, then they'll spot us when we move in close. There's no solution."

"Your pardon, Doctor, but I believe there is."

"Go on, Chekov," Kirk urged him.

The tactical officer warmed to his argument. "We need to emerge from warp somewhere close enough so that Mister Scott can get a direct transporter line on the enemy but sufficiently hidden so that they don't become aware of us. All this talk of dangerous supernovas has got me to thinking. Unless Romulan technology has changed or advanced so much that it is beyond imagining, their detection systems should still be highly sensitive to very strong magnetic fields."

"What are you suggesting?" This time it was Sulu's turn to object. "That we come out inside Jupiter's magnetic field? We can't maneuver in there for the same reasons detectors don't work, and if we emerge on the side of the planet where we can get a transporter sight on the enemy, they're likely to have other long-range detectors that will pick up the distortion caused by our appearance."

Chekov nodded knowingly. "Not Jupiter, Mister Sulu. Saturn."

The helmsman shook his head doubtfully. "Magnetic field is still eight thousand times stronger than Earth's and would play havoc with our instrumentation. And there's still the transporter line problem."

"I was not thinking of Saturn itself." Chekov let his gaze shift among his fellow crew members. "What about Titan?"

"Titan?" Kirk considered briefly, looked toward his helmsman. "Mister Sulu?"

"Already on it, Captain. It might—it just might work. If we come out of warp on the outsystem side of Titan, our presence will not be noticed by the *Narada*. We can then maneuver to get a transporter line on the Romulan ship. We should still be sufficiently masked from detection by Saturn's magnetosphere and by its mixing with Titan's much weaker one. Additionally, the Titanian atmosphere will mask any visual that might alert the Romulans, and the ionization that is continually taking place in its upper atmosphere will further serve to conceal the *Enterprise*'s signature. And unlike emerging behind our own moon, if we *are* detected we'll be far enough outsystem to get back into warp before they can attack." He looked at Chekov admiringly. "I think, Mister Chekov, you picked the one place in the solar system where we can hide and still give Mister Scott a chance to beam an attack team onto the *Narada*."

McCoy wasn't quite ready to accede to the strategy. "Now wait a goddamn minute! How old's this kid?"

"I am seventeen." Chekov sat up straighter in his seat. "How old are *you*, Doctor?"

"Old enough to *shave*," McCoy shot back. "And when I shave, I'm only holding whiskers in my hand—not the fate of worlds."

The dispute might have escalated further save for an interruption by a new voice.

"Doctor—Mister Chekov is correct."

Everyone on the bridge turned simultaneously toward the lift. Striding toward them was a familiar figure, but it was not the same as the one who had left. This Spock was renewed in purpose and clear of eye and voice. What had happened to bring about the transformation none of them could imagine. They only knew they were glad to see him back on the bridge.

Kirk tensed, but the Vulcan's manner was calm, composed—almost serene. And professional. When he spoke, there was a determination in his voice that had not been there before.

McCoy was not in the least intimidated. "How do you know he's correct?"

"I have not just been sitting in my quarters bemoaning recent events, Doctor. That would have constituted an illogical waste of precious and rapidly disappearing time. In the course of my research I reviewed similar information and have come to similar conclusions." He eyed the much younger officer. "Though it remained for Mister Chekov to formulate the exact stratagem."

Chekov did not quite blush. "Tactics are what I was trained for."

Spock turned to face Kirk. There was not a trace of animosity in his tone or posture. "If Mister Sulu can maneuver us into position according to the dictates expressed by Mister Chekov, and relying on Mister Scott's expertise in calculating transporter delimitations, I believe I can be beamed aboard Nero's ship."

Kirk's tone was uncommonly serious. "I won't order you to do that, Mister Spock."

The science officer regarded his former adversary as if nothing untoward had ever passed between them. "Romulans and Vulcans share a common ancestry. Unless, as Mister Chekov suggests, the technology on board the *Narada* has changed beyond recognition, I am probably sufficiently familiar with Romulan scientific and engineering standards to access their ship's functions and thereby locate the device." He paused ever so briefly. "And—my mother was human. Which makes Earth the only home I have left. So I have as much reason and rationale as anyone to want to risk my life in hope of preserving it."

Everyone's eyes remained on him, but his lingered only on Uhura's. No one really noticed—except McCoy. As chief medical officer he was attuned to subtle aspects of crew performance that escaped his colleagues.

"Then I'm coming with you," Kirk declared with conviction.

Spock considered what was, after all, not a request but an inevitable declaration of intent. "I would cite regulation stating that a captain and science officer should not be off their ship at the same time, especially in potentially hazardous situations, but I know you will simply ignore it—as I suspect you are frequently likely to do in the future, should we come out of this alive."

Kirk repressed a smile. "See? We're getting to know each other."

Spock straightened slightly. "It would be foolish to say that continuing contact does not beget familiarity—however intemperate that contact has been on occasion."

Stepping back, McCoy whispered to the newcomer

Scott. "Which is a Vulcan way of saying that they might, just might, come out of this as friends—if they don't kill each other first."

The blue and white matrix of sea and sky that was Earth's most striking feature when seen from space had worked its magic on thousands of visitors ever since first contact had been made with other sentient species. His abhorrent ambition notwithstanding, the effect it had was no less profound on the planet's current observer.

What a pity, he thought as he gazed upon the shimmering panorama spread out below, *that it is about to be wiped from the catalog of worlds forever.*

Staring at the viewscreen, Nero joined members of his crew in admiring the view. *So much water,* he thought. Water in abundance, whereas it was often scarce on other worlds. Vulcan, for example. But now neither water nor anything else was a problem for Vulcan, nor for the feeble remnants of that calculating, perfidious race.

Whose allies, he reminded himself, were about to follow their excessively logical co-conspirators into oblivion.

"It is beautiful, no?" he murmured aloud as he continued to contemplate the glowing image on the monitor.

"Yes, Captain." Having seen to the *Narada*'s safe arrival at its latest destination the helmsman had momentarily moved from his station to stand near his leader. "It is. I wonder why they decided to call it Earth instead of Water?"

There was an awkward pause during which the helmsman found himself, for the first time in a long while, unable to perceive the commander's intentions. A good moment, perhaps, to advance a concern that had been festering for some time now in the minds of all on board.

"Sir, the men and I have discussed this. What we are about to do." He hesitated. "We have to turn the ship around. We can save our home. *Stop this.*"

The intimations of wistfulness that had crept into the commander of the *Narada*'s face as he stared down at the planet he was about to eradicate vanished like the ephemera of a poem unwritten. His features hardened as he turned to face his first officer.

"We can go back," Ayel continued. "That's what we want. We have taken our vengeance on Vulcan. We want to go home now."

Fingering his ceremonial staff, Nero considered the request. "There is no need to threaten me, Ayel. I understand. I understand—but you are wrong."

From the wrong end of the staff, four blades snicked outward. Ayel's eyes grew wide—as he fell backward to the deck. As murmurs began to rise from the rest of those present, Nero rose to confront them. To challenge them. His voice rang out across the bridge.

"We will return to Romulus when the Federation lies in ruins. When those who watched our people *burn* at last understand our pain. Our loss. When Romulus no longer needs to kowtow or defer or submit to dictates from uncaring Vulcans and humans and others. It will be the turn of *Romulus* to command and to dominate. We will not return to our homeworld as the last progeny of an annihilated planet. Any time paradoxes will be resolved. Were such concepts to prove fatal to this time stream, they would already have done so. Think of it! Instead of mourning a lost world and a lost system, you will be able to greet your own younger selves, your own parents, your own friends as you knew them when you were young. They will stand before you awed and amazed, and hail the *Narada* and all those who crew her." He paused for emphasis.

"Because we will return not as the simple exploration miners who once left, but as *conquerors.*"

Whirling back to face the monitor once more, he eyed the dazzling vista like the predator he had become.

"Science, you have pinpointed the location of Starfleet Command?"

"The coordinates are a matter of record, Captain."

Nero nodded with satisfaction. "Deploy the drill."

On the bridge of the *Enterprise* there was no sign of its current captain or science officer. Instead, helmsman Sulu sat in the command chair while Chekov manned the helm.

"Emerging from warp in three—two—one."

On the forward monitor subspace streaking gave way to a thick, roiling atmosphere fetid with suspended hydrocarbons. The *Enterprise* rocked for a moment, then steadied. Penetrating instrumentation revealed a vast lake of dark methane below, the liquefied gas lapping against a stony shore. Other instruments showed an enormous banded shape lying far above them and beyond the atmosphere. The ringed planet Saturn, looming like a mad spherical racetrack in the center of its accompanying moons.

They had arrived at Titan.

"Tactical, report," Sulu ordered crisply.

Doing double duty, Chekov checked his instrumentation. "No sign that we are being scanned, Mister Sulu. No indication that our arrival has been detected."

"Excellent." Sulu nodded, then turned to grin at his fellow crew member. "Remind me when we're on leave to download that advanced course on in-system evasion techniques. That's one seminar I somehow managed to miss."

"I will do so, Mister Sulu. Orders?"

The helmsman returned his full attention to the forward monitor and the task at hand. "Transfer manual control to the captain's chair."

"Aye, sir."

Chekov manipulated his console, and a proxy of the helm appeared before the command station.

"I have projected the parabolic course we must follow to ensure that we are not detected by anyone in orbit in Earth's vicinity. According to Mister Scott's equations, in order for transporter entanglement to be effected we must pinpoint the *Narada*'s position without her finding us." Sulu knew that as well as did the tactical officer, but it was reassuring to everyone on the bridge to have their situation voiced aloud. The helmsman leaned toward his proxy console.

"Give me one-quarter impulse power for five seconds and I'll do the final alignment with thrusters. If they're looking for us or anyone else, they'll never pick up a quick thruster burst at this distance."

"Not in this atmosphere." Chekov allowed himself a smile.

"On my mark," Sulu murmured. "All stop in three— two—one."

Hovering in Titan's dense atmosphere, the *Enterprise* halted all forward movement. "Tactical?"

"Still no indication of scanning, sir," Chekov reported. Murmurs of relief rose from the rest of the bridge crew.

"Communications silent on all channels and frequencies," Uhura added.

Sulu let out a long, deep breath. "I think we've done it, Mister Chekov. Inform engineering."

"Yes, *sir.*" Fully aware it might only be temporary, Chekov proceeded to convey the good news.

In the main transporter room Kirk and Spock were readying themselves for departure. Utility belts, tricorders, phasers—they needed to take enough gear to try and ensure the success of their mission but not so much that it would slow them down. At least they were able to leave behind food and water. If they were on the Romulan vessel long enough to have to either eat or drink, then they likely already would have failed.

When word reached them from the bridge that the *Enterprise* had successfully emerged from warp and had entered Titan's atmosphere without being detected, Kirk was unable to suppress a grin.

"Well done, Mister Sulu, Mister Chekov," he called toward the nearest comm pickup. "Outstanding work. One more thing. If we manage to really kick 'em where it hurts and you think you have a tactical advantage, don't hesitate to shoot to disable, even if we're still aboard. That's an order. If we can't gain possession of the device but you can cripple their ship, then you'll be able to negotiate from a position of strength. Mister Spock's survival and mine is not necessary to the success of this . . . enterprise. Understood?"

"Understood, Captain. Good luck."

Having already equipped Kirk, Uhura was in the process of passing a special translator to Spock. "This goes in place on your uniform, in the chest area. Far enough from your mouth to enjoy some protection, close enough to pick up speech and transmit replies."

"I am aware of the instrument's optimal location," Spock replied quietly.

"Yes—yes, of course you are." She eased it into place. "We don't have a full understanding of Romulan syntax— some of their words and names are hard to pronounce—but I've modified these translators to allow you to speak and to be understood conversationally."

"Thank you, Nyota."

Standing nearby, Kirk reacted sharply. *Nyota?* That was her first name? But how did Spock . . . ?

As he looked on, she proceeded to attach the tiny translator unit to the science officer's uniform. Then he bent forward—to whisper something over the buzz of conversation in the transporter staging area, no doubt.

There was no doubt when he kissed her—of that much a startled Kirk was completely certain.

She put a hand on his chest, letting her fingers drift slowly past the translator unit.

"Be careful. Come back."

"I always endeavor to come back," he murmured with equal tenderness. "Especially when I have something to come back to."

She stepped clear, turned, and exited the transporter

bay. Even at a distance Kirk could see that her eyes were moist.

"Time, gentlemen." From his position behind the main transporter controls, Montgomery Scott eyed both officers solemnly. First Kirk, then Spock, stepped up onto the transporter platform. Turning, they placed their hands behind their backs and positioned themselves in readiness. Spock's mind was focused laser-like on the dangerous task on which they were about to embark. Kirk's was—momentarily distracted.

"Her first name is . . ." He broke off, careful not to stray from the transporter pad on which he stood. "How'd you pull *that* one off?"

Leveled straight ahead, Spock's gaze, like his attention, did not wander. "I have no comment on the matter." Kirk just stood on his own pad, grinning at the science officer.

"If there's any common sense to their ship design and if it relates in any practical way to what we know of smaller Romulan vessels, then I'll be puttin' ye right in the cargo bay," Scott told them. "Big enough open space to ensure you don't materialize inside one of the crew. Considerin' they're not here to pick up a load of souvenirs, there shouldn't be a soul in sight. Good luck to ye."

Kirk nodded. There was little left to say. There was only to do.

"Energize, Mister Scott."

Slower than Spock's or Sulu's fingers but, if anything, more sure of themselves, the engineer's hands moved over the transporter controls. Light flickered within the bay, and in a matter of seconds the two men were gone, taking with them the hopes of every man, woman, and Vulcan on board the *Enterprise.*

And the future of planet Earth.

It turned out that Scott's physics were far more accurate than his suppositions. Kirk and Spock materialized right where the engineer said they should, in the center of the *Narada's* rambling, multicompartmented cargo bay.

It was not, however, empty.

Half a dozen crew reacted with surprise as the two Starfleet officers appeared in their midst, so close that there was barely time to react. Arriving mentally ready for combat, human and Vulcan lit into their foes with a deadly combination of speed, skill, and desperation. Unlike the Romulans, they had nowhere to go if they went down.

Fortunately, only one of the cargo bay workers was armed. Singling him out, Kirk engaged him immediately. Mindful of the difficulty he'd had with hand-to-hand combat atop the drill platform in Vulcan's atmosphere, he made sure to go on the offensive immediately and not let up. Being general crew, this Romulan proved easier to get a hand on than the more highly trained specialist Kirk had tackled high above Vulcan. That left Spock to deal with all the remaining Romulans.

It was difficult to tell, but it was possible that he was pleased.

Fighting the Vulcan was like trying to grapple with a shadow. Spock was a blur—dodging a wild swing while knocking one crew member unconscious, leaning back just out of the reach of clutching hands and then putting his assailant on the deck, spinning around to snap the heel of his palm upward to crack open the nose of yet another. Though the Romulans swarmed him, they might as well have been one instead of five. When one broke away from the fight in an attempt to get within range of an audio pickup, Spock found just the right piece of cargo to fling in his direction. The Romulan reached the wall panel containing the comm unit—and slammed into it, thanks to the cylindrical container that struck him precisely in the back of his head. As the Romulan slid down the wall, a fully energized Spock turned swiftly to confront his next attacker.

There were no more attackers.

Breathing hard but evenly, Kirk surveyed the carnage that had been wrought by the *Enterprise*'s science officer. Everything had happened so fast he couldn't be sure, but it occurred to him that Spock had put down the five Romulans in order of size, beginning with the biggest and finishing up with the least threatening.

He even fought logically, the younger officer realized. Doubtless he played a mean game of three-dimensional chess.

At Kirk's feet the Romulan whom he had been battling emitted a final pained snuffling sound before going motionless. Kirk eyed him, then the five enemy Spock had rendered unconscious.

"Mine had a gun," he pointed out, perhaps a bit self-consciously.

"Indeed he did." There was not a trace of condescension in the science officer's voice. "I am trained in the Vulcan martial art of *Suus Mahna*. Techniques for dealing with multiple opponents are among the first that an acolyte strives to master."

Kirk moved to where one of the Romulans who had challenged Spock was groaning and trying to sit up. "See if you can master the whereabouts of the device."

While his companion stood guard over the dazed Romulan, Spock knelt and placed his hands on the alien's temples and closed his eyes. His fingers appraised—knowingly, precisely. After a long moment he looked up at Kirk.

"I am unable to meld with this Romulan. There are subtle differences in their physiology. Or it may be that my traditional skills are lacking. Whatever the reason, I cannot draw forth the information we need."

"Then we'll have to resort to traditional human skills."

Spock frowned. "In what sense?"

"Punch him in the face. *Make* him talk. *Suus Mahna* his ass!"

The science officer sounded doubtful. "*Suus Mahna* is only intended for self-defense. This individual is no longer a threat."

Kirk rolled his eyes in exasperation. "*Pretend* he's a threat. That's an *order*!"

"Vulcan strictures insist that the techniques of *Suus Mahna* should only be employed on occasions of . . ."

Kirk glared at his fellow officer. "This is one of the people who destroyed your homeworld and is preparing to blow up mine! Excuse me if I mistakenly interpret him as a threat!"

Spock replied softly. "I take your point." Bending over, he proceeded to ram his closed fist square into the Romulan's face while making sure his words were directed as much as

possible toward the tiny translation device Uhura had fastened to his uniform.

"What is your ship computer prefix code?"

Smirking, the Romulan spat green blood at his tormentor. With the methodical precision and relentless con-
sistency of a machine, Spock continued the questioning
session while Kirk divided his attention between the ongoing interrogation and the still unoccupied corridors that
entered the vast cargo bay.

"*Tell* [punch] *me* [punch] *the* [punch] *code*
[PUNCH!] . . ."

The torrent of tightly contained tornadic plasma that roared
forth from the mouth of the Romulan drill platform was
directed with precision. As at Vulcan, it could have been
aimed at any point on the Earth's surface. The most practical place for deployment and the one that would have produced the quickest result was the Mariana Trench in the
Pacific Ocean. There the plasma would have hissed its way
through kilometers of water in mere seconds to strike the
planetary crust at one of its thinnest points.

But the individual behind the drill and the eventual
obliteration of the planet it was piercing was not in a
hurry. It would all be over soon enough, this second induced armageddon, and he wanted to remember it in all
its annihilating glory. There was no rush. Providentially,
the rest of Starfleet was infinitely far away engaging in
pointless maneuvers in the Laurentian sector. The few
armed atmospheric aircraft that took to the clear skies and
made feeble attempts to attack the drill were effortlessly

brushed aside by the *Narada*'s infinitely greater firepower. Earth's multiple automated defensive stations had been electronically disabled, thanks to the codes extracted from the admirably stubborn but eventually responsive prisoner Pike. The captured captain had resisted the interrogation manfully, but he was only composed of flesh and blood. He was not even aware that he had surrendered the information necessary to allow the *Narada* to safely assume its unassailable geosynchronous position above the west coast of North America.

A valiant representative of his species, Nero mused, however futile his efforts at resistance. The commander of the *Narada* had already decided that his brave prisoner would live. Pike would comprise one of several interesting exhibits to be returned to the triumphant Romulus of this time frame.

"Magnification," he commanded. The science officer complied, and the view on the forward viewscreen increased exponentially.

The view showed the plasma stream boring into the rock beneath an extensive saltwater bay. What could be discerned of the surrounding terrain was exceptionally beautiful. It was no wonder, he thought, that Starfleet had chosen this particular coastal location for the site of Starfleet Headquarters and its noisome Academy. Reports from the drill's sensors indicated that the city itself sat atop a major but now stabilized earthquake fault. Doubly ironic, then, that it should be the site for the insertion of the Red Matter that would initiate the reaction that would destroy the planet. Ironic, and also fitting. The commander of the *Narada* was pleased.

He considered himself, in his own megalomaniacal fashion, also very logical.

On the bridge of the *Enterprise* a broad expanse of readouts simultaneously went blank. No amount of effort or attempts at work-arounds were able to restore the flow of information. Several instruments that did continue to function provided the explanation.

"They've activated the drill," Chekov muttered. "We're now subject to the same interference as we were at Vulcan."

Turning in her seat, Uhura added confirmation. "Communications and transporter inoperative. I've broadcast the usual plethora of amplified queries in an attempt to punch through, without any luck. Distortion is across the board."

Seated in the command chair, Sulu studied what limited data was available. "We can't talk to them and we can't bring them back until the drill goes off-line or is disabled." He stared at the viewscreen that was opaque with turbulent brown clouds.

"They're on their own now . . ."

XVII

*T*he speed with which Spock worked not only an alien input device but one whose layout was both different and advanced in design was breathtaking to see. Looking on, Kirk could barely keep track of the flying fingers. He shook his head in amazement.

"How the hell are you doing this?"

The science officer replied without looking up from what he was doing. "I am familiar with the technology of several other space-going species besides that of Romulus. While the design of this instrumentation is different, it is not so radically advanced that I cannot fill in the divergences with intuition. One plus one equals two no matter where one happens to be in the known cosmos, and the means for generating such a result are not beyond inference to one who is familiar with the basics."

"Yeah," Kirk agreed readily. "My sentiments exactly."

Seconds later a pair of images appeared within the projection screen. One showed a small starship of unique design that resembled nothing Kirk had ever seen before. He said as much to his companion.

"I perceive sufficient design elements to identify it as Vulcan in origin." Spock indicated a glowing point within the ship schematic. "What you refer to as the Red Matter device is still located on board. It may be too tightly integrated with the ship's superstructure to be removed." One finger traced the peculiar torus shape that encircled the rear of the singular craft. "This section appears capable of movement independent from that of the rest of the vessel. I suspect it may have something to do with containing the Red Matter when the ship is in motion."

The second image was less heartening. Lying on a platform suspended above a pool of liquid in the depths of a dark chamber was the supine body of Christopher Pike. His eyes were closed, and insofar as they could tell from the remote image, he was not moving. A lack of magnification prevented them from discerning if his chest was moving up and down, however slowly.

Spock's verbal evaluation confirmed what Kirk was seeing.

"We now know that the Red Matter device is on board the small ship in the main hangar—and as you can see, I have also located Captain Pike."

Kirk tried to will his vision to clarify the image on the screen, to no avail. "Is he alive?"

Spock tuned a couple of inputs. The details they supplied were extraneous and immaterial. "Unknown. This is the cargo bay, and we only have access here to minimal visualizations, not medical information."

Kirk nodded. "Let's move."

As the science officer turned from the Romulan console, he nodded in the direction of the still-unconscious half-dozen crew members. One was covered in green blood.

"They will begin to recover within a short time."

"Doesn't matter." Kirk lengthened his stride. "A short time is all we've got. A short time is all everyone on Earth has got. Either we resolve this fast or it won't matter." He smiled thinly. "It's the Matter that matters now."

This time the vastness of the *Narada* worked to their advantage.

Only once did they encounter members of the crew. Having no reason to believe intruders might be aboard, and with their own transporter intentionally disabled to prevent any enemy from potentially making forcible use of it (there being no reason to suspect any Federation vessel in this time frame capable of transwarp beaming), Kirk and Spock managed to avoid being seen before continuing on their way.

Resting in the huge main hangar alongside Captain Pike's shuttlecraft, the strange Vulcan vessel sat open and unguarded. The two officers nevertheless boarded cautiously, not allowing themselves to relax until they stood in the forward cabin. Searching the interior, Kirk was reminded of what Spock had said only moments earlier about utilizing intuition to fill in the blanks in one's knowledge. Because of his studies at the Academy, the basics of Vulcan flight technology were almost as familiar to Kirk as to the science officer. The panel he was looking for should be . . . there.

Sure enough, as soon as he hit the intuited place on the most likely console, a friendly voice responded in basic Vulcan. On command it switched to Federation Standard and repeated what it had said.

"Voice print, face, pheromone, body density, and retinal recognition analysis enabled."

Taking a step back, Kirk gestured to his companion. "Spock, you'll be piloting the ship alone."

The science officer had been studying the extensive command layout intently. "Which may be problematic. While I recognize, as did you, certain essential instrumentation, I have to confess that I am unfamiliar with this particular vessel's design and construction."

Responding to his voice, the ship immediately sent a scan playing across his features. Other less visible security instruments took note of everything from his height to the color of his eyes to his general respiration. It all took only a couple of seconds.

"Access granted, Ambassador Spock. All ship functions are now at your disposal."

Kirk's exaggerated exclamation of surprise did nothing to fool the Vulcan.

"Wow, what a coincidence, huh? Weird."

It took a moment for the science officer to make certain mental connections. *Ambassador* Spock, the ship had called him. "You'll be piloting the ship alone," Kirk had insisted. Vulcan intuition was applicable to more than just instrumentation.

"Computer," he asked, "what is your manufacturing origin and date of commission?"

The ship replied without delay. *"Stardate twenty-three eighty-seven, commissioned by the Vulcan Science Academy under special emergency declaration twelve-oh-eight."*

Spock digested this, then turned to Kirk. "It appears you've been keeping rather important information from me."

Kirk repressed a grin. "You're just going to have to trust me, Mister Spock. Can you do that?"

"Once again you ask for trust. For a deceiving stowaway who advanced in short order from the would-be instigator of a near-mutiny to becoming acting captain of the same vessel, you certainly ask for a lot of trust."

Kirk could no longer hold back a smile. "I'm not the shy type."

Spock considered this, then nodded thoughtfully. "While I attempt to engage with this vessel, I presume you are going to try and find Captain Pike."

Kirk shrugged, as if what Spock had just surmised was the most natural thing in the world. "He told me to come and get him. Just following orders. Like I always do."

The science officer seemed ready to say something else, but every considered comment took time, and time was the one commodity of which they were running short. With a last nod he settled himself into the command seat and resumed his detailed examination of the strange instrumentation. This console should activate the engines, that one communications, the one next to it was new to him but he felt he could puzzle it out, the next . . .

He could have departed sooner, but he had to wait until Kirk had enough time to exit the hangar—or at least until his fellow officer had moved beyond the nearest blast airlock door. When he felt that sufficient time had passed, he began moving his hands over the gleaming, futuristic cabin controls. A few of the elements that sprang to life were unfamiliar to him. But not those that controlled the impulse engine.

Detecting a rising hum where there should have been only silence, a contingent of crew conversed briefly among themselves before advancing in the direction of the captured Vulcan craft. Unlike their now semiconscious comrades lying in the cargo bay, this group was armed. As they approached the now internally illuminated vessel, they cautiously drew their sidearms. While it was impossible for any enemy to have boarded the *Narada,* there was no reason to take chances. Perhaps the captain was running a drill, in which case their need to respond appropriately was self-evident. Or possibly a distraught comrade had finally given in to an overwhelming desire to try and return home, even if only by himself.

Soon the leader of the squad was near enough to the Vulcan ship to see that someone was indeed sitting in the forward cabin—someone far too sallow to pass muster as even the most pallid Romulan. Shouts and sidearms arose simultaneously as the Vulcan craft lifted from the deck. Someone pulled their comm unit and started to shout the alarm.

At the same time, and in lieu of wasting precious moments hunting for the appropriate Romulan command to cease and desist, Spock let loose with the ship's weapons. They opened an exit just as effectively as any hangar command, though with considerably more noise and accompanying destruction. The unfortunate members of the patrolling contingent followed the phaser-shattered airlock doors out into open space.

Blown apart, large sections of the hangar doors were flung outward. They were followed closely by the now fully activated Vulcan craft. Growing more and more familiar with the ship's instrumentation with every passing moment, Spock swooped in and out among the *Narada's* superstructure, firing at close range from within the protective diameter of her defensive shields.

A human would have rocked the fore cabin with jubilant shouts while inflicting such devastation on an enemy. Spock went about the business of disabling the Romulan vessel with surgical silence and precision.

On the *Narada's* bridge, chaos and confusion had without warning taken the place of the previous air of satisfaction. As the ship shook around him, the flustered helmsman reported one constituent failure after another.

"Primary core damage! Warp engines are off-line! Multiple decks report loss of life support. Automatic shutdowns continue to multiply and engage!"

Nero had bolted erect in the command chair to gape at his officers.

"How!?"

A response came from tactical. "Someone has detonated weapons in the main hangar! And"—the disbelief was plain in his voice—"we appear to be under attack!"

"How can we be under attack?" Furious and confused, Nero felt suddenly disoriented. "Our shields are up and there are no Federation starships within parsecs!"

The tactical officer stared at his readouts, trying to make sense of what he was seeing.

"Apparently we are being fired on by a small craft that

has somehow materialized *inside* our shields. Yet no such vessel was detected approaching. It just . . . appeared." He looked blankly at his captain.

"Nothing just 'appears'!" Nero roared. "Identify the attacker and prepare to engage." He shifted his attention to engineering and science. "Restore full power! Engage auxiliary systems!"

Impossible, he told himself as the *Narada* continued to tremble and quake. They were under attack from the impossible.

Which iteration rendered the damage that was being inflicted on his ship no less real for the unlikelihood with which he was investing it.

Leaving the Romulan ship damaged and its crew occupied and reeling, Spock drove the remarkably responsive one-man starship toward the surface of the planet below. A single carefully directed burst from the Vulcan craft's compact but powerful weapons sliced through the complex of cables supporting and powering the plasma drill. The energy vortex shut down, a few remaining lines snapped, and the drill platform, together with the complex of dangling cables above it, plunged downward, falling, falling . . .

On the grounds of Starfleet Academy and elsewhere on the fringes of San Francisco Bay, onlookers scrambled for cover as the heavy drill platform slammed into the cold green water and sent out a wave that drenched the surrounding shorelines.

Fully occupied with trying to track the enigmatic attacking vessel that had seemingly appeared out of nowhere, the *Narada*'s overwhelmed tactical officer now looked fearfully in his captain's direction.

"The plasma drill has been severed and the platform has crashed into the surface!" This news was followed by an even more startling report.

"Ambassador Spock's ship has been stolen and is heading outsystem!"

Nero was beside himself. "Who stole it? I want identification—now! Which traitor . . . ?"

The first officer paused, studying his readouts. "A crew member managed to transmit a portion of a visual at the last moment before severe hangar damage was incurred." He looked up in disbelief. "It is impossible to resolve fine details without further processing, but I believe the pilot to be Ambassador Spock."

Shock rippled through the bridge. Somehow, Nero kept control of himself as he settled back down in the command chair and hissed, rather than spoke, a single command.

"Follow."

Both ships were well on their way outsystem when he finally spoke again to his communications officer. "Open a hailing channel."

The officer complied swiftly. "Channel open." A brief pause, then, "We are receiving a response."

An image appeared on the forward viewscreen. It was of a very young Vulcan officer, remarkably composed given the circumstances. Ignoring for the moment the inexplicable difference in age from the hated Spock he knew, Nero stared at the all-too-familiar visage, his voice cold.

"Spock. It *is* you. I should have killed you when I had the chance. I wanted you to see Vulcan destroyed as you let Romulus be destroyed. But *I should have killed you."*

The subject of the threat stared directly back into his ship's pickup. A human would have reacted differently, perhaps with a counterthreat, possibly with a challenge of his own, maybe with a word-string full of hatred and accusation and foul language. Spock responded purely as Spock.

"Under authority granted me by the Europa Convention of Sentient Species, I'm confiscating this illegally obtained ship and order you to surrender your vessel. No terms. No discussion. No deals."

Nero could only gaze at the screen in wonder. The sheer audacity of the Vulcan. The absolute absurdity of it. "You can't cheat me again, Spock. I know you better than you know yourself. I know what has to happen, what is preordained by the time stream, and you can't stop it!"

The level gaze never flinched, the icy determination did not waver. *"Last warning: unconditional surrender or you will be destroyed."*

The game had gone on long enough. In Nero's mind, fury overcame reason. Whatever happened from this moment on, ensuring the Vulcan's death had become paramount in his mind. Even if it was necessary to destroy the captured ship and its irreplaceable contents, the *Narada* would remain invincible, by far the most powerful warship in this corner of the cosmos. As for the Red Matter device, the science team on his ship had garnered a good deal of information about it. Returning to Romulus and explaining the necessity of building another one would also assure his world's salvation. Then, led by himself and his crew, Romulan rule would still spread across the galaxy.

A galaxy devoid of treacherous Vulcans, and of one Vulcan in particular.

He turned toward tactical. "Fire at will."

His second-in-command was reluctant. "Sir, if a direct hit should occur, either phaser energy or photon torpedoes contain enough explosive force to momentarily duplicate the heat and pressure present in the core of a planet. A strike could cause a portion of the Red Matter aboard the Vulcan's ship to implode and ignite, thereby . . ."

Nero glared at him, his voice rising. *"Don't talk back to me! That's a direct order! This isn't a time for arcane scientific speculations—I want Spock dead!"*

Leaving the command chair, he roughly pushed his tactical officer out of the way and began readying the *Narada's* weaponry himself. He was looking forward to the opportunity to kill someone without an intermediary, for a change.

As a brace of advanced torpedoes launched from the *Narada,* Kirk continued to work his way through the vast and largely deserted reaches of the Romulan warship. Occasionally he would pause to check the information that had been downloaded to his tricorder. Once he had to back up and retrace his steps, another time he took a wrong turn and was forced to correct his course.

Eventually he confronted a closed doorway with specific and unpleasant markings in Romulan. A quick pass with his tricorder identified it as the chamber he had been seeking. It yielded without hesitation to his request for entry, there being no reason to secure it from anyone on board.

The room was dark and damp even for a Romulan interrogation chamber.

He saw Pike still fastened to the slightly tilted platform.
The faint moan that reached Kirk as he hurried toward it was
more uplifting than a whole stadium full of cadets cheering
on their Academy team. The captain was still alive.

There was nothing elaborate about the straps that held
him down. As traditional and straightforward as they were
effective, they yielded rapidly to his determined hands. As
he worked, Pike's head lolled limply in his direction. The
captain's eyes struggled to focus.

". . . Kirk?"

"Came back, sir. Just like you ordered. Hold still—I'll
have you out of this in a minute."

Pike managed a nod to show that he understood.
"How—how did you . . . ?" He swallowed, coughed. "Where
are we?"

"Still on board the *Narada*, sir. A lot has happened
since you were taken prisoner. Some of it I'm still not sure I
believe myself. But believable or not, we have to deal with
it." He pulled hard at the main strap, yanking it free. "One
thing you *can* believe: I'm not leaving here without you."

As more straps were released, Pike fought to move his
arms and legs and reassert some control over his stiff muscles and unused nervous system. "I believe your presence
here constitutes violation of at least a dozen ordinances,
Mister Kirk."

Working above the supine senior officer, Kirk had to
smile. Pike was going to make it, all right. "Guilty as
charged, sir. You can decide my punishment as soon as we're
back on the *Enterprise*."

With his back to the entrance, he failed to notice the arrival of several heavily armed guards. Kirk's presence hadn't been detected by ship security; the guards were simply carrying out a time-scheduled check on the prisoner. Eyes widening in surprise, the Romulans perceived what was taking place and started to raise their weapons.

In a tribute to a lifetime of hard work, and demonstrating to the utmost the efficacy of Starfleet training, Pike pulled Kirk's own sidearm and shot them in perfect sequence before a single one of them could trigger their weapons. They went down as Kirk whirled. Exhausted, Pike let the phaser fall from his fingers. Kirk caught first it and then his superior officer.

"Thanks, Captain. Don't worry—I've got you. Can you stand?"

Gritting his teeth, and with Kirk's help, Pike was on his feet a moment later. Once he was sure he wasn't going to fall, he nodded to his rescuer.

"Not only can I stand: if circumstances require it I think I can run." He gestured past the dead guards in the direction of the only exit. "The question is, where do we run to? I don't know how you got on this ship, but from what I've seen, there's no way off it."

Draping one of Pike's arms over his shoulders, Kirk helped the older man stumble toward the portal. "I don't suppose, Captain, that you've by any chance heard of a disgraced Starfleet engineer named Montgomery Scott?"

Having unleashed the first volley of torpedoes at the fleeing smaller ship, Nero had subsequently returned tactical to the officer in charge. He could not direct the *Narada's* firepower if he also wanted to bathe fully in the moment of destruction.

The Vulcan's evasive maneuvers were carried out with exceptional skill and his small but advanced ship was proving difficult to hit, but the number of weapons the much larger Romulan warship could bring to bear could not be avoided forever. Detonated by a proximate program, one torpedo finally ripped into the hull of the Vulcan craft. Though it self-sealed, Spock's vessel had unmistakably suffered some permanent damage. The *Narada's* tactical sensors confirmed the partial hit.

Observing the ongoing pursuit via the forward viewscreen, Nero whispered to himself with satisfaction.

"You should have entered warp when you had the chance, Spock. You should have fled." Looking toward tactical, he raised his voice. "Sight target for final destruction and *fire.*"

Spock's ship was far more advanced than any vessel he had ever served upon, seen, or studied, but it was not from a thousand years in the future and it was not immune to equally sophisticated and no less deadly weapons. Particularly when those weapons were fired on it in multiples. One of the first lessons students in warfare were taught was that club plus force plus trajectory achieves the same totality of death as a properly aimed phaser burst.

"*Warning,*" the ship announced in deceptively calm tones, "*all shields off-line.*"

This was it, then, he knew. The end. But not the end just for him. He steeled himself. At such moments logic and reason offered a great comfort that was unknown to all but a few humans who found themselves trapped in similar circumstances.

"Computer, prepare to execute General Order Thirteen."

"General Order Thirteen," it repeated. *"Self-destruct sequence confirmed."*

Strange, he mused, how the computer and he sounded so much alike.

"Execute," he finished with hesitation as he redirected the ship's course.

Straight back toward the pursuing *Narada*.

Their quarry's abrupt reversal of direction did not go unnoticed on board the Romulan warship. There was pandemonium as tactical, science, and the helm fought to react appropriately. Somehow, the Vulcan ship managed to avoid every weapon that was flung in its direction. Nero's second-in-command wasn't worried about the damage a collision might cause. The *Narada* was large enough to overcome such an impact.

There was, however, the not-insignificant matter of a certain quantity of the galaxy's most volatile known substance being held in stasis on board the Vulcan vessel. And the two ships were too close for evasive action to be taken, so that . . .

It was a great relief when, an instant later, one of the numerous torpedoes the Romulan warship had unleashed struck home and the Vulcan craft was blown to bits.

XVIII

*P*ressure. Heat. The machinery on board the smaller vessel that sustained the stasis shell collapsed under the force of both. Driven inward by the intensity of the torpedo explosion, within nanoseconds they compacted the contents of the inner containment bubble, forcing it in upon itself.

Igniting that which lay within.

A tiny anomaly appeared in space. It was pure luck that when it was created it was on a trajectory that would take it out of the solar system on a course nearly perpendicular to the plane of the ecliptic. It would not pass by any of the eight planets—which meant that said planets would remain intact.

Anything caught in its immediate vicinity, however . . .

"Full reverse course!" Nero was screaming as an expanding darkness blacker than space itself appeared on the viewscreen. "Get us away—now, now! Prepare to engage warp drive!"

"Warp drive activating, Captain," the helm reported. "Warp one in four—three . . ."

The *Narada* shuddered violently. Crew members found themselves thrown from their chairs. Throughout the great ship longitudinal rips lacerated her hull as phaser bursts tore through the superstructure. Crew members barely had time to wail in despair as they were sucked out into space. One blast after another tore at her components, her weapons systems, her engines. As her wild-eyed commander struggled to retain his seat, the cause of the devastating and unexpected disruptions was revealed on another screen.

Fully occupied in the pursuit of Spock's vessel as it reached the vicinity of Saturn, its crew and tactical arm had failed to notice the appearance of another ship behind it as it had risen from within the distorting depths of Titan's atmosphere.

It was *possible* there was someone on board the *Enterprise* who was not at that moment fully engaged in one critical task or another, but only among the wounded in sickbay. Every other member of the crew was on station, their entire being devoted to a particular task at hand. Tactical was engaged in pouring as much debilitating fire into the Romulan warship as possible while the helm controllers undertook a ferocious combination of evasive and assaulting actions.

Nowhere was activity as frenetic as in the main transporter room, where a focused Montgomery Scott was directing two equally perilous and life-threatening actions at the same time. It was not an impossible feat to pull off, but it was difficult enough to make everyone involved sweat profusely despite the presence of fully functional climate control.

A figure began to materialize on one of the transporter pads. As it started to flicker dangerously, Scott's attention darted from platform to instrumentation to those assisting him.

"Hold it, hold it," he muttered tensely. "Full power—now!" At the same time as the first shape began to solidify, two more started to appear. Fingers raced over controls as telltales on the main console flashed warningly. The second pair of silhouettes began to steady. Off to one side Uhura looked on apprehensively while McCoy and a full medical team stood by in case their skills were needed. Despite the new chief engineer's evident expertise, the doctor was not optimistic. But then, whenever a transporter was in use, he never was.

The three shapes tightened, opaqued, and began to take on the appearance of something more substantial than refulgent hopes. Spock was the first to be recognized. From Uhura's throat there emerged a small sound that McCoy would forever keep private. Then the other two figures steadied and he was able to identify both—Kirk and Pike.

Rapidly regaining full control of his neuromuscular system, Kirk was the first to step off the platform and congratulate the engineer.

"Nice timing." He looked to his left. "I'm beginning to think you could beam anything from any place to anywhere, Mister Scott, if only someone gave you the right coordinates."

The engineer stood a little taller. "Never beamed two targets from two places onto the same pad before. And both targets in motion, at that. Have to try it one day with something smaller and more stable over a greater distance. A bottle o' fine malt whiskey, for example."

Kirk grinned. "I hope you get the opportunity— Scotty." He turned. "Captain?"

As the seriously weakened Pike finally gave in to exhaustion, Kirk caught him as he slumped forward. The medical team took over immediately. Playing a scanner over the captain's barely conscious form, McCoy barked orders to a senior medtech.

"We're gonna need neurogenic stimulators and"—he made a face as his scanner locked onto a small dark shape pressed tightly against the captain's spine—"cord sheath protection. Let's prep him for surgery. We're gonna have to do repair, rejuve, *and* an extraction at the same time."

As the other two just-transported arrivals headed for the bridge, the briefest of glances was exchanged between the *Enterprise*'s science officer and its communications chief. No one noticed it but Kirk. Varying from the sly to the snide, several suitable comments took shape in his mind. Ultimately, he voiced none of them.

Like lightning, maturity can strike anyone unexpectedly and at the most peculiar moments.

On board the *Narada* the situation was degenerating with a rapidity that made it impossible for its personnel, dedicated and highly skilled as they were, to keep up. It was not their fault. Confronted with not one but two potentially deadly unexpected events, even the best of crews could not have coped any better.

Unfortunately for those on board the Romulan warship, rapidly worsening circumstances suggested their best was not going to be good enough.

Another phaser blast struck home, jolting the bridge violently. Vital instrumentation began to go dark, only some of which was compensated for by the activation of auxiliaries or backup. Discharges flared from consoles even as their operators sought to sustain their functions. On one side of the bridge, fire broke out, consuming not only instruments but precious atmosphere.

"Captain," the communications officer shouted, "it's the *Enterprise*!"

"Activate all weapons systems and raise shields!" Nero directed.

The officer fought to stay seated at his station, his eyes widening as he struggled to reconcile the information his console was providing with the *Narada*'s rapidly shrinking list of options.

"Engines using all our power, sir!" As he turned toward his captain, his expression was one of desperation and despair. "If we divert to shields we'll be drawn into the new singularity." Checking his readouts, he saw numbers that continued to fall steadily despite the best efforts of the *Narada*'s drive. "We're barely maintaining position as it is!"

The instant Kirk and Spock reappeared on the bridge, the acting science officer moved away from his post and Sulu surrendered the captain's chair to return to his own post at the helm. Chekov was reporting excitedly even before Kirk had resumed his seat.

"Keptin! The enemy ship is losing power and . . . its

shields are down!" He looked toward the command chair. "All of them! They're defenseless."

All eyes turned toward Kirk. There was no uncertainty in them now, no qualification in those glances. They no longer hoped for him to render decisions—they expected it.

Would he issue the directive to resume firing on the Romulan craft whose commander was responsible for so much death and destruction? Or . . . ?

"Hail them," Kirk snapped. "Now."

It took longer than usual for contact to be established, and when the screen finally produced a picture, it was not the best. Static occasionally distorted the image and it shifted or doubled unpredictably. The commander of the *Narada* took a moment to try and stabilize his own pickup. Despite the continuing disruption, there was no mistaking the identity of the human who was presently gazing back at him.

"This is Captain James T. Kirk of the *U.S.S. Enterprise.* Your ship is compromised. You are sacrificing power fighting a losing battle against a growing gravitational anomaly. The closer to it you fall, the more inexorable its pull becomes and the less the likelihood that you or any of your crew will survive. In the absence of full warp power there is no possible way you can attempt to escape by utilizing the anomaly to attempt a time shift—you have no maneuverability. None of you will survive without assistance—which we are willing to provide."

Of all the possible responses to the current state of affairs Kirk could have articulated, this was one none of his fellow crew members had anticipated. Spock's reaction was no different.

"Captain—what are you doing?"

"We show them compassion. It may be the only way to secure a permanent peace with Romulus. It's logic, Spock. I thought you'd respond positively to such an offer."

The science officer measured his words even more carefully than usual. "Captain, he destroyed my home planet. As a human might say—to hell with logic."

As it turned out, further discussion and possible dissension was obviated by an unequivocal retort from the *Narada*'s commander. Pushing his face toward his pickup, Nero glared unapologetically across space at his human and Vulcan nemeses.

"I would rather suffer the death of Romulus a thousand times than accept assistance from you!"

That was all Kirk needed. *No,* he told himself—it was more than he needed. When the history of this encounter was written, no one would be able to say that he had not acted with consideration and forbearance.

He was much relieved.

"You got it," he shot back as he turned toward Chekov. "Lock phasers. Fire everything we've got!"

Swinging around in a wide arc, the Federation starship unloaded a massive burst in the direction of the struggling *Narada.* Already weakened by previous attacks, its shields down, and succumbing to the relentless pull of the anomaly, one detonation after another began to tear the huge ship to pieces. As it lost what remained of its drive it began to disintegrate, collapsing into the singularity. The main bridge screen offered a final glimpse of the Romulan commander they had known as Nero: defiant, half-mad, and ultimately frustrated as he joined his ship in being crushed down into his subatomic components.

The *Narada,* Nero, and everyone else on board who had taken part in the destruction of multiple Federation starships and the planet Vulcan—were gone.

There no longer being any need to address tactical, Kirk directed his attention and his command elsewhere. "Kirk to engineering—get us out of here, Scotty!"

"Aye, Captain!" came the immediate report. A slight quiver ran through the length of the *Enterprise* as her weapons systems and shields were drawn down so that all power could be directed to the engines.

On screen and behind them, the last vestiges of the warship *Narada* collapsed inward and upon themselves as they passed the gravitational point of no return and vanished into the mini–black hole. Seated squarely in the captain's chair, Nero had less than a second to let out a final defiant scream as his life, body, and fanatic's hopes were compacted out of existence.

On board the *Enterprise* full power was directed to ram her into warp. Dilithium gave up its incredible matrix in ever-increasing quantities in response to the command from engineering central. And . . .

Nothing. The ship's position relative to the system-departing anomaly did not change. It did not fall inward in the wake of the *Narada,* but neither was it able to pull away. The fabric of the ship itself began to vibrate as it threatened to succumb to the enormous gravitational forces that were clawing at its superstructure.

On the bridge, Kirk stared at the main monitor. The

view aft showed the all-devouring monster to which Red
Matter had given birth.

"Why aren't we at warp?"

"We are!" Sulu reported even as he struggled with a re-
calcitrant helm.

"Captain!" Scott's voice resounded over the bridge
speakers. *"We're caught on the edge of the gravity well! It's got
us!"*

"Go to maximum warp! Push it, Scotty!"

From deep within engineering, Scott raised his voice to
a shout in order to make himself audible above the straining
whine of the engines.

"I'm givin' 'er all she's got, Captain!"

"All she's got isn't good enough!" Kirk shot back.
"What else have you got?"

Scott's thoughts were awhirl. *"If we eject the core, the
wave front when it detonates against the singularity might be
enough to kick us clear—if it doesn't kill us. And if that fails,
then we'll be without drive power! We'll be sucked in for
certain!"*

Kirk looked over at the helm. "Mister Sulu! Status!"

"Still holding position relative to the anomaly, Captain, but we can't break the impasse. If we don't break free
soon, we'll begin to lose ground incrementally until we pass
the gravitational point of no return!"

Kirk didn't need to hear anything else. "Do it, Scotty!"
he yelled into the command chair pickup. "We're dead anyway!"

In engineering Scott slammed a series of controls, un-
keyed a protective security cover, entered the catastrophe
code all chief engineers are required to commit to memory

in the course of their initial studies, and then struck simultaneously two parallel and now flashing deep-set switches. The entire central engine compartment shook once, violently, as the warp core was expelled from the stern of the ship.

Ejected at speed, the activated core sped backward. Impinging upon the singularity, it released *all* of the energy contained within it in a single titanic explosion. Light too bright to look at directly illuminated a tiny corner of the solar system and flared outward. There was no sound.

That was not the case within the *Enterprise*. The shock wave enveloped the ship that was now fleeing as fast as possible in the opposite direction on impulse power alone. On multiple decks, anything not fastened down was jolted loose. Artificial gravity was momentarily disrupted, sending airborne anyone not strapped in place or failing to grab onto something fixed. The instant gravity was restored, bodies fell to the floor or onto surrounding furniture or equipment. A collective moan of pain seemed to wash over the ship as nearly every crew member suffered bumps or bruises. Paradoxically, those who came through without injury of any kind were the patients confined to sickbay, who were secured in their beds. In a single instant the entire crew had been battered and beaten. So had their ship.

But it had not come apart.

And in spite of the pressure, the pain, and the threat of near annihilation of themselves, their ship, and the world whose survival had ultimately rested entirely on them, neither had they.

EPILOGUE

*I*t is astonishing how quickly people can go from imminent catastrophe to the boredom of daily routine. Back
on the ground, back at Starfleet, there was still much to do.
Final courses so rudely and urgently interrupted still required completion. Personal matters left unfinished demanded the attention of the hastily dispersed. Seminars
paused in a convulsion of emergency were resumed. At the
Academy, orders of mundanity swiftly and smoothly replaced the desperate attempt to save a planet.

The individual upperclassmen and -women who had
been hastily assembled to crew the *Enterprise* were no exception. Having gone from students to saviors and back to
students again in the space of days, certain leeways and
dispensations were granted when one newly promoted officer was a little late completing an assignment, or another
pleaded a date with a counselor as an excuse for missing a
simulation.

No such handicaps affected Spock. As on previous

mornings the science officer was busy in the main Academy hangar supervising the allocation of supplies. Any demons tormenting his soul were held tightly in check, forced down into the darkest depths of his psyche, where only he would have to deal with them. Inwardly as well as outwardly he was in complete control of himself.

Or so he thought, until a glance across a delivery path revealed the presence of another Vulcan in the hangar.

The man's dress was unusual, more affected than practical. An odd choice for a Vulcan, especially for one as elderly as this individual appeared to be. Heading toward the figure who stood quietly surveying his surroundings, Spock knew of only one person who might logically be so clad as well as present in the hangar at this moment in time.

Still, as he drew nearer, something about the shape was not quite right. Familiar, yes, but not quite right.

"Father?"

At the sound of his voice the figure turned. Expecting Sarek, Spock was more taken aback than at any time in his life. The circumstances were understandable.

"I am not our father," the visitor replied gravely.

Spock found himself staring at . . . himself. Only older, much older. Older than he would care to be, except he self-evidently was. Thoughts rose and fell with the speed and force of wave crests in a storm. What to say? Then he wondered why he was worrying. Obviously, whatever he said would be the right thing.

"Fascinating."

His senior self nodded agreement. "There are so few Vulcans left—in this time frame. We cannot afford to ignore one another. The knowledge each of us carries must be treasured and shared, not only with each other but hopefully for generations yet to come. Especially the knowledge that I, unwillingly but unavoidably, hold. I intend to devote the remainder of my life—not yours—to committing for posterity everything that I know."

His younger self was plainly puzzled. "If you know so much, then why did you send Kirk back onto the *Enterprise* when you alone could have far more persuasively explained the truth to its crew? To me?"

The elder Vulcan turned reflective. "Because of so many things that happened and so much that transpired in a future that you will now—perhaps for the best—never know. A future that will remain forever closed to you, now that the past has been altered. In that future, James T. Kirk and I developed a personal and working relationship that resulted in many achievements, in the doing of great things. All such now lies open before you, in ways and along paths neither of us can imagine.

"But one thing I do know for certain. To perform at your highest level and achieve your full potential, you and James Kirk will need each other. You boast opposing yet complementary personalities and minds. When pooled, when set to solve a problem or face a difficult situation together, you will invariably accomplish far more than either of you could separately. It was that balance between us that often made the impossible possible." The barest suggestion of a smile tweaked one corner of the elder's mouth. "This I know from often fractious experience."

"So forcing me to learn how to deal with Kirk, how to

function beside him, how to . . . trust him—it was a test?" the younger Spock concluded.

"Nothing so formal. But I felt it was the best way. Had I imposed myself on the two of you, with my knowledge and experience, you could not possibly have developed the working relationship that has resulted. Such an understanding between two disparate personalities cannot be imposed from without. It must occur, it must happen, naturally. I will not deny that there was risk in such an approach. I am happy to see that my assumptions were justified." He turned away from his younger self.

"I am in no position to pass judgment on anyone for anything. As I said, my actions have robbed you of much if not all of the future that I know. Please understand when I say that I could not also deprive you of the revelation of all that the two of you can accomplish together. Of a friendship that will define you both in ways you cannot yet realize. If I have proceeded wrongly, I beg your forgiveness. After my capture and marooning at the hands of Nero, I did not think I would have a chance to redeem myself."

The younger Spock regarded his elder self in surprise. Explanation he had expected. Such a naked expression of emotional vulnerability was something of a shock. He tried to shift the conversation elsewhere.

"How did you persuade Kirk to keep your secret? The knowledge of your existence in this time frame?"

"I implied universe-ending paradoxes would ensue should he break his promise."

"But that did not turn out to be even remotely true." The young science officer spoke with conviction. "Perhaps if the displacement had taken place much farther in the past, yes, but not in the course of so recent a period. No such paradox occurred, nor was likely. You lied."

Spock senior shrugged.

"A gamble," his younger self surmised. "Many things could have happened to change or interfere with the course of events. I nearly killed him, for example."

"Call my actions an act of faith. Or if you prefer, one of trust. One I hope you'll repeat in the future. I came to trust implicitly the James Kirk of my time frame. I felt, I believed, that despite your initial differences you would come to do the same here." He paused for emphasis. "I still feel that way."

The response of his younger self was not entirely positive. "I can foresee such a development, though perhaps one devoid of the modifier 'implicitly.' "

"All good things come only through the passing of time," the elder Vulcan replied. "A subject with which I have been forced to become more conversant than ever I thought possible."

"Good things?" Spock queried.

"No—time." The elder paused, studying the much younger face of himself, and then gave a nod. "Ah. I see. You essay an attempt at humor. Your half-human side coming out. A mildly commendable attempt."

"I appreciate your restrained approval."

They regarded each other for another long moment before the younger Spock once again broke the contemplative silence.

"The future clearly is not what it used to be. In the face of possible extinction it is only logical that I resign my

Starfleet commission in order to contribute all my efforts into helping to rebuild our species."

His elder self looked thoughtful. "And yet, you are in a unique position. You can be two places at once. I urge you to remain in Starfleet. In discussion with other Federation science departments I have already located a suitable uninhabited world on which to establish a Vulcan colony."

"I believe I understand you," declared the younger science officer. "My future cannot be determined by your past. We are one, but not the same. I must make my own future independent from yours. Yet, I hope that from time to time, should circumstances allow, that I may call on you for advice."

"Why not?" his senior self replied. "Who better with whom to debate decisions affecting yourself than yourself? The society you've inherited lives in the shadow of incalculable devastation—but there is no reason you must face it alone." Pivoting on one foot, he strode purposefully toward the nearest exit. Only there did he halt and turn for a last look back.

"As my customary farewell would appear oddly self-serving, I will simply say—good luck."

They exchanged salutes, heavily wrinkled and aged fingers rising to the exact same height and distance from the body as their younger counterparts. Anyone witnessing the display of perfectly matched gestures would have been forgiven for thinking they had been made by the same person.

Resplendent in dress uniform as formal music played behind them, the four hundred stood at attention. Each row was perfectly aligned, each crew section sharing the ancient private wish to outshine the other. So it had been since the time of the Phoenicians. So it was now in twenty-third-century San Francisco.

Standing alone at the speaker's podium, Admiral Barnett—the Academy commandant—gazed out over the sea of expectant young faces. How many times had he presided over such a gathering before, on how many equally momentous and gratifying occasions? But even for him, this one was special. Before him, awaiting their final commissions and their assignments, was a crew that had already done great things. He was confident they were destined to do more. He cleared his throat. Throughout the amphitheater, the last whispers died away.

"This assembly calls Captain James Tiberius Kirk."

Pivoting smartly, a single figure broke from the formation to march down past rows of fellow officers. His progress was tracked by numerous pairs of eyes. Uhura—Scott—Chekov—Sulu. No one tried to repress what they were feeling and it shone forth in the smiles that filled their faces. Ascending the stairs to the podium, Kirk turned sharply and halted at attention. He too was smiling. The commandant forgave him.

"Your inspirational valor and supreme dedication to your comrades are in keeping with the highest traditions of service and reflect utmost credit upon yourself, your crew, and the Federation. By Starfleet Order Two-eight-four fifty-five, you are hereby directed to report to commanding officer of *U.S.S. Enterprise* for assignment as his relief."

Snapping off an acknowledging salute that would have brought a tear to his first-year instructors, Kirk turned and walked past the commandant to halt in front of another officer. Admiral—formerly Captain—Christopher Pike saluted back from the autochair in which he sat. The trauma he had suffered had turned his hair permanently gray. Easy enough to cosmetically reverse the coloring, but not a choice a proud Starfleet officer would necessarily take. Experience was a badge of honor that neither Pike nor any other senior officer would casually discard.

"I relieve you, sir." Kirk's words rang out over the assembly—loud, precise, and Starfleet formal.

Pike was the one who smiled. "I am relieved," he responded quietly. Then he too lapsed into procedural formality as he opened the box that was resting on his lap. Inside was a medal; its composition distinctive, the words engraved on it memorable.

"And as fleet admiral, in acknowledgment of your . . . unique solution to the simulation, it's my honor to award you with this commendation for original thinking."

Kirk advanced closer. Restraining a smirk, Pike reached up to secure the medal to the younger officer's chest. "Congratulations—Captain."

"Thank you, sir."

He turned to face the crowd, not entirely certain of what to expect. The subsequent roar of appreciation and thunderous applause brought a moistness to his eyes. He stood there for as long as he thought proper, not wanting it to end but not wishing to overstay his approval.

It was a long way from Iowa.

Near the back of the assembly a lone figure looked on in silence. He did not applaud—physically. He did not cheer—verbally. But his appreciation was none the less for his silence and his poise. He did not stay for the aftermath, for casual conversation and idle chat. There was far too much to be done.

Remaining any longer would not have been logical.

The gold shirt and appropriate insignia fit well, Kirk decided as he entered the bridge. Evidently his crew thought so as well, if one were to go by the admiring looks that greeted him as he strode toward the captain's chair and settled himself into the command seat. As soon as he nodded toward the helm, Lieutenant Sulu responded crisply.

"Maneuvering thrusters and impulse engines at your command, sir."

"Weapons systems and shields on standby," Chekov reported confidently. The ship's chief tactical officer had aged remarkably fast—as had they all.

"Dilithium chamber at maximum efficiency, Captain," came a broguish report from engineering.

Uhura swiveled slightly in her chair. "Dock control reports ready for departure. Yard command signaling all clear on chosen vector."

From where he was standing between the command chair and the lift, the ship's chief medical officer grinned wryly. "Same ship, different day."

Kirk smiled at that. His expression changed as he spared a fleeting glance for the empty science station. Along with everyone else on the bridge, he hoped the position would have been filled before departure. By a particular science officer. But it still sat vacant, and they could delay no longer. The galaxy is forever in motion, he knew resignedly, and time waits for no man.

Lately, he had been forced to think a lot about time.

"Mister Sulu," he announced as he swung back toward the helm, "prepare to engage forward thrus—"

The order was interrupted by a soft *whoosh* as the turbolift doors parted to admit a single figure onto the bridge. Displaying the insignia of a senior science officer on his blue uniform, Spock moved toward the command chair and halted halfway between Kirk and the empty—but no longer vacant—science station.

"Permission to come aboard, Captain." Admiration gleamed in the eyes of every other officer present. Quite appropriately and as would have been expected, Spock ignored them all.

Well, perhaps not all.

Kirk struggled to suppress a broad smile. "Permission granted. Your purpose in presenting yourself here, Mister Spock?"

"As you have yet to select a first officer, I would respectfully like to submit my candidacy. If you decline, there is still time for me to disembark. I ask that you fully consider all candidates and qualifications before rendering a final decision in this important matter." He paused a moment, his expression never changing. "Should you desire, I can provide character references."

It was all Kirk could do to keep from bursting out laughing. As he met the Vulcan's gaze, one of the science officer's eyebrows rose prominently. Little more needed to be said.

"It would be my honor, Commander. The science station is yours." Turning, he addressed the helm briskly.

"Maneuvering thrusters, Mister Sulu. Take us out."

"Aye, Captain." Sulu's smile matched those of everyone else on the bridge.

The *Enterprise* began to move. Slowly at first, but without hesitation and with the subtle intimation of purpose that would define her own future. As it slipped clear of the dock, Spock remained by Kirk's side.

"Before assuming my formal duties, I must know one thing. The *Kobayashi Maru*—how did you break the encryption code?"

Looking up at his friend, Kirk was finally unable to repress a smile that harkened back to an earlier time. To a simpler, younger, far more innocent time. He lowered his voice conspiratorially.

"Orion women talk in their sleep."

Spock considered carefully before responding. "I suppose I may never understand cheating."

Kirk nodded slightly. "Give it . . . time."

No one was in the transporter room when it unexpectedly and fleetingly energized. The figure that emerged on the pad closest to the rest of the chamber did not hesitate, but made straight for the nearest open portal. The blip engendered by its appearance was too transitory and insufficient to alert security. It did not matter, because the unexpected arrival's appearance on board caused only consternation and not alarm.

For the life of them, as it sped outsystem and entered warp space, no one on the *Enterprise* could figure out where the beagle with the very peculiar ears had come from.

Space—the Final Frontier